PRAISE FOR
Murder on Ice

"Alina Adams gives a g
mosities and the bickeri
ateur figure skating. The
the better leads to come
delightful sense of humo
her quest to find a murde
amateur sleuth tale star
heroine."

—*The Best Reviews*

"If you are even a casual fan of figure skating, you will love this book. The author . . . really knows the behind-the-scenes dish . . . The character of Bex is one of the best amateur sleuths to come along in some time . . . The mystery is interesting, and the investigation is so entertaining that you'll be glad you're along for the ride. I'm already impatiently awaiting the next book in this series."

—*The Romance Readers Connection*

"Adams uses her extensive knowledge of the real life world of competitive figure skating to create a very realistic background for this murder—and possible blackmail—mystery complete with hints of dark humor. A likeable, down-to-earth heroine makes this a must-read for cozy mystery fans with a fascination for figure skating."

—*Romantic Times Bookclub*

"Adams's style is light and breezy, and the book moves right along. She wickedly portrays the behind the scenes backbiting and jealousies of television personalities, both on and off the screen. Readers who enjoy a lighter mystery and those who are intrigued with the rumored infighting in the world of competition figure skating should enjoy this one!"

—*Books 'N' Bytes*

"*Murder on Ice* mirrors events from the last Winter Olympics. Corrupt judging, cutthroat battles between the skaters, and the behind-the-scenes viewpoint all help to add depth to this unique mystery . . . This marks the first book in the new Figure Skating Mystery series. It is shaping up to be an addicting collection of books."

—*Roundtable Reviews*

Berkley Prime Crime titles by Alina Adams

MURDER ON ICE

ON THIN ICE

On Thin Ice

ALINA ADAMS

BERKLEY PRIME CRIME, NEW YORK

ON THIN ICE

A Berkley Prime Crime Book / published by arrangement with the author

PRINTING HISTORY
Berkley Prime Crime mass-market edition / October 2004

Cover design by Lesley Worrell.
Cover illustrations by Teresa Fasolino.

Text design by Kristin del Rosario.

For information address: The Berkley Publishing Group, a division of Penguin Group (USA) Inc., 375 Hudson Street, New York, New York 10014.

ISBN: 0-425-19884-7

Berkley Prime Crime Books are published by The Berkley Publishing Group, a division of Penguin Group (USA) Inc., 375 Hudson Street, New York, New York 10014

PRINTED IN THE UNITED STATES OF AMERICA

10 9 8 7 6 5 4 3 2 1

One

"He is the best young skater in the United States," the voice on the other end of the phone receiver unequivocally pronounced. "And you are never going to see him."

As the Senior—all right, only—researcher for the 24/7 Sports Network, Rebecca "Bex" Levy was used to out-of-the-blue phone calls praising this or that previously unheard of athlete. What she was not used to, however, was being told that she wouldn't be allowed to see him. After all, the point of said phone calls was usually to convince Bex to convince the 24/7 Sports top brass that said athlete was worthy of a 24/7 up-close-and-personal feature, preferably in prime-time. Rarely was the point of the phone call to taunt her about a feature she wouldn't be able to do.

Which was why, rather than following her first instinct, which was to politely offer, "Well, thank you very much for sharing that with me," and hanging up, Bex, instead, stayed on the line, waiting for the explanation that she could only hope would be forthcoming.

Oh, and Bex had another reason for continuing to listen.

The voice on the other end of the telephone receiver belonged to one Mrs. Antonia Wright.

Bex had met Toni a year ago, before Bex started working as the "24/7" researcher, back when she was just another struggling, freelance sports reporter, newly out of college and still barely earning enough to simply get by (granted, she was trying to do the getting-by thing in Manhattan, a borough where "simply" and "get by" couldn't even acquiesce to sharing a Central Park bench), much less begin making any sort of substantial dent in paying back her rather substantial student loans.

Bex had written a cover feature for *Black Maturity Magazine* (she refused to let a little fact like being neither black nor mature stand in her way; Bex's other freelance clients included *Boys' Life, Parents,* and *Cats,* and she wasn't any of those things, either), chronicling Toni's struggle as the first African-American ice-skater to attempt competing within the United States Figure Skating Association (USFSA). It truly was a fabulous and inspiring story, ranging from the first time seven-year-old Toni tried to pay her admission to a local ice rink and was told, "No niggers allowed," to her breaking the color barrier by joining a skating club so that she could perform at a local competition, to her triumphant win of a U.S. Pairs title with—oh, the scandal of it!—a white pairs partner. Afterwards, Toni went on to a rather successful professional career in a series of splashy and sequined ice shows before settling down to coach at the Connecticut Olympic Training Center in Hartford. These days, she was past sixty years old and still lacing up her skates to get out onto the ice with her students. The woman was a marvel. And, when she talked, Bex listened. Even if, at the moment, Toni wasn't making a heck of a lot of sense.

"I have this student," Toni backtracked. "His name is

Jeremy Hunt. He is thirteen years old, and he's terrific, a prodigy. He started skating at eight—most people will tell you that's too late, I know I thought it was. But, then, he got all of his double jumps in six months, started landing triples within a year, passed his Senior test at eleven, and now he's doing quads! Quads, Bex! Good ones, not cheated—fully rotated. The Salchow, the Toe Loop, and even the Loop three out of five times. A quadruple Loop, can you believe it?"

A year ago, Toni's words would have sounded like gibberish to Bex. A year ago, she hadn't been able to recognize an Axel on the ice from the one on her ten-year-old car. But, in researching and writing the article on Toni, she'd paid careful attention. And the older woman was an excellent teacher.

So excellent, in fact, that Bex had no trouble running her current words through the Universal Skating Translator in her head, to come up with the following interpretation: While eight years old would still seem to be a rather young age on most normal planets, in the world of competitive skating, this Jeremy Hunt might as well have been named Grandpa Moses. Popular wisdom dictates that, in order to succeed at the sport, the potential Olympic and World Champion ought to begin his serious, daily training preferably by the age of eighteen months, private lessons by age three, and lessons with a top-ranked coach by no later than five. A boy who only takes up the discipline at age eight might as well scrape "Loser" onto his forehead with a rusty skate blade and prepare for a future as Eeyore's fuzzy rear end in the European company of "Disney on Ice." However, it seemed that Toni's student, Jeremy, had beaten the prognosticators by being somewhat of a talented fellow, and precociously mastering his double jumps—meaning he could take off from the ice, rotate twice in the air, and come down on one foot without his other foot, hand, chin, or chest also slamming into the ground beside him. Mastering the double jumps—Salchow, Toe Loop, Loop, Flip, Lutz, and especially double Axel, which, in spite of its name, actually required two and half revolutions in the air—was a process that some skaters took years to perfect. The fact that Jeremy did it in under six months was impressive. But, not as impressive as the fact that he then went ahead and mastered all his triples, as well. Mastering all of the triple jumps—Salchow, Toe Loop, Loop, Flip, Lutz, and especially a triple Axel, which, in spite of its name, actually required three and half revolutions in the air, was a process that took some skaters—well, never. Most skaters never mastered all of their triple jumps. And they especially didn't do it in one year. At the age of eleven. Of course, when it came to quadruple jumps, there were only a dozen men in the world who could actually land one successfully, much less land two-almost-three of them (and at least half of those who claimed to be landing quads cheated them somehow, either taking an extra half turn on the ice before they jumped, or after they'd landed). When it came to men doing clean quads, that is, four full revolutions in the air—no cheating—there were only a handful. And none of them were thirteen years old, that was for sure.

"Oh, and Bex, this is the best part." Toni sounded almost religiously ecstatic as she unveiled her piece de resistance. "He can actually skate!"

Come on, Universal Skating Translator—Bex cheered on her brain—do your stuff! Sure enough, after a moment, it kicked in with the code-breaker. What Toni actually meant to say was: "When Jeremy Hunt gets on the ice, he doesn't look like he is trudging from place to place through gravel, and he doesn't just perform like an acrobatic monkey, he actually knows how to stroke, to glide with a semblance of smoothness, to float the way you're supposed to if we're to keep this sport from becoming tumbling on ice, instead of the art it was always intended to be."

All right, so maybe Bex embellished a little on that last part. But, it was exactly what Toni meant. She could tell from the excitement in her voice.

Still, Toni wasn't as over-the-moon excited as Bex would have expected a coach to be when talking up a supposed find of this boy's caliber. There had to be a catch. Something Toni intended to tell her, but couldn't quite find the right words.

Bex tried to guess, offering up her version of "Skating Twenty Questions." She asked Toni, "So, what's the problem? Does he leave it all on the practice ice?"

In human language, what Bex meant was, "Is he good in practice, but then can't deliver in competition?"

"Not at all," Toni assured. "If this boy can do it, he can do it, doesn't matter when or where."

"Meaning he doesn't freeze up under pressure?"

"Nope. Solid as a rock. Two minutes before competition, he's grinning and waving to his friends and clapping for the competition and jabbering about which little girl he's planning to invite to his eighth-grade dance. Nothing fazes him. I swear, when results went up at Sectionals last week and we saw he'd placed first, the smile he had is the same one he'd have had if he finished last."

Translation: Sectionals were a qualifying competition. There were three in the country, divided into geographic regions—Pacific Coast, Midwestern, and Eastern. The top four skaters from each discipline advanced on to the U.S. National Championships. If Jeremy Hunt won his Eastern Sectional, it meant he had a very good chance of winning a medal—even a gold one—at Nationals. And a U.S.

National Champion, traditionally, had a very good chance of going on to win a medal at the World Championships, or even at the Olympic Winter Games.

"Not bad for a thirteen year old," Bex noted.

"Except that there's a problem."

Aha! Chalk one up for Bex's instincts. Of course, there was a problem.

"It's Jeremy's father."

Oh, yes, here it came. Bex took mental bets with herself on exactly what sort of cliché "problem" parent Mr. Hunt would prove to be. There was a limited number of types, and none of them was a barrel of monkeys. "What's wrong with him?"

Toni took a deep breath and, in a voice that suggested she couldn't believe it herself, revealed, "Jeremy's father won't let him compete at Nationals."

"What?" Bex sat up in her office chair, rubber wheels scraping the floor with a squeak equal in volume to her dismay.

This was certainly a new one for her. Usually, when one said there was a problem with a skating parent, one meant that Mommy Dearest (and it was usually a Mommy Dearest, though a Daddy or two did sneak into the party once in a while) was beating her Skating Sweetie in the back bathroom with a hairbrush while screaming that Skating Sweetie messed up her combination jump on purpose. Or it meant that Mommy Dearest was keeping her Skating Sweetie on a diet so strict, gaunt Ethiopian children were sending Skating Sweetie humanitarian relief, or, at the very least, that Mommy Dearest had taken to calling up judges at their regular place of employment to demand an explanation for why Skating Sweetie hadn't qualified for Nationals, when anyone could see that she was the superior child in her flight, if not in the entire world.

Although Bex had only been in the formal research business for a little over one season (last year had been her first and she was just three months into her second), she'd been writing about sports of all kinds for almost ten years now, going back to her high-school paper. And she'd never, ever heard of a parent trying to keep their child OUT of a competition.

"Does the dad say why?"

"He says that he has no problem with Jeremy skating for fun, but he doesn't want it consuming his life."

Oh. Well, that certainly was a new one. Bex almost didn't know what to say. She stammered, "I, well, Toni, he's not exactly wrong in that, is he?" This was truly unprecedented. On the other hand . . . "But why did he let Jeremy enter Sectionals if he wants him to do it just for fun?"

"I asked him the same thing. Mr. Hunt—his first name is Craig—he said to me that local competitions are still fun. Nationals are where it gets crazy."

Well, he was right and he was wrong about that. From where Bex sat, she'd seen some pretty crazy behavior at local interclub competitions for skaters between the mature ages of five and five-and-a-half, but, okay, let Mr. Hunt have his opinion.

Bex said, "This Jeremy though, he sounds to me like the type of kid who can handle big-time competition. Especially if he's got no pressure coming from the homefront."

"Personally, I don't think it's that at all. Personally, I think Mr. Hunt is afraid of Jeremy losing. He dotes on that boy, he's afraid to see him hurt."

"Again, Toni," Bex, as a civilian, was treading carefully now. You never knew with these skating people what exactly would set them off. One time Bex watched a skater go mental because someone mistook his teal costume for being blue. There were certain things these people took extra-special seriously. And you'd darn better take them seriously, too, if you wanted them to keep talking to you.

Still, Bex bravely pressed on, "Is that so wrong?"

"When you've got a boy of this talent, yes!" The fervor in Toni's voice reminded Bex that no matter how generally reasonable the older woman sounded, she was still a skater down to the freon in her veins. Of course, to her, Craig Hunt was spouting heresy. "Jeremy Hunt is the most talented male skater I've seen since Robby Sharpton. Do you want him to end up throwing his potential away the same way Robby did?"

Actually, Bex had no idea who this Robby Sharpton was. She made a mental note to act out her job description and actually go research it. How hard could it be? She already had a pretty big clue. Apparently, the said Robby Sharpton never lived up to his potential.

Toni went on, "What if someone had kept Fred Astaire from dancing? Or Caruso from singing? What if someone had taken away Van Gogh's paint brushes?"

"He might have ended up with better hearing?" Bex was being flip, she knew she was being flip. But, she just couldn't help it sometimes. Not when it was this easy.

Toni said, "This boy could be the star of the next Nationals. Doesn't 24/7 want to be the first one to tell his story?"

"Not if he's not going to be there, Toni, which, right now, it sounds like he's not."

"I need you to do something for me, Bex."

Ah, only sixteen digressions later, and here they were, finally arriving at the point of this conversation. Bex immediately felt more comfortable. This was an arena where she was the star, where she knew what to do. As 24/7's only researcher, anyone who had a story to pitch had to come to her first. Only after Bex decided whether or not it had any merit or dramatic potential, would she take it to her Executive Producer, Gil Cahill. If Gil agreed with her assessment, he would dispatch a producer to shoot the story, based on her research notes. If Gil disagreed with her assessment—which was usually—he made her feel like she was exactly three centimeters tall and ready for the bird-brain remedial classes.

Bex did not enjoy that sensation. Which was why, before Gil had the chance to shoot down the ideas she brought him, Bex took the time to shoot down most ideas herself. She was a sort of Gil in training. God, but that was a horrifying thought.

Still, Toni wasn't just any coach trying to sell Bex on a story. She was a classy lady who deserved to be listened to and treated with respect. Before she was shot down.

"What can I do, Toni?"

"I think you should send a camera crew here to the Training Center to shoot Jeremy practicing. Once Mr. Hunt sees that a major sports network like 24/7 thinks his son has enough potential to be profiled as an up and comer, I think he'll realize just how truly exceptional Jeremy is, and he'll agree to let him live up to his full potential."

Unlike, apparently, this Robby Sharpton person.

"I.e., he'll let him go to Nationals?" Bex just wanted to make sure they were all on the same page here.

"Where he'll steal the show, I guarantee it. And 24/7 will have gotten the first exclusive with him!"

Leave it to Toni to do her homework. She was up on all of her TV buzz-words. Still, Bex truly doubted that Gil could be talked into shelling out the expenses for a producer and two-man crew, camera and sound guy, to travel to Connecticut to shoot footage of a boy who, in all likelihood, wouldn't even be at Nationals. And, even if he was, Bex still suspected Toni was doing a bit of the over-hype dance. No thirteen-year-old boy could be as good as she claimed this one was. Jeremy Hunt may have had a ton of potential he was in danger of not living up to, but Bex doubted a thirteen year old at his first major competition had a chance in hell of qualifying for the top five at Nationals. And, as far as the always compassionate television world was concerned, if you weren't in the top five, you were never even entered in the event.

Toni must have sensed Bex's hesitation. Because, before Bex had the chance to purse her lips in anticipation of politely but firmly offering up a "no," Toni interrupted to say, "How about if I send you a tape of Jeremy skating? You can see for yourself how special he is. Just watch him skate for a couple of minutes. Then tell me whether or not you'll go to Gil Cahill with the piece."

She'd been all set to say "no." Bex's lips were all pursed and everything. See?

But, Toni was a sixty-year-old sports pioneer. Bex was just a twenty-four-year-old figure skating researcher whose mother had taught her to be polite, especially with older people. And, oh, yes, Bex also suffered from a terminal gastro condition known as gutless.

"Sure." Bex sighed, knowing that she was merely putting off the inevitable task of saying "no" for a few days at most, and feeling both like a first-class coward and yet oh so relieved at the same time. "Go ahead, Toni. Send me the tape."

"It's already in the mail, honey."

Oh, great, now Bex was not only gutless and a procrastinator. She was also predictable.

Two

While waiting with dread for Jeremy Hunt's tape to arrive, Bex tried to keep the inevitable at bay by continuing to doggedly plug away at other parts of her job, like compiling biographies of all the skaters 24/7 was scheduled to cover in the upcoming season. As a network devoted to sports twenty-four hours a day, seven days a week (hence the catchy title), 24/7 had an exclusive contract to show the entire year's skating season from October to February, starting with several invitation-only international competitions set to take place all over the world, followed by the U.S. Nationals, and then, in this non-Olympic year, the culminating World Championships.

This meant that Bex was in charge of finding out everything there was to know about every single skater, Man, Woman, Pairs, and Dance, that had even the remotest chance of showing up on the air, and then digesting and summarizing that information into easy-to-read sound-bytes the announcers could pithily read on camera while sounding as if this was stuff they just happened to know off the tops of their heads. It was the most horrible kind of drudge work. Because it was drudge work that was also incredibly hard. (Kind of like skating itself. One elite ice-dancer once described the process of mastering a compulsory pattern as, "boring, yet really difficult.")

Bex had trouble enough compiling pertinent information on the American skaters, since they repeatedly lost the questionnaires she sent them, or, once she got them on the phone, answered everything she asked in monotonous monosyllables, punctuated by equal parts giggles, "likes," and "you knows."

But, at least—and thank God for small favors—most of the American skaters were more or less in her time zone. Which meant Bex didn't have to drag herself out of bed at five A.M. and, teeth still unbrushed, eyes half pasted over with sleep, attempt tracking down, by phone, a renegade Pairs skater in Lithuania. Also, American skaters, monotonous monosyllables, giggles, "likes," and "you knows" aside, usually spoke English. Not so for a majority of their competitors. Japanese, Chinese (both Mandarin and Cantonese dialects), Russian, French, German, and Serbo-Croatian, that they could speak. But not English.

Naturally, this meant that Bex passed a good portion of her day dialing four-hundred-digit international phone numbers, arguing with overseas operators, wrestling with telephone wires that only worked during a full moon after an eclipse as long as there wasn't a sudden regime change, and, once she finally got through, shouting questions ranging from, "Could you please list for me, in order, all the elements in your short program, plus the name of your music, its composer, and your choreographer," to "Is there any connection between your father's death last year and your decision to skate to a traditional Irish funeral dirge this season?" Only to receive in response a string of incomprehensible Japanese, Mandarin, Cantonese, Russian, French, German, and/or Serbo-Croatian, always shouted at the highest possible decibel. To help Bex understand them better.

After a few months of this "Which Jump's on First?" routine, Bex could state with absolute certainty that shouting did not, at any time, help her to understand them better.

Granted, Bex wasn't so ethnocentric that she ever thought that citizens from other countries should be able to speak English. She didn't expect them to, any more than she expected herself to speak Japanese, Mandarin, Cantonese, Russian, French, German, or Serbo-Croatian. Although Gil did; he always looked so surprised each and every time Bex reminded him that she didn't. The fact was, Bex had been honest about her linguistic skills when she applied for this job. She told Gil that she'd studied Esperanto in college because she'd been fascinated by the concept of an international language (and also because she'd thought it was funky and weird, and Bex naturally gravitated toward funky and weird the way normal people gravitated toward, well, normal; but she hadn't told Gil that part. She'd really needed the job, after all, to pay off all those pesky student loans she'd accumulated while studying the aforementioned funky and weird). Alas, Gil heard "international language" and, in Gil-logic, assumed that it meant Bex could speak the language that everyone else spoke . . . uh . . . internationally. Gil was wrong.

When she first started at 24/7, Bex hired translators to help her with the phone calls. This was a good plan up to a point. Its flaw came in that most people fluent in a foreign language didn't necessarily speak skating, which, as demonstrated by the Universal Skating Translator, was necessary even while speaking English. When Bex tried to use The Universal Skating Translator to go from English (Bex) to, say, Russian (interpreter) to Skating (skater) to Russian (interpreter) and then back to English (Bex), she ended up facing a confused Russian speaker who covered the receiver with one hand while turning to Bex with a quizzical expression to report that, "He says he will end his short program by sitting in a sailboat."

It took quite a bit of heavy research on Bex's part before she learned that the Russian word for a "Spread Eagle" skating move literally translated to "sailboat."

That's when she sort of gave up on translators.

And, after her third incomprehensible international telephone game of the day ("My music choice, she to symbolize my love of goat cheese,"), Bex temporarily gave up calling, too, deciding instead to take a break (or, as Gil called it any time he walked by her office to see Bex engaged in such unproductive activities as eating lunch or breathing, "goofing off") by researching something easier. She figured now would be a good time to satiate her curiosity about this Robby Sharpton guy that Toni mentioned in her phone call. Bex figured if he was some sort of skating boogeyman, the one about whom parents told their children, "You'd better practice hard, or you'll end up just like Robby Sharpton," then it would probably behoove her to know exactly who he was.

That's why, instead of trying to dial Taiwan, Bex instead dialed the four-digit extension for the 24/7 records department, and asked them to bring up Robby Sharpton's file, presumably compiled by one of Bex's many, many predecessors (it often disturbed Bex to learn just how high of a turnover rate this job had, but she thought it best not to ask any questions as to why that was exactly. All she knew was, at 24/7, a skating researcher's tour of duty lasted approximately as long as the lifespan of your average Vampire Slayer, or red-shirted security guy on *Star Trek*).

Once the file was delivered, Bex leafed through the top few pages. At first glance, she wasn't even sure she'd gotten the right info. She checked the name on the folder, "Robert 'Robby' Sharpton," so yes, she had the right guy. But, if this was Toni's definition of a skater failing to live up to his potential, then perhaps Bex needed an adjustment to her Universal Skating Translator.

Because, as far as she could see, ol' Robby had done pretty well for himself in skating. He was the 1985 and 1986 U.S. Junior Pairs Champion with Felicia Tufts, a (according to their official photo) ballerina-tiny blonde with no breasts, her hair up in a bun, a big Miss America smile, and tasteful golden studs in her ears, and the 1987, 1988, and 1989 U.S. Senior Pairs Champion with Rachel Rose (they were called R&R by their fans), a ballerina-tiny blonde with no breasts, her hair up in a bun, a big Miss America smile, and tasteful golden hoops in her ears.

And, if that weren't enough, once that latter partnership broke up, the one-time Novice and Junior Men's Champion went back to his Singles career, qualifying for both the 1990 and 1994 Olympic teams, finishing fourteenth at the former, and fifth at the latter. To Bex's untrained eye, Robby Sharpton's looked like a pretty darn respectable career.

She was about to log on to the Internet to see what else she could find out about this man to help explain what Toni meant by his wasted potential when—speak of the devil—the perpetually sullen mail clerk (he always looked like he was writing a screenplay in his head and really resented being disturbed by this job thing) came by to carelessly lob a videotape-sized package wrapped in brown paper into her in-box. Not surprisingly, it turned out to be a videotape wrapped in brown paper. From one Mrs. Antonia Wright. The attached note read: "This is Jeremy Hunt. And it wasn't even one of his better days."

Bex sighed. Then she figured she might as well get it over with. The sooner she watched the tape, the sooner she could call Toni and tell her they wouldn't be doing a feature on her student.

Oh, that would be fun.

Bex popped the tape into the VCR atop her filing cabinet, and used the remote to turn on both it and the television set, automatically adjusting the tracking as she waited for the images to start. The first thing she saw was a fuzzy, upside down view of the Connecticut Olympic Training Center's main ice surface, which, no surprise, looked exactly like every other ice surface anywhere else on the planet. And, even though she'd heard from dozens of skating professionals about how ice could be too hard, or too soft, or too slick (apparently, if skaters were to be believed, their lives were a perpetual retelling of *Goldilocks and the Three Bears*), to Bex, ice was still ice was still ice. It was white, it was wet, it was cold. Let's get on with the program.

As if heeding her unvocalized command, the camera straightened itself out and pulled into focus. And then it proceeded to whip nauseatingly about the entire rink, weaving in and out and around two dozen kids in brightly colored warm-up jackets trying to land jumps and center spins, until coming to a sudden and abrupt jerk-stop upon finding the one kid it was looking for.

"Jeremy Hunt, I presume," Bex mumbled at the now centered preteen. Had Toni said he was thirteen? He looked closer to eleven, definitely pre-adolescent, and, while not precisely scrawny—Bex could see the toned muscles in his arms and especially his thighs and calves—he was definitely on the slender side.

His haircut made him look younger, too. His hair was extra-fine, blond, straight, and looked as if it had been cut by someone putting a ceramic bowl on his head, then trimming everything that stuck out. Although he did have a sparkling smile, just like Toni said. After seeing the scary, phony smiles in the photos of both Felicia Tufts and Rachel Rose, it actually made Bex happy to see a skater for whom a childish grin looked natural, rather than like a carefully practiced part of the choreography. The most striking thing that Bex noticed about Jeremy, though, was that he wasn't nearly as pasty as the traditional skating drone. Despite his naturally light complexion, Jeremy actually seemed to be flaunting the remnants of a summer tan. Like maybe he didn't spend his entire life in a rink. Like maybe he had some wholesome outside interests, too.

Not that any of it mattered for the task at hand. Bex was paid (if you wanted to call it that) to research stories about potential, break-out stars. Not wholesome, well-adjusted Boy Scouts and the Fathers Who Want to Keep Them That Way.

"Alright, kiddo, do your stuff," Bex said. "Make Toni proud."

His music began. Bex recognized the opening bars to *Warsaw Concerto*. An interesting choice, as it was an awfully powerful piece. Wasn't Toni afraid a kid Jeremy's size would be crushed by the grandeur of the building chords?

Bex wondered what Toni was thinking.

Until she saw Jeremy land his first quadruple Salchow.

It went by so quickly, and looked so smooth and easy and clean that, for a second, Bex was sure she must have miscounted the turns in the air. He must have only done a triple. It couldn't have been that simple. Bex reached for the remote control so that she could rewind the tape and put it in slow motion to make sure it had really been a quad.

But, that's when Jeremy landed his quadruple Toe Loop.

Bex put down the remote.

And she just watched.

She watched him land a triple Axel.

Combination Spin.

Serpentine Footwork into a triple Lutz.

The difficult tricks seemed to flow out of him as smoothly as water from a straw. No. No, it was more than that. The difficult tricks seemed to flow out of his music. They seemed both inevitable and unpredictable and utterly natural, as if every triple jump was a part of the boy, who was a part of the notes. It was impossible to tell where one ended and the other began.

Oh, and by the way, Toni was right. The kid didn't just jump. He could actually skate, too.

Bex finished watching the entire program.

Then she rewound and watched it all again, this time carefully counting each of the revolutions on each of the jumps.

And then she grabbed the tape out of the VCR and tore down the hall to Gil Cahill's office.

She didn't even turn off the TV.

Three

Gil Cahill's office was all the way down the hall. It was the last one you came to and it was the only one around that particular corner, which meant that, once you got there, there would be no chickening out and claiming you'd come to see someone else. Gil's office was the office of no escape. A few months ago, in a fit of whimsy, Gil's secretary, Ruth, hung a little sign on her desk. It read: "No one gets in to see the Great and Powerful Wizard. No way. No how."

When Gil saw it, he said, "Good," and closed his office door behind him.

This was the sign Bex always tried to avoid looking at as she cowered in front of Ruth's desk, feeling very much like "Bex, the meek and the small," every time she asked to see Gil.

It was, actually, a very schizophrenic experience. The fact was, the only time Bex ever asked to see Gil was when she thought she'd found someone or something worth profiling. Which usually meant she was bursting with excitement and eager to run in there and wow Gil with what she'd discovered. Which meant she hoped he wasn't busy and would see her. On the other hand, seeing Gil was . . . well . . . seeing Gil. It was rarely a lot of fun. Which meant she also hoped that he was really busy and couldn't see her.

"Gil can see you right now," Ruth said, and gestured toward his office.

Yahoo, Bex thought. Followed by, *Drat.*

His office was the only one on the entire floor with windows. He had them on all three sides, an Eastern, a Southern, and a Western exposure. Gil usually kept the blinds closed. His desk was the size of a horse coffin. And it was located in the farthest corner of the room, so that a visitor had to cross what felt like miles of hostile tundra, while Gil just sat there, looking at you expectantly and not saying a word as you trudged past all the photos on his walls: Gil with the current president of the International Olympic Committee (IOC), Gil with the organizer of the Kentucky Derby, Gil with Arthur Ashe and Muhammad Ali and Mark Spitz and Joe Namath and Joe DiMaggio and Arnold Palmer and lots of other people with big, white, perfect teeth.

Gil, himself, had perfect teeth. And perfect hair. And the most stylish, dapper clothes. And a perpetual tan. Having started his career as a radio announcer, his diction was also perfect. In fact, Bex might have been tempted to pronounce Gil Cahill the most perfect human being ever assembled inside the human being factory. Except that, in addition to his teeth, hair, clothes, tan and diction, he was also . . . well . . . Gil.

"What is it, Bex?" he asked. "I'm very busy."

She never knew whether or not she could sit. Gil never asked her to sit, and yet, she felt awkward standing for the duration of her entire presentation. So, Bex compromised. She reached for the chair that was facing his desk, ran her hand tentatively along it's back, and, when he didn't bark for her to unhand his furniture, kind of casually leaned against it, so that she no longer looked reverential or awkward. Just stupid.

Of course, once she realized that her posture was stupid, it was already too late for Bex to modify it. And so, half standing, half leaning there, Bex at least tried to look casual as she shifted her weight forward, hoping not to topple over while she handed Gil the video tape of Jeremy, and, in as few words as possible, summarized his story.

"So the kid is good, so what?" Gil shrugged. "If the old man isn't letting him go off to Nationals, why do we care?"

"Toni thinks if we can convince Craig Hunt of how good Jeremy really is and what a shot he has at doing really well at Nationals, then he'll let him go."

"Is this our job, now? I don't think convincing parents to send their kids to Nationals is our job, Bex."

"But telling the best stories at Nationals is." Bex wondered where the fine line between informative and condescending was drawn, and how many times she'd already crossed it. "It's a great story, Gil, you have to admit that. I mean, this kid's come out of nowhere, he's going to be the youngest boy in the field, he's landing jumps skaters twice his age are still struggling with, and he might very, very well win."

"I am not spending a thousand dollars to send a crew and a producer down to Connecticut to waste film on a kid with a big old question mark stamped across his behind."

"Okay," Bex conceded, "that's fair."

"Then why are we still having this conversation?"

"Because. Gil. I—I have a thought."

"Oh, this should be good."

"I thought . . . I thought, what if I go down there?"

He looked at her as if IQ points were falling out of Bex's ears like leaves in a storm. "You go with the producer? Explain to me how that's saving me money."

"I—See, I thought—I thought that I, maybe, I could produce it."

"Wonderful." Whenever Gil said "wonderful," he never really meant "wonderful." So Bex patiently waited for the other shoe to drop. "Except we've got one minor problem." Ah, here came the high-heeled sandal now—aimed, as usual, at Bex's head. "You're not a producer, Bex."

Thanks, Gil. She already kind of knew that.

"I—I could be."

"Oh. Did I promote you and forget?"

"No. But, I've worked with the producers. I know what they do, I know how they do it, and the stories are mine to begin with. I write the story and they just sort of put pictures to it."

"It's harder than it looks," Gil said dryly.

"Oh, I'm sure it is. That's why—that's why I thought, we could kind of do it like this: I'll go down and shoot Jeremy and his dad and everything with just a Beta camera."

"You have a Beta camera?"

"I thought I could borrow one. From the network . . ." When Gil didn't respond one way or the other, Bex pressed on, figuring if she couldn't convince him with her words, maybe she could simply bury him in a blurted pile of them. "Then, I'll come back and I'll screen what I've got to a producer—a real producer—and he and you and everybody can see if it's any good and if we can use it. By then, we'll know if Craig is letting Jeremy go to Nationals or not, and, if you decide the story is worth doing, you can send a real producer down again to get shots I've missed."

Bex had to stop now. Not because she was out of words. Because she was out of breath.

"Oh, good idea, Bex. This way it will cost me twice as much."

"No. It won't. I mean, you don't have to pay me a producer's fee or anything."

"I wasn't planning to."

"Right."

"But what about the double travel fee? The double hotel fee? The extra edit time, and the tape-stock and the missed days of you doing your real job? What about that?"

"I'll pay for all that," Bex blurted out, before she'd even thought it through. Obviously, if she'd thought it through, she wouldn't have blurted it out.

Gil cocked his head to one side. "Did I also give you a raise along with your promotion?"

"What I mean is," Bex was still babbling, but at least now she had a better idea of what she was trying to say. "I'll pay all my travel expenses up front. You only have to reimburse me if you like the footage I bring back and if you end up using the story."

Gil stared at her, eyes narrowed, for what felt to Bex like an eternity. She imagined that, if the drapes were actually open, she could watch day slowly turn to dusk then dark then dawn, and Gil would still be staring at her.

Finally, he snapped, "Fine," and reached to pick up his phone even though Bex could see that it wasn't ringing or even blinking.

Obviously, this was a symbolic, dismissive phone call. "Just don't come back with crap, you got that?"

"Right," Bex said, trying her best to barrel out of the office without looking as if she were trying to barrel out of the office. In other words, she was attempting to barrel . . . casually. "No crap. I'll write that down."

Bex drove her own car down to Hartford. She figured she could have taken the train or rented a vehicle that didn't begin coughing like the third reel of *Camille* whenever she so much as thought of raising the speed limit to seventy. But, considering that the cost for this entire quest might end up coming out of Bex's own pocket, she figured it was in her best interest to keep all expenses down to a minimum.

That was why she didn't so much pull in, as shudder into the Connecticut Olympic Training Center's parking lot, wrestling her ancient wheels into the only free spot left, right between an SUV boasting the bumper stickers, "Skaters have the best figures" and "I used to be rich—then my child took up figure skating," and a Honda with the vanity license plate, "GLDCOACH." Bex guessed they weren't talking about the carriage Cinderella arrived at the ball in.

She unlocked her (well, 24/7's) Beta-Cam from the trunk of her car, swung the carrying case over one shoulder, and after a few quick steps across the parking lot, stepped through the two swinging doors and into the snack bar just outside the OTC's main ice surface.

She was immediately assaulted on two fronts by two equally formidable sensations: the wet, dank smell of freon, and the nearly unbearable brightness of being. The rink was painted white. The ice was, obviously, white. The girls' skates were white, and so they wore equally white practice dresses to match. Add to all that a ceiling full of fluorescent lights radiant enough to illuminate a hairpin dropped onto the ice, and the bridge of Bex's nose went into a *Gremlins*-worthy "bright light, bright light!" spasm. She gasped and winced, looking instinctively down at the floor, and covering her eyes with one hand for good measure. Pressing on and bracing herself for the gust of cold to come, Bex bravely stepped out through the swinging snack bar doors leading to the ice surface. She paused by the rink's waist-high barrier. The bracing did a limited amount of good. Within a minute, Bex was freezing. But, hey, at least she'd been prepared for it.

Bex spotted Toni right away. Dressed in dark gray leggings and a knee-length padded coat with matching wool hat, she stood out easily among the sea of tiny white, pink, yellow, and other pastel outfits. Bex raised her hand to wave, and Toni enthusiastically waved back. Grabbing the hand of a boy Bex recognized from the video as Jeremy Hunt, she gestured that Bex should stay where she was, and they would both skate over to where she was standing.

"Jeremy, this is Ms. Levy from 24/7 Sports, I told you about her yesterday," Toni rested her hand protectively on the boy's arm. "She's here to film you skating."

"How do you do?" Jeremy pulled his hand out of the jet black glove he was wearing and offered it to Bex for a shake. "It's nice to meet you. Thank you for coming to see me."

Quadruple jumps, and manners, too. The perfect young man. It should have been impressive. Instead, it kind of creeped Bex out. A little too *Stepford Wives* for her taste.

She told Jeremy, "Toni's told me a lot about you. She thinks you've got a lot of potential."

"Toni's a good coach. Real encouraging." He smiled the same eager smile Bex had first glimpsed on the videotape, and she felt a bit of her reserve melting. Maybe she was jumping to conclusions. Maybe the charm was natural, after all.

Bex asked, "Are you in the middle of a lesson? I was hoping we could talk a little bit before I started shooting."

"We just finished," Toni said. She told Jeremy, "Why don't you take a break, kiddo, and then we can do a run-through of your long program for Ms. Levy and her camera."

"Okay. Thanks for the lesson, Toni." Jeremy rested his hand on the barrier and clanked—as gracefully as one could while wearing knives strapped to one's feet—off the ice. He plopped himself down on a nearby bleacher and asked, "What do you want to talk about?"

"Um," Bex rubbed her goose-pimpled upper arms with her hands, teeth chattering, "You think we could do this inside?"

"Sure." He stood up, still waddling awkwardly on his skates as he attempted to walk on the threadbare carpeting. "Let's go."

Once back in the snack bar, Jeremy hopped onto a nearby bench, settling next to a green duffle bag with *Jeremy* stitched on the side. He reached inside to pull out a dingy, gray square cloth, and, raising his foot to rest on his knee, began carefully wiping the accumulated sludge off his skate-blade. Bex took the empty seat next to Jeremy. She looked around and asked, "Is your dad here today?"

"He's at work. He'll be by to pick me up at the end of this session and take me to school."

"You go to school full-time?" A rarity in the skating world. Most kids were either home-schooled or did correspondence classes.

"Yeah. I get first period off because of the skating, that counts as my gym class. But, I do everything else."

"Sounds like a full schedule."

"It's fun. When I don't have anything to do, I get a little crazy, you know?"

"What about your mom? What does she think of all this?"

Jeremy lowered his foot back onto the floor. He looked down at the cloth, kneading it between his fingers. Softly, he said, "She's dead. She died a long time ago. When I was a little kid. Before we moved to Connecticut." Still not looking at Bex, he bent over, untying the skate he'd just dried. "It was an accident. Like in a car. She died. It was before we moved here."

"So it's just you and your dad, then? No brothers, sisters?"

"Just us." Jeremy finished unlacing and took off his boot, dropping it on the floor with a thump. "We don't need anyone else. My dad and I, we're each other's best friends."

Newly unsheathed from the cumbersome leather, Jeremy stretched out his foot and flexed his toes, rotating his ankle this way and that, then letting out a satisfied "ahhh. . . ." Noting Bex watching his ritual, he grinned and mischievously explained, "It's skating's big secret, you know. The only reason we go through the torture of learning to jump and spin is because it feels so great to take the boots *off*!"

Bex laughed. His deadpan delivery really did make the joke. A regular Jerry Seinfeld, this kid. She said, "You know, if this skating thing doesn't work out for you, you could always get into stand-up comedy."

"That's what my dad says. He says it's important to have a fall-back plan."

"Your dad really doesn't like your skating, does he?"

"Oh, no. No, that's not it," Jeremy said, unlacing his other boot and repeating his ecstatic stretch. "My dad doesn't mind my skating. He says, as long as it makes me happy and I like it, I should be allowed to do it as much as

I want. He doesn't even mind the money. What my dad doesn't like is my competing."

"He let you compete at Sectionals."

"That was kind of an accident. I begged him and begged him to let me skate in Regionals. I've been wanting to for such a long time and he always said no. He said just skating for enjoyment and to pass all my tests would be enough. But, I passed my Senior Freestyle and my Moves in the Field test two years ago. I've got no more tests to take. I got bored."

"And you hate being bored, right?"

"Right. So I begged and I begged, and since Regionals were happening right here at the OTC and we wouldn't have to travel or anything, he finally said okay. But, it was supposed to be just Regionals. He didn't think I'd win it and qualify for Sectionals."

"But, you did. And he let you skate in them, too."

"More begging, Ms. Levy." Again with the deadpan delivery. "I'm very good at it."

"So it seems." Bex rested her elbow on the bench, leaning her head on her palm so that she and Jeremy were eye-to-eye. "So how come a master beggar like you can't break his dad's resolve when it comes to skating at Nationals?"

"My dad doesn't believe in competition. He doesn't like what it turns people into. He says it makes them crazy. Like really sick in the head. He doesn't want that for me."

"And you don't mind?"

"I mind it a whole lot. I like competing. I especially like winning. I mean, skating a clean and perfect program is great and all, and I like skating and everything. But, I can skate well on a practice session, you know? When I come to a competition, I like to win."

"Spoken like a true champion."

"Well, that's the plan. Someday. But, see, the problem

is, my dad thinks that to be really good in skating, you have to go crazy. He thinks I'm not good enough to win Nationals, and, since he knows I really want to win, he thinks that if I go and see how much better everyone else is than me, then I'll go crazy trying to become as good as they are. Does that make any sense?"

"Actually it does." If Craig Hunt was a lunatic, he was a very reasonable, logical one.

"That's why Toni and I decided you could change his mind."

"Yes, so Toni tells me. I'm not exactly sure how you two expect me to do that, though."

"Toni says you're an expert. Figure skating expert, that's your job. You know who's good enough to be at Nationals and who isn't. So, all I need is for you to tell my dad that I'm just as good as any other guy who's going to be there, and that seeing them, it won't make me crazy. I'll just keep training the way I always have. Going to Nationals won't make me nuts, even if I don't win. 'Cause, you know, I'm not expecting to win my first year and everything. I just want to get out there and, well, I just want to show off a little. That's not so bad, is it?"

Bex smiled. "Actually, Jeremy, the truth is, you're not as good as any other guy who's going to Nationals."

"I'm not?" His previously chipper voice sunk to a whisper, complete with adolescent crack on the word *not*. He did his best to fight it, but Bex thought she saw tears springing to the edges of his lashes. "Oh."

"Jeremy." Bex lowered her head to make sure he could see her face. "You're better."

"I am?" In a split second, the tears were gone, and his eyes beamed a combination of relief and cockiness.

Oh, Bex, thought, *to be a bipolar teen again.* She

wouldn't relive those days for all the ice-chips in the Zamboni.

"Yes, you are. That's why I'm here. I think it would be a crime if you didn't get to skate at Nationals. And, if I want to keep my job, it would be a crime if 24/7 didn't have exclusive rights to your story."

"You can have them!" Jeremy shouted, even though Bex was pretty sure the boy had no idea what that meant. "You can do anything you want with me!"

"As long as your dad approves," Bex reminded.

"Well, yeah, but, you'll convince him, right?"

"We'll see . . . ."

Jeremy didn't seem to have heard her. As soon as she uttered the word Nationals, he was a whirling dervish, rif-fling through his bag, looking for his skates and yanking them back on.

"Come on," he jumped up, pulling Bex by the hand, leading her back towards the arena. "I want you to see my long program."

Four

While Jeremy warmed up on the ice and Toni stood by the tape player, waiting for his turn with the music, Bex leaned against the barrier, fiddling with her Beta-Cam to make sure everything would be working perfectly as soon as Jeremy was ready to skate.

As she cleaned the fragile lens with the sleeve of her sweatshirt (very professional, Bex, very producer-like), a heavyset, forty-something woman in a red and white OTC official jacket inched her way down the multiple bleachers until she had moseyed up practically to Bex's elbow. She didn't say a word, and Bex wasn't sure if she was supposed to notice her or not, so she stayed quiet, waiting for her new lurker friend to make the first move. It came soon enough.

"It's Bex, isn't it? Bex Levy? Do you remember me from last season? I'm Amanda Reilly. Lian Reilly's mother."

Lian Reilly was last season's U.S. Ladies' Bronze

Medalist. Bex had met them briefly at both the Nationals and the World Championships the previous year.

"Hello, Mrs. Reilly." Bex tried to convey both genuine sincerity and subtle dismissal in the same breath. "Nice to see you again."

"Are you here shooting b-roll for Nationals?" Mrs. Reilly asked.

Shooting b-roll? This woman sure knew her TV jargon, just like Toni. Did everybody in skating these days? Was it as much a part of the program now as learning backward crossovers or a camel spin?

"Yes, for Nationals, and for other events, too."

"Oh, that's wonderful. I'll let Lian know you're here."

"Actually, Mrs. Reilly—"

"Please call me Amanda."

"Actually, Amanda, I'm here to shoot Jeremy Hunt."

Somehow, Bex suspected that if it were at all possible, Lian's mother was about to ask Bex to start calling her Mrs. Reilly again.

Naturally, she didn't. But, she sure did look like she wanted to. Instead, she managed to sputter out, "But—but, Jeremy Hunt, he's one of Toni Wright's students."

"Yes, I know."

"Toni Wright doesn't coach champions."

"I'm sorry, what?" Bex turned around, giving the woman her full attention for the first time since this sycophantic dialogue began. Apparently, her Universal Skating Translator was on the fritz again.

"Oh, you didn't know. Well, that's all right."

"Didn't know what?"

"That Toni Wright is strictly B-level. I mean, don't get me wrong, she seems to be a lovely woman, and I'm sure her life has been full of all sorts of challenges and handicaps and restrictions—I understand that sort of prejudice, myself, of course, because of my own situation."

Bex considered Mrs. Reilly's strawberry blonde hair and blue eyes. "You do?"

"Naturally, I do. And I relate to it wholeheartedly. My own Lian, she's Asian, you know."

Bex resisted the urge to point out that it was sort of hard to miss.

"My husband and I tried to have children for years, and then we tried to adopt domestically and that never worked out. Finally, when we adopted Lian from China, it truly was the happiest day in my life. That's why I named her Lian. *Lian* means, 'my joy,' you know."

Bex resisted the urge to point out that Mrs. Reilly had already told her all this last year. Instead, she asked a question that had actually been nagging at her since the last time she'd heard the story. "Does it mean 'my joy,' in Chinese?"

"Well, no. I didn't like the Chinese word for *joy*. Too hard to pronounce. And it was too foreign sounding. *Lian* is actually Hebrew for 'my joy.'

"Are you Jewish?"

"Irish. But, I liked how it sounded. You know, sort of Chinese, without actually being—"

"Chinese?"

"Exactly."

"Ah."

"But, you see, because of Lian's being Asian and all, I like to think myself particularly sensitive to issues of prejudice. I understand that while it was most likely racism that probably kept Toni from reaching her full potential—"

Toni Wright single-handedly broke the color barrier in American figure skating and went on to win several U.S. titles plus headline a half-dozen ice shows. What was it with these people and their bizarre definition of reaching one's potential?

"—But, the fact is, Toni is a fine coach for beginners and for people who just want to skate for fun or whatever. But, when it comes to training champions, anyone with any kind of potential eventually gets noticed by one of the elite coaches. Gary Gold, or Igor Marchenko. My own Lian, she was five years old when I took her out of lessons with Toni and put her with Gary. I mean, she wouldn't have gotten anywhere taking lessons from Toni."

Bex couldn't believe what she was hearing. "Have you seen Jeremy Hunt skate?"

"It doesn't matter," Mrs. Reilly waved a dismissive hand in the boy's direction. "Everyone knows he isn't champion material."

"Really? And why is that?"

"Well, for one thing, he hasn't hit his growth spurt, yet. No one can judge what kind of skater anyone is going to be until they finish growing and we see the body God has given them."

Well, okay, she did have a point there. Adolescence did tend to wreak havoc with a skater's timing and agility. But, why did Bex think there was more to this than just that?

"And then there's that father of his."

All right, now Mrs. Reilly had Bex's full attention. "What about his father?"

"Well, I'm not one to gossip . . . ."

"Oh, come on," Bex did her best to rein in the irony currently dripping from her every word like a superfluous coat of wet paint. "Just this once."

Mrs. Reilly narrowed her eyes and looked around her, first right, then left, then right again. She was either being very conscientious because she was about to cross the street, or she expected Craig Hunt to suddenly materialize out of thin air, like a Count Dracula of the skating world.

Once she was satisfied that neither was about to happen, Mrs. Reilly stood on her tiptoes so she could reach Bex's ear, and whispered, "There is something seriously wrong with that man."

Oh, that was very helpful. Talk about a lot of drama for absolutely no information. Bex couldn't help thinking of her father, a high school science teacher, who used to lob such bromides both at work and at home as, "*Lots* is not a number." Bex used to roll her eyes whenever he said it. Except that now she felt a mad urge to tell Mrs. Reilly, "*Seriously wrong* is not an actual piece of information."

But, seeing as how she was still hoping that Mrs. Reilly might actually bring forth a relevant bit of knowledge, Bex once again restrained her natural tendency toward irony and sarcasm to offer the more neutral, "For instance?"

"Well, for instance," Mrs. Reilly lowered her voice again. "I think he hates skating."

"And this qualifies as something being seriously wrong with a person?"

"With a person whose son is a skater? Yes."

Okay, again, Mrs. Reilly had the beginning of a point.

"What makes you think he hates skating? Have you observed him burning effigies of St. Ludwina?"

Mrs. Reilly stared at Bex strangely. Fortunately, Bex got that sort of thing a lot, so she knew that it meant, "What the heck are you babbling about now, Bex?"

She explained, "St. Ludwina is the patron saint of skaters."

"Oh."

"You can look it up in a book. I'll send you a copy. But, anyhow, you were saying?"

The woman clearly needed another moment to get over

her Bex experience. Once she had, though, she promptly launched into, "Mr. Hunt isn't like the other skating parents. For one thing, it's so rare seeing a father bringing his child to the rink. Usually it's the mother mostly. Now, I understand him being a widower and all, what with Mrs. Hunt dying from breast cancer like that, so tragic, really, I understand—"

"Jeremy's mother died of breast cancer?"

"That's what Mr. Hunt told me. But it was many years ago, before they moved to Hartford. I always got the feeling that's why they moved, actually, to get away from the bad memories."

"Where did they come from?"

Mrs. Reilly looked like she'd been blind-sided. "What?"

"You said that Jeremy's mother died before the Hunts moved to Hartford. Where did they move from?"

Mrs. Reilly actually had to stop and think about that. Bex could tell she was thinking because her brow was furrowed and also because, for once, she wasn't talking. Finally, she said, "You know, I don't think he ever mentioned it."

"Okay," Bex said. "I was just curious. Go on."

"Right. Well, anyway, like I was saying, he's a very peculiar man. He brings Jeremy to the rink, but he takes no interest in skating. He never asks questions or talks to the coach about how Jeremy is progressing. It's like he doesn't care."

"Maybe he doesn't."

"Well, it's unnatural. And so is the way he behaves toward the other parents. It's always a polite hello and nothing more. He never stops to chat, he never carpools, he never asks how our children are doing—"

"Do you ever ask him about Jeremy?"

"What? Jeremy? No. How could we? It's not like Mr.

Hunt behaves like a normal parent. A normal parent comes in, has a cup of coffee at the snack bar, a little chat, a little conversation. No, it's just in and out with Mr. Hunt, in and out, like some kind of factory time-clock. That's why Jeremy, no matter how talented he is, is never going to make it in skating."

"Because his father doesn't drink coffee?"

"Because his father isn't a part of the community, Ms. Levy. Skating is a very small world. Word gets around when a parent is surly or thinks he's better than the rest of us. Word gets around, and judges take that sort of thing into consideration."

"It can't matter that much. Jeremy won Sectionals."

"Oh, that. That was simply because he skated better than the other boys."

Again, Bex felt like her translator was in the shop. "That's not the name of the game?"

Mrs. Reilly looked at Bex as if she couldn't decide whether to enlighten or pity her. She apparently settled for a combination of both. "Reputation matters in our sport. That's something Mr. Hunt doesn't seem to understand. Keeping Toni as Jeremy's coach when he could have Gary or Igor—I know they've both asked about Jeremy, but Mr. Hunt refuses to switch—is not good for his boy. Plus, there's that patronizing attitude, the aloofness, the indifference. If I didn't know better, Ms. Levy, I would swear that Craig Hunt is deliberately going out of his way to sabotage his son's chances for success in skating. That's why I say Jeremy isn't championship material. He's never going to make it. His father will see to that."

Bex was thinking about what Mrs. Reilly said—the stuff that made sense, not the self-centered rambling, though her

Universal Nonsense Sorter was working double-time to make sure she assigned each utterance to the correct group—when Jeremy waved to her from center ice, signaling that he was ready to begin his long program. Bex waved back, to show that she got the message. She noted where his starting pose was, and got into position to film. Bex raised the camera to her face, centering Jeremy in the middle of the frame, taking care not to chop off either the top of his head (very amateurish) or the bottom of his skates (there was nothing more frustrating than trying to watch figure skating when you couldn't see the performer's feet). After all, this might very well prove to be her first piece of professional camera work. This could be her shooting and directing and producing and editing debut. The least she could do was make sure it didn't look as inexperienced as she actually was.

Toni flicked the switch on the tape player, filling the arena with the *Warsaw Concerto.* As soon as she did, the other skaters got out of the way. It was rink etiquette that whoever's music was playing got the right of way. Although Bex did notice that some skaters did the skedaddling thing a bit quicker than others. Ms. Lian "My Joy" Reilly, for instance, did it only at the very last second, when it looked like Jeremy was literally about to skate on top of her, and she did it so slowly that she looked liked she was being dragged off by a giant hand against her will. As it was, while Lian did ultimately move, her taking so long to do it forced Jeremy to slow his speed to make sure he avoided hitting her, and it messed up his timing entering the quadruple Salchow. Still, there was something catlike about the boy. Even though he went into the quad slower than usual and tilted at a precarious angle, some feline instinct prompted him to straighten out in the air so that, by the time his right foot touched the ground, he was in perfect position again.

If Bex hadn't been taping the program for posterity, she would have allowed herself an impressed, "wow." But, as it was, she never even got the chance to suppress it.

Because, the instant Jeremy flung both his arms out to their sides to stop the rotation of his quadruple Salchow jump through a technique called "checking out," Bex felt a strong, masculine hand grab her wrist and, without warning, yank it so hard that she not only lost Jeremy in her shot, she practically dropped the expensive camera, as well.

Furious, Bex spun around to demand an explanation for this inexcusable interruption, only to come face-to-face with a total stranger in his mid-thirties, dressed in a neatly pressed black suit and tie, his olive complexion darkened by anger, a lock of sienna hair from his bangs falling haphazardly into his face—the better to emphasize the absolute fury in his mahogany eyes.

"What the hell," he wasn't shouting, but the quiet steel in his voice was somehow more frightening, "do you think you're doing shooting video of my son?"

Five

Bex's traditional, premeditated, spontaneous response to such rude interruptions was, "Mr. Craig Hunt, I presume?" Or, at least, it would eventually be her response if said rude interruptions didn't traditionally, and in an utterly unpremeditated manner, discombobulate her to the point of not being able to saying anything at all, witty or otherwise.

"Um . . . I . . ." Bex stammered.

But, she was *thinking*, "Mr. Craig Hunt, I presume." So that had to count for something.

"Who are you?" Craig held Bex's digital camera in both hands. Was it her imagination, or was he actually squeezing it ever so slightly? Not unlike Clark Gable, whose idea of foreplay in *Gone With the Wind* was to tell Scarlett that he could squish her skull between his palms.

"I . . . uh . . ."

"Dad!" Jeremy called out, interrupting Bex's train of thought. And right when she'd been asked a question that, if given a bit more time to collect herself, she probably could have answered, too. Bex usually got her name right. Especially after a few tries. "Dad, this is Bex Levy."

"Bex Levy!" she repeated. There. She knew she'd had the answer to that one.

"She's with 24/7 and—"

"The network?" Craig demanded.

"I called her, Mr. Hunt." Toni skated up and joined the conversation at the barrier. Craig looked from her to his son, seemingly undecided about whom to glare more at first.

"Toni thought that if Bex saw me skate—"

"Bex is the 24/7 researcher, Mr. Hunt. She knows world-class skating when she sees it."

"Toni thought maybe Bex could convince you to let me skate at Nationals because I'm just as good as anyone else who's going—"

"He really is, Mr. Hunt. In fact, like I keep telling you, our Jeremy is actually better than a lot of the boys who'll be at that competition."

"Bex thinks I'm really good, Dad. She thinks I could win. Or at least get on TV. And I wouldn't have to go crazy or anything. I promise. I double promise."

"I see," Craig said. He was still calm. He was still squeezing the camera.

Bex had nothing to add. So she just nodded. Fervently. And wondered if it was too late to answer the question about what her name was.

"Ms. Wright," Craig decided Toni would be the first proud recipient of his glare, "Jeremy's lesson is over. Jeremy," he shifted his gaze over an inch and down four, addressing his son. "I will see you in the parking lot in five minutes. Ms. Levy," he flipped her camera over, gently tapping the red release button and popping out her tape. He placed it in his pocket and politely returned the camera to Bex. "Have a nice drive back to New York."

And then, without another word or a single raised syllable, he turned around and walked out of the ice rink.

Bex stared at his retreating back.

And she was out in the parking lot, already calling his name, before she realized that she'd followed him.

"Mr. Hunt, Mr. Hunt, wait!" Bex shouted, even as she wondered what she would actually say if he, in fact, heeded her request.

He heeded her request.

Craig Hunt paused, one palm resting on the trunk of his several-years-old blue Toyota. He turned around. "Yes, Ms. Levy?"

"Wait," she repeated.

"I'm waiting."

She caught up to him, also resting her hand on the trunk, facing him. She'd read that this was called "mirroring." It was supposed to make people like and trust you more. She wondered how it was working.

"Your son," she said, "he's a really good skater."

"Thank you."

"He has an excellent chance of medaling at Nationals."

"Not if he's not there."

"I don't understand," Bex wondered if whining made her mirroring more or less effective. "I mean, Mr. Hunt, I really would like to know why you won't let Jeremy go to Nationals."

"I'm sure that's true. I, however, don't have to tell you."

A valid point. With not a lot of leeway for a rejoinder. So, instead, Bex said, "Jeremy's a great kid."

"Thank you, again."

"You've done an excellent job raising him. Especially all by yourself."

Craig crossed his arms and just looked at her. Apparently, she'd reached the end of either her flattery or his politeness rope. "Toni said you were a skating expert, Ms. Levy. Is that true?"

"Um . . . yes?"

"Answer me this, then, from an expert's point of view: How many of the skaters that you interview, on average, would you say are happy? And I mean honestly, truly happy, not just temporarily appeased by a piece of gold hanging around their anorexic necks?"

"I . . . I don't know. I mean, that's not really my judgment to make, is it?"

"I walk into this rink here every day, and I see a baker's dozen of daytime talk show guests waiting to happen. Lian Reilly walks around like a zombie, mumbling, "If you believe it, it will happen" to herself every moment that she isn't on the ice. She has to say it exactly a hundred times every day and if you interrupt her she has to start all over again. Jordan Ares sued to be legally emancipated from her parents so she could skate more. She's been living alone since she was twelve. Our defending national champions in ice dancing have given each other, in no particular order: a severed finger, a dislocated shoulder, a broken jaw, and two concussions. And that's off the ice, Ms. Levy, not on it. The Junior World Champion is on Prozac, but that hasn't kept him from ripping his hair out of his head and eating it. He says it relieves stress. And I presume I don't have to tell you, of all people, about what happened to our National Champion from last year? Erin Simpson?"

No. No, he didn't have to tell Bex about it. She'd actually been the one who broke that story, live on 24/7, during their broadcast of the World Championships. It was her first attempt at a murder investigation. Bex would even say it had gone rather well. Except for the number of lives destroyed in the process.

"And that," Craig continued, "that's the snake pit you want me to let Jeremy triple-jump his way into? You just told me what a great kid he is. How long do you think that will last once big-time skating gets its paws on him?"

Mrs. Reilly had accused Craig Hunt of knowing nothing about their sport. It sounded to Bex like he knew quite a bit more than he needed to.

"But, it doesn't have to be that way," Bex insisted. "Some people leave this sport very happy and well adjusted."

"Like who?" Craig smirked. "Robby Sharpton?"

Again with Robby Sharpton. Bex made a mental note to look into this guy further. She didn't need to do a feature on him, she just needed to satisfy her own curiosity.

Craig continued, rattling off a whole list of names, from which Bex only recognized Rachel Rose and Felicia Tufts, Sharpton's two Pairs partners. The other dozen or so just wooshed over her head. The only thought that stuck was the question of why, for a man who cared so little about skating, did Craig Hunt seem to know so much about it?

"I wish you'd reconsider," Bex said, and then, since she didn't think her own reason of *because I've got a good bit of money and most of my career riding on this story* would prove particularly compelling, added, "because I think you're really hurting your son's chances of doing something fantastic with his life."

"You know what, Ms. Levy?" Craig looked over Bex's shoulder, saw Jeremy coming out of the rink, his heavy skate-bag slung over his shoulder, and gestured for him to hurry up. He waited for Jeremy to silently and with a plaintive look at Bex, drop his bag in the trunk and slide into the passenger seat before telling her, "I really don't care."

And drove away without another word.

"Well," Bex said, plopping down on a snack bar bench next to a resting Toni, "I'd say that went well."

Toni smiled. "Is it time for me to apologize for dragging you into this?"

Bex shrugged. "I let you drag me. How can anyone see that kid skate and not want to make him a star?"

"Did you ask Mr. Hunt that?"

Bex sighed. "He certainly has his reasons all nicely enumerated, doesn't he? I take it he's had lots of chances to practice his speech-making?"

"Craig Hunt and I have been having the same conversation for five years. At first, I didn't want to press it too hard. I'm not proud to say it, but I was too scared."

"Of Craig Hunt? Is he dangerous?" Bex recalled Jeremy's plaintive expression as he got into the car with his dad and, for a moment, wondered if the story here was a lot more twisted than just a father and son disagreeing over a teenager's hobby. "Is he abusive?"

Bex felt a little sick just thinking about it. Here she'd been so focused on getting the story she needed to keep from getting fired, she might have totally overlooked a desperate kid in need of salvation having nothing to do with skating.

"Oh, no, no." Toni shook her head. "Well, at least not that I know of. Sad to say, but I've worked with kids who were being abused. Jeremy doesn't show any of the symptoms. He's too sunny, too good natured. Not that I'm an expert or anything. God knows, I've missed danger signs before and lived to regret it. But, no, no, I was afraid of

Craig Hunt for a completely different reason. A rather, I'm sorry to admit, selfish one."

Bex didn't know what to say. But, if there was one crucial thing she'd learned from sitting, cramped, on the floor of a room where a seasoned feature producer was doing an interview, it was to keep quiet. Because it was amazing what a person would say to fill up the silence, rather than in response to a direct question.

"My first six months coaching Jeremy," Toni continued, "I couldn't believe what a major talent he was. I'd never seen anything like it, and I've been doing this for a lot of years. I was convinced it was just a matter of time before Mr. Hunt realized what amazing potential his son had and promptly switched him to a better-known coach. Gary, perhaps, or maybe even Igor. I was, frankly, resigned to it before our first year was even up. But, then an amazing thing happened. Mr. Hunt never said a word about switching coaches. He just paid my bills and made polite small talk and never even asked how good did I think Jeremy was? Some parents, they ask me that every blessed day. Every day, every lesson, can you imagine? 'How's he doing? How's she coming along? When do you think that Axel might be ready for competition?' Mr. Hunt never said a word. Finally, even though I was scared of losing Jeremy as a student, I figured I should say something to them both. One morning, I got up my courage, and I laid it out for them. I told Mr. Hunt that he had a very talented kid, that I honestly thought Jeremy could go all the way, that the Olympics were not outside of the realm of possibility; and I never, ever tell anyone that. It makes the parents too excited and the kids too lazy. Except, in this case, I thought I should make it clear that I wasn't just blowing smoke. Only, you know what, Bex? It was like I'd never spoken at all. Mr. Hunt just thanked me for my kind words, smiled that noncommittal smile he has, and walked out of the rink. Never brought it up again. I was the one who kept pushing for Jeremy to compete. And he just kept giving me that speech of his. I didn't push him too hard the first few years because, like I said, I was terrified of losing Jeremy to another coach. But, now . . . now it's just ridiculous. That boy has exceeded my wildest expectations and his father . . . his father. . . . Oh, I am sorry I got you into this, Bex. This is hardly your problem."

Bex asked, "Do you think everything is on the up and up with those two?"

"What do you mean? Granted, Mr. Hunt is a very strange man, yes, but, well, this is skating. Normal people don't choose to spend their lives falling down in the cold at four A.M., so the standards are a bit different."

Bex smiled. That's what she loved about Toni. The woman at least had some sense of perspective about where and who she was. And who she was working with.

"Mrs. Reilly told me that Mr. Hunt told her Jeremy's mother died from breast cancer. Jeremy said it was a car accident."

"Mrs. Reilly," Toni said, "*has* chosen to spend her life in the cold at four A.M. I would not count her as my most reliable source of information. She could have misunderstood. Or, most likely, miseavesdropped."

"Hmm," Bex said. Because it was the sound that best matched her mood. And then she asked, "So what do we do next?"

"We?" Toni stood up, balancing with some difficulty on her skates upon a carpeted floor. "You still want to be involved in this, Bex?"

"Well, I kind of, sort of staked my career on it."

"Oh, Bex . . ."

"I know. Not one of my shiniest moments. But, hey, I

suppose I could convince myself that I'm one of those people who loves a challenge."

"In that case, what can I do to help keep you from the unemployment line?"

"I want to try talking to Craig Hunt again. Maybe away from the rink and Jeremy and everything, he'll be more reasonable. Do you have his home address? I could go there. I've got nothing but time on my hands, right now."

"I presume he's at work at this time, Bex. Although how do you figure barging in on him at home might make him more reasonable?"

"Well, where does he work?" Bex hoped that by asking another question she could cover up her lack of an answer to the first one. The one where Toni wanted to know just how exactly did Bex figure that barging in on Craig at home—or at work—might make him more reasonable?

Toni hesitated. She looked at Bex for a long beat, thinking God-knows-what, and all of it probably accurate. She sighed. And then she said, "I'll write down both addresses for you."

Craig Hunt, Bex learned, worked for a small, mom-and-pop electronics store, Hiroshi Electronics, as a sort of jack-of-all-trades salesman and Mr. Fix-It on call for the customers.

"The man can fix anything. He touches an appliance or a computer and it just hums back to life, like magic," Mrs. Jennifer Hiroshi, a slender redhead in her mid-fifties standing behind the cash register, told Bex in response to her questions about their employee. "If we could only count on him to show up when he says he will and actually tell us when he won't, he'd be perfect."

"Son-of-a-bitch skips out with no notice so regularly, I

tell Jenny—consider his being in one day notice that he won't be in the next." Mr. Michael Hiroshi, his graying jet black hair tied into a ponytail at the base of his neck with a rubber band, laughed at his own joke, then admitted, "It's not that funny. But we put up with it. Why? Because he's friggin' good. When Hunt's here, he gets more stuff done in a day than two guys I hired last summer for a test run did in a week. And, besides, Jenny feels sorry for him. Single dad, blah, blah, bring out the violins."

"Did Mr. Hunt come in today?" Bex asked.

"Ha!" Mr. Hiroshi barked. "Today is what? Wednesday? He worked Tuesday, Monday, and yeah, even last Friday. I'd say he figures he deserves a break today."

"That," Jenny laid a vaguely restraining hand on her husband's arm, "would be a 'no.'"

He winked at her affectionately in response, then turned his attention back to Bex. "Why are you looking for him, anyway? He owe you money? Because Craig Hunt is just an employee here. We've got nothing do with where he goes or what he does. Or who he owes."

"It's a . . ." Bex faltered. "It's a private matter."

"Well, then, we've certainly got nothing to do with anything like that."

"So, even though he was supposed to be at work today—I mean, Jeremy told me his dad was going to be at work today—you've got no idea where Craig Hunt is?"

"Not a clue."

"Thanks for your help," Bex said. And tried to suppress a mild feeling of panic.

Driving from Hiroshi Electronics to the address Toni gave her for Craig Hunt's home, Bex told herself not to panic. There was no reason to panic. Why the heck was she panicking? After all, she'd heard it herself from the no-reason-to-lie Hiroshis: Craig Hunt didn't show up for work all the time. There was nothing strange or suspicious about today. In fact, considering his record, wouldn't Craig's actually showing up for work be *more* suspicious, under the circumstances? So why was Bex panicking? There was no reason to panic.

That is, until her buzzing the Hunts' door elicited no answer.

But, still, no reason to panic.

Why was Bex assuming that a man who regularly skipped out on work would then spend his free day at home? That was silly. There was no reason to assume that. Bex was sure that Craig and maybe even Jeremy were probably playing hooky somewhere on the streets of the great city of Hartford. It was probably a family tradition. Something they did all the time. A bonding thing. There was no reason to assume that Craig and Jeremy not being around meant anything at all.

That is, until she found the presence of mind to call their building's superintendent. And was informed that, a mere hour ago (probably while Bex was talking to the Hiroshis) Craig Hunt had asked the super to cancel his cable TV and throw away (not hold; throw away) his mail.

And took off for parts unknown, Jeremy and two suitcases in tow.

The super didn't remember if Jeremy had been carrying his skate-bag.

Six

Now, Bex thought, might be a good time to panic. It was, after all, one thing not to get an interview. It was quite another to drive the subject into hiding. Actually, maybe she should feel proud of herself. She bet that didn't even happen to the *60 Minutes* guys that often. But, then again, the *60 Minutes* guys had other people they could interview. Bex's only two options had just fled the scene. And taken her one, pathetic little reel of tape with them. She wasn't just back where she'd started. She was now also down a piece of 24/7 digi-beta stock. Which Bex had a very strong feeling Gil would make her pay for.

Sitting on some rung of the depression ladder that fell a notch below doom, gloom, and pestilence, Bex did the only thing she could think of. She returned to the rink. To whine.

But first she asked Toni, "Is this maybe something Craig and Jeremy do all the time? Just take off for vacation in the middle of the day? In the middle of the week? In the middle of the school year? With their cable turned off and their mail in the trash?"

"No," Toni said.

"Oh," Bex said.

"But, they do travel a lot," Toni admitted. "All over the world, too. Though they always tell me about it in advance. It's not like Jeremy to just not show up for a lesson. They know it's my livelihood. They're very considerate about giving me plenty of notice. And Jeremy is always bringing back souvenirs from Europe and Asia. They even went to Africa on safari last year. Mr. Hunt may not want Jeremy's life disturbed by skating, but he certainly has no compulsions about pulling the boy out of school whenever he gets the whim to take a trip."

Bex thought about it. "Maybe Mr. Hunt is an international drug dealer."

Toni looked at her funny.

"Or a spy. Maybe they're both spies. That's why Jeremy can't go to Nationals or ever be photographed. Because it will blow his cover. He's not really a thirteen-year-old skating prodigy. He's a fifty-five-year-old Lithuanian ex-National champion turned double agent."

"Yes," Toni said. "There's a lot of spying to be done at the ice rink. Is he exploring the possibilities of triple Axels as a weapon of mass destruction?"

Now, normally, Bex was a major fan of sarcasm. In fact, she suspected that, sans sarcasm, the bulk of her conversations would be limited to simple declarative sentences like, "See Jane run." Alas, Bex's overall love of sarcasm had a teeny, tiny little caveat: She really only liked it when said sarcasm flowed from her to someone else. She wasn't so big on the vice-a-versa.

So, rather than admit when she'd been outsnottied, Bex

changed the subject. She asked Toni, "But don't you think their lifestyle is a little weird?"

Toni pointed to Lian Reilly through the glass separating the snack bar from the ice surface. She said, "Lian's father lives alone in the family's dream house in San Jose, California. Lian's mother lives in a one-bedroom apartment down the street so that Lian can train here. Lian gets up every morning at three A.M., skates for three hours, does an hour of stretching, an hour of home-school, an hour of ballet, then three more hours of skating. She goes to bed at six P.M. And, you know what, Bex? I don't see anything wrong with what she, her mother, or her father are doing. So, under the circumstances, what exactly would I know about defining weird lifestyles?"

"I see your point," Bex said. And then she added, with less sarcasm, lest it come bouncing back and smack her on the nose, "I'm sorry it looks like I cost you a student, Toni."

Toni shrugged. "I told you, I've been expecting to lose Jeremy from the first lesson I gave him. I never expected to have him for five years. It always happens that way. Let them show an ounce of potential and it's bye-bye, Ms. Wright. The saddest part is, sometimes I really grow to like the kids. Not as skaters, necessarily. Just as kids. Those are the really tough ones to let go."

"Like Jeremy?"

"He's a good boy. And, I know this sounds egotistical, but I just don't trust that any other coach will really care about him as much as I did. I mean, they'll care about the medals he can win them and the money he can pay them, but as soon as he isn't useful anymore, they'll drop him like the technical mark after a fall in the short program."

Universal Skating Translator: The short program required a mandatory deduction for every element not completed. Dropping someone like the technical mark of a short program meant dropping them down really far and really fast. What, in the real world, would be called a "hot potato."

Toni continued, "I've seen it happen—coaches dropping a kid they've practically raised without a word of warning, and it's tragic. The more sensitive kids don't know what hit them." She looked out onto the ice and spied a girl of about seventeen, her chestnut hair tied back into a ponytail, her knee supported by a cloth brace as she slowly skated around the rink, biting her lip either in determination or pain. Toni said, "That's Sondra. She and her partner were fourth at Nationals last year. They had a really good chance of making the World Team. But, then Sondra got injured and, while she was still in surgery, her coach had a new girl lined up for her partner—someone younger and smaller. The worst part was, Sondra had been living with her coach, sharing a room with the coach's daughter, for Pete's sake, traveling with the family for vacations—for the last six years. She called her 'my other mom.' Well, her other mom sold her down the river."

Bex said, "You know, Toni, I have a feeling Craig didn't take Jeremy out of town so he could find him a better coach. I really think there is something more going on here."

"Oh, I know, I know. I was just . . . just thinking out loud, I guess. When you get to be my age, the kids sometimes blend one into the other. But, there are some you remember. And wonder if there was anything you could have done to change the situation."

The look on Toni's face suggested she was having a rather wistful moment. A combination of "Regrets, I've had a few" and "The Road Not Taken," thrown into a blender with "Thanks for the memories." The woman had led a fascinating life, and Bex was sure that even her regrets were more interesting than most people's achievements.

But, they were talking about Bex's future now, not Toni's past. So Bex mentally promised to respect her elders in a little while. Just as soon as she got this whole potential-for-losing-her-job situation under control. She pressed on, "Do you have any idea where Jeremy and Craig might have gone? Did Jeremy ever talk about their having, I don't know, a vacation home somewhere?"

"No. No vacation home." Toni came out of her reverie with relative ease, apparently having reached the conclusion that, no, there wasn't anything she could have done to change the past, so let's move on with it. "It was mostly the exotic vacations that they took. I can't even think of any place they went to more than once, to be honest."

"Exotic vacations to Europe and Africa cost a lot of money. Craig Hunt was practically a repairman. And he was paying for daily skating lessons on top of that. How much are those?"

"About a dollar a minute for five twenty-minute lessons a week. Plus ice time."

"And the cost of his skates?"

"Four hundred dollars for good boots, about the same for blades."

"Right, so let's say a thousand dollars a year just for equipment, and another," Bex did the math quickly in her head, happy that five times twenty made such a malleable number and rounding off the weeks in a year to make her life easier, "plus five thousand dollars for lessons, then ice time and rink admission and clothes and other incidentals, and this is easily costing Craig Hunt almost ten thousand dollars a year. So, how does a guy who fixes toasters and computers for a living—when he feels like showing up, that is—how does he afford skating, and safaris in Africa, and jaunts to Europe at the drop of a hat?"

"I don't know, Bex," Toni said.

"Aren't you curious?"

"I wasn't until this moment."

"Did Jeremy have any friends at the rink? Someone I could talk to about if Jeremy maybe said anything about where he and his dad were heading for next?"

"Jeremy was a pretty friendly boy, you could try talking to any of the kids. But, honestly, Bex, if information is what you're looking for, there's really only one all-knowing source."

Toni moved slightly to the side so that Bex might have a better view of the cabal of which she spoke. And there they sat. In the furthest corner of the rink, an even half dozen. Some wore fur coats, some clutched a cup of steaming coffee for warmth, still others sat on a specially heated cushion. All stared intently at the ice, their lips poised in concentration, their brows furrowed in contemplation, their toes tapping with agitation.

"You really should talk to the skating mothers, Bex."

A frigid wind blew through the rink and all around them it went pitch black. A glaring spotlight shone itself on the group from above, and a dramatic musical sting—like a soap opera organ announcing something particularly dire—filled the air.

Well, all right, maybe what really happened was that someone opened the door from the rink to the lobby and raised a slight chill, the overhead lights briefly blinked when the candy machine in the corner was turned on, and the boom of theatrical music was just the dramatic beginning of yet another *West Side Story* program. But, this was Bex's world and she was allowed to interpret it in any way she saw fit. Toni had just suggested that she go talk to the skating mothers. That certainly warranted a dramatic sting.

And a nervous gulp.

"Um, okay," Bex said, figuring that showing fear would just throw the fur-lined gang into even more of a killing frenzy. "Which one of them, you know, which one of them is which?"

"Well," Toni counted off from the woman closest to them, the one in the central, prime seat. "I think you know Lian's mother, Amanda Reilly. She's kind of the undisputed queen, here. What with Lian being the reigning Senior National Bronze Medalist. Usually, you'd expect Jordan Ares's mom to claim the best seat—it's the only one with an unobstructed view of every corner—because Jordan medaled at Worlds last year and Lian didn't. But Jordan is actually an emancipated minor, so the spot is Amanda's by default. And then next to her are Mrs. Keller-Dakota and Mrs. Stein. Their children are the Center's top-ranked dance team."

"Wait, wait," Bex said. "Those two parents hate each other. I remember because last year at Nationals I was trying to interview the kids, and Mrs. Keller-Dakota spent fifteen minutes telling me how they're being forced to pay more than their share of the bills since Mrs. Stein refuses to pitch in for travel expenses, because she thinks, since they have the boy and there are a lot fewer boys to go around than girls, the Keller-Dakotas should be the ones to pay for travel. Mrs. Keller-Dakota called Mrs. Stein a . . . let me see if I remember exactly, a 'miserly, morose mental case with delusions of grandeur and more hair on her upper lip than Stalin.' I remember because it's so rare that I get a good alliteration and Communist Party leader reference in the same sentence. It was definitely a 'miserly, morose mental case with delusions of grandeur and more hair on her upper lip than Stalin.' And those two sit together?"

"Every day, every practice."

"Why?"

"It's how things are done, Bex."

"I see . . . ."

"The other three women . . . Mrs. Bosley's son lost to Jeremy at Regionals and Sectionals, so she hasn't let the boys speak since; I don't think she'll be able to tell you much. Mrs. Knox tried to convince Jeremy to skate pairs with her daughter, and when he turned her down—rather politely, I think, and besides, it's not Jeremy's fault, I'm the one who advised him against it; the girl is too big for him—she kind of erased him from her universe. Finally, Mrs. Hernandez, I don't think I've ever heard her say a word to any of the other parents. She just sits there and watches and yells at her child in Spanish periodically. I have no idea what she thinks or knows. She doesn't really need to be involved with the club beyond the coaches. Her husband works for the embassy, they're not American citizens. Her daughter doesn't compete on the same U.S. track as the other kids. She's already qualified for Junior Worlds representing Spain."

Bex tried to absorb the plethora of information, wishing she'd thought to take notes when Toni first started. She asked, "And you really think these are the people who can help me find Craig and Jeremy?"

Toni smiled grimly. "These are our Oracles of Delphi, Bex. If there is something worth knowing around here, they know it. You just have to ask them the right questions."

Oh. Was that all? That didn't sound so hard. Sort of like roping a bull. Without a rope.

Approaching the pack gingerly, Bex dragged her feet

along the threadbare carpet, trying to come up with a pithy opening line that wouldn't make her snooping too obvious.

"Hi," Bex said, swallowing the urge to add, "Hi . . . skating moms."

Six heads swiveled in her direction. The neat trick was, they all somehow managed to plant one eye on her, while keeping the other on the ice.

"Hello, Bex," Amanda Reilly chuckled brightly. "I guess that feature you were planning on Jeremy went up in smoke, so to speak, didn't it?"

The boy and his father had been missing for less than a few hours. How did this group already know all about it?

"You wanted to do a feature on Jeremy Hunt?" The woman Toni identified as Mrs. Bosley—mother of Loser Boy—tried to chuckle as merrily as Amanda had. It proved a bit tricky, what with the practically visible venom squirting through her front teeth. "What was your angle, Ms. Levy? Fluke wins that can never be repeated?"

Bex asked, "Didn't Jeremy win both Regionals and Sectionals this season?"

"Only because he skated better," Mrs. Bosley sniffed. "If Jeremy had missed his quad and Eric landed both his triple Axels, Eric would have been the clear winner."

"Eric has lovely presentation. It's world-class. Head and shoulders above Jeremy," Mrs. Reilly chimed in and patted Mrs. Bosley's hand reassuringly.

"Just like your Lian," Mrs. Bosley chimed back, and the two women beamed at each other.

Oh, how cute, Bex thought, *ice-based, delusional co-dependency*. Live and in color.

Bex asked, "Do any of you have any idea where Jeremy and his dad might have gone?"

"They probably ran away because they couldn't handle the competition," Mrs. Bosley mused. "Winning Regionals and Sectionals because the competition didn't skate up to their ability is one thing. Nationals is a whole new ballgame. Craig Hunt was terrified of Jeremy going head-to-head with my Eric at Nationals. He knew Jeremy didn't have the skills to compete on that level."

"It happens quite a bit," Mrs. Keller-Dakota piped up. "Quite a few skaters reach a certain level, and then they just don't have the fortitude to go on. It's just as much of a mind game as it is a physical one. Kids crack. They can't take it."

"Like Rachel Rose," Mrs. Stein said. "Do you remember Rachel Rose? She trained here as well, but many years ago. I think she was Lucian Pryce's girl. An exquisite skater. Born to skate pairs. A true, blooming flower on the ice. But, she was too fragile. She and Robby Sharpton could have been World Champions. Instead, she just up and ran away, disappeared without a trace at the height of her career. I hear she's living in seclusion somewhere. A commune, I think."

"Oh!" Mrs. Reilly exclaimed. "That's just like Gabrielle Cassidy. The girl who slashed her wrists at Worlds a few years back after missing a step in the *Yankee Polka*. I hear she gave up skating, too. Went to school and got a degree in psychology, or some other such nonsense. It's so sad, she had so much potential."

"Or that girl, what was her name?" Mrs. Bosley put in. "The one who they forced to quit because she got so skinny and her front teeth rotted out from all the vomiting? Oh, what was her name? Because I don't think she got a fair shake. Who cared what was going on in her personal life, that's no one's business, in my opinion. She looked so lovely on the ice. Long and lean and toned. It was a thrill to watch her."

"Or how about that boy with the temper? Didn't he end up going to jail finally?"

"Or the one who was his main rival? I think it was drugs in his case. Irony is, of course, he skated much better high than he ever did sober."

"How about that brother and sister team who had the total meltdown at Nationals after he dropped her on her head?"

"The national champion who got knocked up right before Worlds . . ."

"And Erin Simpson, of course . . ."

"Oh, God, yes, Erin Simpson . . . I doubt we'll ever see her on the ice, again. . . ."

"Focus!" Bex wanted to shout. Naturally, she did not. Primarily because, despite her oft-stated aversion to gossip and voyeurism, this was actually kind of interesting. Bex had no idea so many seemingly promising people had dropped out of skating for one reason or another.

"But, about Jeremy Hunt . . ." Bex prompted.

"Good riddance," Mrs. Stein said. "He was a nice enough boy, but that father of his . . . ."

"I'm not sorry to see him go," Mrs. Keller-Dakota agreed.

"Creepy. Wouldn't you call him just creepy?" Mrs. Bosley looked around the cabal for support. "Always just lurking, not saying anything."

"And the way he obsessed over that poor child," Mrs. Reilly vaulted into the lead of Bex's unofficial "Delusion of the Day Poll." "I've never seen anything like it. He acted like Jeremy was the most precious thing in the world. Like we were all out to kidnap him or something!"

"Did you say kidnap?" Bex perked up as a possibility she'd never previously considered bloomed before her in all its obviousness. "Craig was afraid of Jeremy being kidnapped?"

"He certainly acted as if he was. Always watching him, keeping their address secret in the club handbook. I once asked him, trying to be polite, to make conversation, it's not like Mr. Hunt gave you a lot to talk about, he never opened his mouth except to answer a direct question. I asked him where he and Jeremy were from, before Hartford. 'Out West,' he said. Well, where out west, I asked. He just walked away. Just walked away! Can you believe the rudeness?"

"What about Jeremy's mother?" Bex asked.

"She's dead," five women answered in unison. Even Mrs. Hernandez nodded firmly. Bex guessed this was the one fact they knew for certain, and each was eager to be the first to share it.

"Did Jeremy ever talk about her?"

"No."

"Never."

"Not at all."

Bex nodded. And smiled. And had her answer.

Seven

"It's obvious," she told Toni triumphantly. "I'm surprised I didn't see it right away. I've been watching *Lifetime* movies for practically all my life. Craig and Jeremy's mother are divorced. The mom has custody and Craig kidnapped him and went on the run. That's why he's so secretive about where they're from and why he doesn't want Jeremy to go to Nationals. His mom might see them on TV and figure out where her son is."

"It's a good theory," Toni agreed. "But, where does his money fit in?"

"His money?"

"Wasn't one of the reasons you suspected him of being an international drug dealer and/or spy because Craig Hunt seems to have a lot more money than a man in his alleged situation should have? If he's on the run from the law, wouldn't he lose access to his bank accounts and whatnot?"

Bex said, "Maybe his wealthy family is bank-rolling

him. Secretly. Craig is probably very rich. I mean, it's always the rich parent that wins custody, isn't it?"

"If Craig is the rich parent who got custody, why would he need to kidnap Jeremy from his mother?"

"You know, you're sucking all the fun out of this for me, Toni." Bex sighed. She rested her chin on her hands and looked up at Toni. "You're not buying my theory, are you?"

"To be honest, Bex, at this point, any answer is as good as another. I taught Jeremy for five years, and I have no idea what went on in his life. It's a bit too late for me to start guessing now." Toni crossed her arms against her chest and surveyed Bex from head to toe. "Besides, the way I see it, you're the one with the more pressing problem these days."

"Me?"

"You, Bex. Do you have any idea what you're going to tell Gil Cahill?"

As a matter of fact, Bex did. She polished her speech on the drive back to New York and added the crowning touches while riding the elevator up to 24/7's corporate offices. She did the final edit while waiting for Ruth to tell her if Gil was available. And, upon crossing the threshold into his palatial office, she promptly forgot it all.

"Gil . . ." Bex said, hoping to cover her stage fright with salutations. Every gear in her brain creaked like the sound effects for a cheap horror movie.

"Where's my footage, Bex?" Gil didn't even look up from the stack of yellow sticky-note covered papers he was reading. He merely gestured at the VCR in his corner.

"I don't have it."

Now, he looked up. Not that Bex preferred it that way. "Where is it?"

"I—Jeremy Hunt's father. He took it."

Gil actually looked amused. He put down his pen and everything. For over a year, Bex had submitted story after story idea to Gil in the hopes of amusing him. She failed miserably each and every time. Who knew all it would take was her utter humiliation. "The kid's dad mugged you?"

"In a manner of speaking."

"That's really funny, Bex."

"I suspected you were amused." *The smirk kind of gave it away.*

"So, you've got nothing, is that what you're telling me?"

"Not exactly." The microscopic thought jumper cables she'd dispatched into her cerebral cortex at the first sign of brain freeze finally kicked in, and the reluctant gears began spewing out the speech Bex had so painfully rehearsed all during her journey home. Alas, it was now spewing at a pace faster than Bex's mouth could keep up with it; but them was the breaks, was them not?

"Gil," she tried to keep from tripping over her tongue while still getting out everything she'd intended, "did you know there was a girl who slit her wrists at Worlds a couple of years ago? And another one who ran away to live in a commune? And a National Champion who got arrested for drugs, and a brother who dropped his sister on her head—or the other way around, I'm not sure about that one, yet . . . . And then, there was some guy named Robby Sharpton, who everyone says never lived up to his potential, and a girl who ruined her teeth from throwing up too much, and—"

"Bex?"

"Yes?" She felt like a *Top Gun* jet abruptly stopped by those cords they strung across Navy aircraft carriers.

"Are you pitching that we interrupt our regularly scheduled programming to run random episodes of *The Jerry Springer Show?*

"No," Bex said. "I'm pitching that we do a piece for Nationals about all the skaters who abruptly dropped out of the sport. A sort of "Where Are They Now?" with a twist. The way I figure, we've got footage of all these people on file. We track them down and get the real story about why they quit. It could get us a lot of attention. Skating fans have been wondering for years about what really happened to, for instance, Rachel Rose or Gabrielle Cassidy or Robby Sharpton. We'll be the first ones to provide them with real answers."

Gil leaned back in his chair. He picked up his pen and made a swish mark in the air. But, he didn't say anything. He just looked at Bex expectantly, waiting for some mysterious "more."

"Because half the footage will be historical from our own archives, this piece will cost half the price of shooting a brand new one, from scratch."

Gil said, "Hop to it, Bex."

She very much wanted to commence hopping. A sign-off on a feature project from Gil was the equivalent of winning a lottery the grand prize of which was the Holy Grail. Bex was very, very happy. She was also very, very nervous. Because, all the while Bex had been blithely telling Gil, "We'll track them down and get the real story about why they quit," she'd also had not the slightest idea about how one—or more importantly, she—might actually go about doing that.

On the one hand, Bex was a professional researcher. Her job was to find out stuff, and she was pretty good at it. On the other hand, these were people who had made it clear that they did not wish to be found.

Gabrielle Cassidy proved to be the easiest one. Knowing that she'd gotten a Ph.D. in sports psychology, Bex simply did an academic search of dissertations, located her university, and, from the alumni director, got Gabrielle's current phone number. When Bex called, she learned from Gabrielle herself that the formerly suicidal ice-dancer had started her own training center, where the focus was on a nonpressured atmosphere for the young athletes. Apparently, the children were all deliriously happy and well adjusted. Alas, not one of them had managed to win a medal above the Regional level. It was sweet as hell and might have made a wonderful Disney movie. But, Bex seriously doubted this story would prove dramatic enough to hold Gil's attention.

Her next subject was Rachel Rose. Here, it seemed, they might actually get something juicy. From the clippings in their 24/7 file, it really did seem like R&R (Rachel and Robby) were headed for the major big time. And then, all of a sudden, it wasn't an injury, it wasn't a coaching problem, it wasn't even, as far as Bex could tell, an official partner break-up: Rachel Rose simply fell off the face of the earth.

She didn't issue a press release wishing Robby and America's future pairs all the very best luck in the world. She didn't hold a press conference, explaining how the decision to go on their separate ways was utterly mutual and that she and Robby were still the best of friends. Even her coach, Lucian Pryce, seemed mystified. In every newspaper article, his only quote seemed to be, "None of us are really certain what the heck happened here. It's been like a bomb going off, we're shocked and we're trying to make sense of the whole thing." Rachel's parents (who, probably just to make Bex's life more difficult, had both since died) told the press, "Rachel hasn't shared with us her reasons for quitting or for so suddenly leaving town. We are as disappointed as her many fans. We, too, were looking forward to many more years of her wonderful performances." (One of the tabloids also had the chutzpah to print how much money in endorsements and ice-show appearances Rachel's disappearance would cost her parents and coach, who were comanagers of her career. A bomb of disappointment, indeed). As for Robby Sharpton, his authorized statement was limited to, "I've switched partners before. I can do it again. I don't need Rachel Rose to be a champion. I can do it without her." There was also a picture of him with his supportive wife and the ex-partner he'd apparently referred to, Felicia Tufts Sharpton, by his side. She gazed upon Robby adoringly with an expression obviously cribbed from Nancy Reagan.

And, according to Robby's file, Felicia's support wasn't limited to just the adoring glances. When Rachel disappeared, so did Robby's sole source of funding (the Rose family had been paying his expenses, as wasn't uncommon in the skating world. Since male partners, especially talented ones, were so much harder to come by than females, it was assumed that the girl would bear the bulk of the costs. After all, at a certain point, buying a partner was really no different than buying the best skates or costumes or coaches. It was just another career necessity. And investment in the future). Without Rachel and her parents, though, Robby couldn't afford to continue skating at the level he'd become accustomed to (Bex briefly wondered if he shouldn't have sued for some sort of skater's alimony). He could have presumably found himself another sugar-partner, but from what Bex read, it seemed as if Robby had been pretty badly pissed off by Rachel's defection and wasn't about to risk putting his career in another person's hands again. He decided to return to the Singles career he'd abandoned after winning the U.S. Novice and Junior Championships. Which is where Felicia came in. She single-handedly took on the full, financial support of her husband, hustling for sponsors, taking out bank loans, working odd jobs, begging her own (not very happy looking, if the newspapers were to be believed) parents, all to facilitate Robby's traveling to the then U.S.S.R. for a chance to work with a legendary Russian coach. Whether or not all that intense work paid off, Bex supposed, depended primarily on your definition of "Potential," with a side dish of "Living up to." Robby won a U.S. Bronze Medal his first year competing as a Senior Man. He went on to win two silvers and even a gold. He qualified for the 1990 and the 1994 U.S. Olympic team. At the latter event, he finished fifth. Out of the medals. What did an ice-dancer she'd interviewed tell Bex last season? "Fourth place might as well be forty-fourth." What did that say about fifth place, then?

Especially since, after that Olympics, Robby Sharpton just disappeared. Well, not the way Rachel had. Robby actually followed protocol and held the perfunctory press conference, reciting how much he'd enjoyed his many diverse years as a competitor but how it was now time to move on to new challenges. His monotonous tone and lack of sincerity practically leapt off the page. In the picture, he looked shell-shocked. As if the whole time he was reading his carefully prepared statement, he was wondering where all those life plans he'd made had gone. After that lackluster performance, there were no more records on Robby Sharpton.

That was the problem with the 24/7 files. They weren't intended to be complete. They were intended to give the announcers something to talk about before and after (and, according to many skating fans, unfortunately *during*) the time the skater was on the ice. As soon as Robby stopped competing, 24/7 stopped keeping records on him. How very, very inconsiderate of them. Didn't they know that, what, ten years down the line, Bex would be trying to track down the missing man in the hope that he could shed some revelatory light on what had happened to his Pairs partner five years earlier? Couldn't Bex's researching predecessors have planned ahead or something?

Stuck now without any tangible leads, Bex prepared to engage in some Basic Research 101 (no, Basic Research 50—the one for Mr. Kotter's Sweathogs). The one which screamed that the logical person to call first would be Lucian Pryce, Rachel and Robby's coach at the time of the infamous disappearance. Fortunately, Bex already had a tentative, professional relationship with the man, having interviewed him a year earlier for her feature article on Toni. Lucian was the white Pairs partner with whom Toni won her National Pairs titles all those years ago. They used to teach together at the Connecticut Training Center before Lucian got an offer to head up the faculty at the Colorado OTC and left about a decade earlier. A few years after Rachel's disappearance.

When Bex initially interviewed him, he'd been very complimentary about Toni, about her skating, especially praising her perseverance and bravery in the face of obvious racism from the judges, the other skaters, and their Federation ("Can you imagine it? There were coaches who not only wouldn't dare train her, they wouldn't even let their students share the same ice! Imbeciles! She was the most talented creature in their midst and they were letting stupid politics get in the way of success! Morons! Fools! Losers!"). But, at the same time as he was going on and on about Toni's incredible courage and unequalled skating ability, he also managed to take several swipes at women skaters in general, noting how, in the past twenty years, they hadn't pushed their technical skills nearly as far as the men had, how they had a tendency to crumble in competition, how trying to seriously train one was the equivalent of riding a perennial hormone train destined for Tantrumville. In short, Lucian Pryce may have given Bex several laudatory quotes about Toni, but overall, a cloud of general misogyny appeared to hover, like smog, around each compliment. At the time, Bex wondered what else she should have expected from a man who married his first Olympic Gold Medal–winning student, despite her being ten years younger, and, shortly after she was killed in a car accident, married his second Olympic Gold Medalist—this one barely older than his daughter.

Which was why, speaking to him now by phone, Bex wasn't at all surprised to hear, after the perfunctory hellos and "Oh, yes, yes, I remember you, the girl doing Toni's piece. I saw that. Read it. There wasn't enough about me," Lucian Pryce told her. "You know what the main problem is with Pairs skating, Bex? You're absolutely required to have a girl in it."

Bex wondered if now would be a good time to tell Lucian about the new International Gay Games, which actually offered competitions for same-sex pairs and dance teams, but then she decided he wasn't the sort of man who would find the information useful or even amusing. In the year Bex had spent swirling about the skating whirlpool, she'd made one key observation: The men of figure skating all tended to fall into the categories of One: Gay, Well Adjusted, and Open; Two: Gay and Closeted, Thus Coming Off as Strangely Asexual; Three: Gay and Prone to Macho Posturing to Convince People That They Weren't; and Four: Straight and Prone to Even More Macho Posturing Lest Anyone Think They Might Belong in any of the Previous Categories. Lucian Pryce, she suspected, was definitely a Type Four kind of guy. And no, for the record, she had never, as of yet, met a skating man who fit into a possible fifth category: Straight and Secure Enough Not to Beat You Over the Head With It.

But, enough about Bex and her observations. The one thing all of the men had in common, no matter what their category, was that none of them wanted to be blatantly confronted with which segment they actually fit in. And so Bex swallowed her urge to enlighten Lucian about Dance and Pairs requirements for the International Gay Games, and instead stuck to the topic at hand, asking him, "You weren't a fan of Rachel Rose then, I take it?"

"Rachel Rose," Lucian scoffed. "She could skate, I'll give you that. A natural. Everything looked like it came easy for her. Well, I suppose being rich will help with that. She never had to work for a single thing in her life, why should skating have been any different?"

"Was she a better skater than Felicia Tufts? Did you agree with Robby's decision to change partners and skate with her, instead?"

"Agree? It was my idea! I told Robby to switch from Felicia to Rachel. You want to talk about being a natural? You take whatever Miss Rachel had, you double it, then you multiply it by a hundred and one, and you might come close to what my Robby had in just the tips of his fingers. We've got a problem here in America, Bex. I'm sure you know, you've been to Nationals. Our boy skaters, they're horrible. Putrid. Oh, not all of them. Just most. And you know why that is?"

"Um? Why?" Bex was having a hard time figuring out which questions were rhetorical and which ones required at least a grunt on her part. This seemed to be the latter.

"It's because we all grow up being taught to think you can't be masculine and graceful at the same time. Bullshit! You ever see a boxer dancing around his opponent? A football player outrunning an entire defensive line? A basketball player hovering suspended in midair for a slam dunk? That isn't grace? It's poetry in motion! But try to convince a boy to do the same thing on the ice, and suddenly you're putting him on a one-way train to Faggotville!"

Now Bex really did have to physically bite her tongue to keep from asking if Faggotville might be on the way to Tantrumville, and what sort of thesaurus-challenged people were naming all these fine towns, anyway?

"So who do we get in our figure skating programs? The best of the best? The boys with the most athletic potential? The gifted ones who could have just as easily been champion boxers or football and basketball players? No! We get the kids too spastic to stay upright in hockey, so their parents stick them in figure skating to use up the lessons they already paid for! Oh, well, them and the actual fags, of course, but there's nothing you can do about them, and at least those boys have some potential, if only as costume designers farther down the line. But the rest? The rest? The ones who've failed at absolutely every other athletic endeavor? These are the ones we're supposed to turn into champions? It's a travesty. It's a national disgrace!"

"Except for Robby Sharpton," Bex prompted. Much as she enjoyed listening to right wing rants on a variety of subjects, she did have a reason for making this call. And she was paying for the long distance, too.

"Except for Robby Sharpton. Pure talent and a real man's man, to boot. He was lucky I rescued him from Toni when I did. A few more months with her and . . ." Lucian sighed. "Don't get me wrong, Toni is a fine enough coach for girls. She's got a lot to teach them, if maybe not all about skating, at least about being a lady. Toni's an honest-to-goodness lady and that's important, a lot of those spoiled brats would do well to take a lesson. But, give her a boy to teach and, what do you know, a couple of years down the line, she's turned him into a girl as sure as if she'd taken a pair of scissors to his balls!"

Bex winced at the vivid imagery. And thought of Jeremy Hunt. He certainly hadn't seemed castrated to her.

"You took over teaching Robby from Toni?"

"I had to. Couldn't let her turn a boy that good into a girl. Besides, Toni doesn't train real champions. Everyone knows that."

Yes, apparently . . . .

"I taught Robby singles for a couple of years. Took him to National Champion in Novice and in Junior, too. But, the problem is, you want to make that jump to Seniors, you need money. A lot of it. And Robby didn't even have a little. Kid practically slept and ate at the rink, and I don't think I ever saw his parents around. I gave him lessons for free. Got the club to throw in free ice-time, too, on account of his being so good and representing us at Nationals. But, when it came time to move up to Seniors, I didn't know what we were going to do. That's why, when the Tufts came to me and asked if Robby would be interested in doing Pairs with Felicia—them picking up all the expenses, of course—I had to say yes. Only way Robby could keep skating, really. And Felicia, she was a good little skater. Hard worker. Got too nervous, though, in competition. Robby really had to put up with a lot from her. She'd cry and make herself sick practically every day. And she could never really take some constructive criticism.

High-strung, that was the thing. Rachel was better in that respect. Cool. Too cool, I suppose. That Grace Kelly I'm-above-it-all sort of thing. Mommy and Daddy's little Princess. You should have seen her—them. The Roses thought, since they were paying for the lessons and the costumes and the ice and the travel, that meant they owned Robby. Like he was a puppy they picked up from the pound. They told him what to wear and what to say and how to stand up practically. It was sickening. They didn't appreciate what they had. A partner that good comes along maybe once in a lifetime, and Rachel treated him like garbage. She barely let him get a sentence out. Rachel picked their music, Rachel picked their costumes, Rachel had approval over their pictures for the programs and any publicity shots. Also, she wouldn't let him touch her unless they were on the ice. Even then, for a split second, she'd get this look on her face, like he made her skin crawl."

"How did he stand it?" Bex asked.

"Well, first of all, he knew she was his only shot at hitting it big. It wasn't just the money, we might have been able to get another girl to pony up the money, Robby was a hot property and practically everybody but the Roses knew it. The problem was, despite her attitude and her fancy airs, the girl—damn it—the girl was a good skater. Nerves of steel, perfect in practice and perfect in competition. And they looked like magic together. Both blonde, both lean. Their legs matched, their arms matched; hell, in the middle of a program, they even breathed in sync. They were the perfect pairs team. It wasn't fair, but it was true."

"So Robby kept skating with Rachel, even though he hated her, because he didn't think he'd ever find another partner as good?"

Lucian sighed. Bex imagined she could feel the phone wire between them trembling from the weighty angst he managed to infuse into that one exhaled breath. He said, "Robby kept skating with Rachel because the poor, deluded boy was madly in love with her."

"He was? Really? Even after the way she treated him?"

Another sigh. Another trembling wire. And then, the final profundity. "Bex, I'm afraid the reason the boy was so mad for that little bitch was precisely *because* of the way she treated him."

At that point, Bex suspected that Lucian Pryce's general misogyny had just slipped over the rim into a general distaste for the whole human race.

Things were definitely getting psychologically interesting, but at that point, Bex really had only one more pertinent question to ask him. "Mr. Pryce, do you have any idea why Rachel Rose disappeared the way she did fifteen years ago? And where she might have gone?"

"She disappeared, Bex, because Rachel Rose always did whatever she damn well pleased whenever it damn well pleased her, regardless of who it affected or hurt. And where she went, I can only say I hope it was straight to hell, for what she did to Robby."

Well, wasn't that terribly pleasant? It was even enlightening, if one didn't fancy the word *enlightening* to mean "shedding some light on the particular issue at hand," rather than on the state of the union in general. Lucian Pryce was certainly a wealth of information. Bex only wished some of it was useful in helping her track down an errant skater or two. Or three. Because as long as Bex had no idea how to go about finding Rachel Rose, she figured the least she could do was go for the next best thing and try to track down either Robby or his partner turned adoring wife, Felicia.

As a child of the new millennium, it never occurred to Bex to look in the phone book or to call 411 to check on contact information for either a Robby or Felicia Sharpton. For Bex, hitting the obvious meant hitting the Internet. Was there another way to find things out?

Bex typed *"Robby Sharpton" & Felicia & skating* into her favorite search engine, knowing that, without the latter word, she'd be flooded with results on anyone who happened to share their names. She waited for a fraction of a second, wondering how, in the olden days, people survived being put on hold, or worse, waiting for a letter to arrive. And then, she got her results.

The link on top was an extract from a nine-year-old newspaper article. Detailing how ex-skating star Robby Sharpton had just been sentenced to an eighteen-month prison term.

For assault.

Eight

And not, it seemed, just any old assault. This wasn't some bar fight or an argument gone bad over who had the better Salchow. The charge was assault and spousal abuse. According to the newspaper article, Robby had beaten Felicia violently enough to put her in the hospital. It wasn't the first time, either, just the first time that charges were pressed.

According to the article, Robby Sharpton had quite a problem keeping his temper and his fists to himself when it came to women.

The article did not happen to mention that Robby's last Pairs partner had disappeared without a trace. But, it was the first thing that flashed through Bex's mind.

And, on the spot, she had a new theory: Robby killed Rachel. It was obvious.

Now, all she had to do was prove it.

And how hard could that be?

* * *

Two hours later, Bex was willing to concede that it might be a little trickier than she initially assumed. Despite diligently poking around on the Internet, typing in every relevant word she could think of and following up on what seemed like the most obscure but possibly relevant links, she had yet to turn up any irrefutable evidence to back up her latest conjecture. Imagine that! Who would have thought she'd have trouble turning up a Web site conveniently called, "YesRobbyDidIt.com."

Well, all right, so Bex hadn't really expected to come across "HeresWhoKilledRachel.com" (it would have been nice, but there was no breath-holding involved). Nevertheless, a clue, or, at the very least, a phone number (in a bow to tradition, Bex had eventually turned to 411—well, 411 on-line) would have been helpful. Instead, at the end of the fruitless two hours, Bex gave up and decided it was time to turn retro and actually contact a human being for the information she needed.

Bex called Toni.

It was a cop-out and she knew it. It didn't feel like real research if, whenever you needed something, you went running to a source. Even if that was how the old muckrakers and Pulitzer Prize winners did it. But, what did they know? Bex bet, if they'd had the Internet, they'd have never left their comfy homes to dig around in slaughterhouses and war zones and whatnot.

Bex called Toni and asked if she knew how to get in touch with Robby Sharpton. Wasn't there some ex-skaters' newsletter everyone subscribed to? Like an alumni bulletin?

And while they were talking, she asked, "Why didn't you tell me that when you mentioned Robby Sharpton's wasted potential, you meant as a human being, not just a skater?"

Toni sighed, "You know about what happened to Felicia, then."

"It's a matter of public record, hardly top secret stuff."

"I don't like to gossip," Toni said. Unlike the skating mothers who'd started off their diatribes with the same disclaimer, Bex actually believed her. Toni didn't gossip. She shared facts, and only when asked. Sometimes, she even had to be asked several times. Salacious was not her cup of ice chips.

"I know," Bex conceded. "And I'm not trying to make you uncomfortable. It's just that, don't you find it a bit of a coincidence that Rachel Rose disappears and later it turns out her old partner had a little violence-with-women problem?"

"It wasn't then, and it isn't now, any of my business," Toni said. The silent implication being, "And it's none of yours, either."

Bex pretended she suffered from a hearing disorder that made her unable to hear subtext. Kind of like dog whistles.

She said, "So, do you think you could track down Robby Sharpton's number for me, Toni?"

"I'll try," Toni said.

And, by the end of the day, she had.

God bless the skating grapevine.

Robby Sharpton, it turned out, was currently living in New Jersey. That bothered Bex on some level. She'd been hoping for a dark, decrepit, possibly Southern-gothic mansion covered in creeping half-rotted vines and shadows as the location for her confrontation with a potential killer.

Somehow, she doubted she would be finding that in New Jersey.

Instead, Robby Sharpton lived in a third-floor walk-up on the outskirts of a quasi-industrial neighborhood, where the sun shined particularly brightly off the hoods of a half-dozen parked cars on the day that Bex drove up for their appointment. He hadn't sounded surprised to hear from her, which also unnerved Bex somewhat. Was he lying in wait for her, ready to make innocent Bex his next victim in a tri-state, skate-themed killing spree?

Or, "Toni Wright called and told me she'd given you my number."

Oh. Or that.

He agreed to see Bex and to be interviewed on camera, even as he told her he wasn't sure why she would want to do it. "Been away from skating for a long time. Bet no one remembers me anymore."

"Actually, your name has come up quite a bit lately."

"Oh," he sighed. "That's a shame."

The man who opened the door to his one-bedroom apartment and let Bex in with a shrug was, no doubt about it, the same one who'd stared so belligerently up from the newspaper photos reporting on Rachel Rose's disappearance. Fifteen years later, his so-blonde-it-could-seem-white hair showed no signs of thinning. It still fell into his eyes the same way it had back when he was executing a blur-worthy sit-spin that made him look temporarily like the sheepdog always in conflict with Wile E. Coyote in the *Bugs Bunny* cartoons. He was so blonde, even his eyelashes and brows were white. They made his blue eyes seem nearly translucent and his nose and chin even sharper. Robby was dressed in jeans and a black tank top. The latter showed that his upper arms were still as developed as they'd been in the years when lifting one hundred pounds of girl over his head was all in a day's work, and the former emphasized that his thighs still benefited from the fact that, while lifting said girl, he'd also been turning at top speed, all the while balancing on a pair of sharp blades no wider than a sliver. In other words, the man was still fit. Heck, who was she kidding? The man was still buff. And not bashful about showing it off.

On the other hand, when it came to talking, bashful wasn't merely the moniker of Snow White's Least Remembered Dwarf. Robby, after sitting patiently while Bex adjusted her camera for maximum light and framing, proved to be the king of the monosyllabic answer.

While she was still setting up, in a combination of making conversation to fill the awkward silence and genuine curiosity, Bex noted, "You're in pretty good shape. Do you work out?"

As soon as the words were out of her mouth, Bex got a flash image of a cement-covered prison exercise yard and large, sweaty men in bandanas lifting heavy objects while snarling. She considered the possibility that she really didn't want to hear the answer to her question, especially if it included a guy named "Bubba."

Alas, it was too late to hit the rewind button.

"Broomball," Robby said.

Bex relaxed. No prison yards or bandanas, thankfully. Broomball was merely the bastard-child offspring of hockey and . . . um . . . sweeping. Basically, grown men who found hockey too harmless got together, usually in the middle of the night, to play a game that followed more or less the same rules, but, instead of sticks, featured brooms and, instead of skates, used regular sneakers. And they wore no protective padding of any kind. From the few games Bex had seen, bleeding and bruising seemed to be a big part of the schedule.

Sure sounded like the perfect game for a wife-beater, Bex thought. What she said, however, was, "Oh. That sounds like fun. So you're still skating in a way?"

Robby shrugged. Silently.

He looked somehow smaller on camera than he did in person. (And no, it was not because the camera's viewfinder was only three inches high; Bex did hate it when even her own mind got sarcastic on her.) In person, Robby stood up straight, shoulders over hips, hips over knees, his chin jutted forward. Bex figured two decades of correct posture conditioning would be hard to shake—even after a stint in prison. But, sitting down for her camera, he slumped. His chest caved in and he couldn't stop looking at his fingernails. Bex could barely catch his eyes from underneath the bangs. It did not make him look like the most forthright or honest of interview subjects. Not that, for what Bex had in mind, that was necessarily a bad thing.

She decided to start gently. After all, leaping right in with, "Did you kill Rachel Rose?" seemed like it would tip her clever hand a little earlier than Bex intended. So, instead, she offered, "You know, Robby, there is still quite a bit of interest in you in the skating community."

"I bet." Bex tried to figure out if Robby sounded angry or sarcastic. Mostly, though, he just sounded tired.

"You were a great skater. Probably one of the best Pairs partners ever."

"I didn't make it."

"Well, I guess that depends on what your definition of making it is."

"Olympic Gold," Robby said. His tone made it clear there would be no room for argument.

"Is that why you and Felicia broke up your original

partnership? Because you didn't think you could win the Olympic Gold with her?"

"Rachel was the better skater. It was Felicia's idea."

Okay, now Bex was sitting squarely in disbelief-land. The idea that a skater would urge her partner to skate with someone else was a fantasy even skating's version of J.R.R. Tolkien wouldn't dream of trying to peddle as true. She thought of the ice-dance mothers back at the training center, who sat side by side every day, swallowing their mutual loathing, all so that their children wouldn't lose their partners and a shot at . . . whatever. And now Robby wanted Bex to believe that it was Felicia's idea he skate with Rachel? Besides, Lucian Pryce had already told her the notion was his.

"Look," Robby's head suddenly shot up, forcing Bex to jump and jerk while still holding the camera. Not a very smooth shot, but certainly one indicative of the force with which Robby sprang to life. "I know why you're here."

"You—you do?"

"This is about my jail time. That's all anybody is interested in about me. No one gives a fuck how I skated. It's about me and Felicia and what I did to her."

"Well, I—"

"I'm not denying I did it. I'm not. I beat her up. I loved her, but I hit her and I deserved to go to jail for it and I deserved for her to leave me after."

Bex nodded emphatically, not sure what he was looking for her to say but pretty certain that whatever it was, Bex wouldn't be able to think of it in time. So rather than ruining everything, she kept quiet. Which was kind of a first for her.

"I did my time, though," Robby continued, going from Bashful to (Really) Grumpy in the blink of a video frame. "It's funny. After skating for twenty years, jail just wasn't that hard. It's all about do this here and do this now, and keep your mouth shut and follow directions and stay cool, don't let anybody rattle you."

Well, that was certainly a unique perspective on the United States penal system. Prison is just one big ice rink, with wardens instead of coaches and . . . Bex didn't want to speculate on what instead of medals.

"I'm sorry about what happened," Robby said. "I wish I knew where the hell Felicia was these days, so I could tell her myself." As fast as he'd revved up, he seemed to peter out. Grumpy was gone. Bashful was back. Robby peered into Bex's camera, blinking like she'd just woken him up and his eyes weren't adjusted to the bright light yet. "That's why I said I'd do this interview, you know. Because I thought, maybe, if you showed it on TV, maybe Felicia, she would see it and she'd hear how I really am sorry."

"What about Rachel Rose?" Bex figured if he could bounce from mood to mood without so much as a warning, she could certainly do the same from subject to subject.

Robby stared at Bex queerly. "Rachel?"

"Your ex-partner . . ." Bex reminded helpfully.

"What about Rachel? Rachel took off years before any of this happened."

"Well, yes. I know. In fact, I wanted to ask you about that. I mean, you've admitted that you had a bit of problem with women and with hitting and everything, and, you know, with Rachel disappearing so suddenly, I was wondering if, possibly, did you, when you were skating together, did you . . . did you . . . hit . . . Rachel? Maybe? Once or twice?"

There. Bex wasn't sure if she'd actually gotten her question out, but she was pretty certain she'd set some sort of record for the most rambling words ever without actually getting to the point.

"Hitting your partner is stupid," Robby said.

Well, yes. Actually, Bex pretty much thought any kind of hitting was stupid, so she really couldn't argue with him there.

"You hit your partner, you hurt her bad, you can't skate anymore. Everybody loses. It's dumb."

Made perfect sense to her. But somehow, Bex suspected that abuse and logic rarely went hand in hand, especially in the heat of the moment. "Well, if it wasn't anything you did, why do you think Rachel disappeared like that, right when it looked like you two were about to hit it big?"

"Who the hell knows?"

"Well, actually, I was hoping you would. Did Rachel maybe say anything or do anything in those last few days that, in retrospect, offers a clue to—"

"Look, why don't you just ask her yourself?"

What? Was he recommending she hold a séance?

"Robby, I—do you . . . do you know where I can find Rachel Rose?"

Shrug. Back to looking at his fingernails. Not even Bashful anymore. More like Dopey. "No clue." And, then, just as Bex was getting ready to put away her camera since she clearly wasn't about to get any more useful footage and/or information here, Robby's head popped back up. Suddenly he was Happy, (or at least Happy's long-lost cousin, Pleasant), and certainly no longer monosyllabic. Robby asked, "If you do manage to track Rachel down, would you mind passing her whereabouts on to me? I really would like to get in touch with her again."

Bex had never actually met a psychopath before. Yet, walking down the stairs of his apartment building, Bex didn't let that lack of experience in any way stop her from classifying Robby Sharpton as one. Well, what else could it be? He had all the classic symptoms. At least, in as much as Bex understood them from that time she watched the middle half-hour of a Discovery Channel documentary on mental illness. There were the requisite mood swings (from reticent to confrontational in the time it took him to raise his head; plus all those Dwarf personas). The lame, false modesty ("Bet no one even remembers my name anymore.") mixed with macho bravado ("Jail wasn't hard."). The condescension ("Hitting your partner is stupid."). And the classic cat-and-mouse mind game he insisted on playing with Bex ("Why don't you ask Rachel yourself?"), obviously toying with her ("If you do manage to track Rachel down, would you mind passing her whereabouts on to me?"). It was text-book.

Plus, on top of everything else, Robby was a plain old liar. Even if Bex overlooked her instincts and the soon-to-be-discovered evidence and believed that Robby had nothing to do with Rachel's disappearance. Even if she believed that he'd never laid a hand on Rachel. Even if she believed that they were the best matched, most harmonious Pairs team since Caveman and Cave-Woman first strapped bones onto their feet, held hands, and allowed their fellow Cave-People to pass judgment on them. There was still no way that Bex could believe that Felicia Tufts had voluntarily passed her husband and partner over to Rachel Rose without so much as a twitch of resentment and a Rachel voodoo doll with a blade stuck into its heart. That was simply a skating impossibility.

And, since Bex knew without a shadow of a doubt that Robby was lying about this, logic dictated that he was also lying about everything else he'd told her.

Luckily, Bex also knew that she didn't have to take his word as gospel for anything.

Prior to even making the appointment to see skating's answer to Killer Bluebeard the Pirate, Bex had run another Internet search, and, this time, easily came up with the contact information for one Felicia Tufts (one-time Sharpton). Ms. Tufts lived in Manhattan on the Upper East Side. And Bex was on her way to see her now.

On her way to get some honest answers, for a change.

Nine

Felicia Tufts was not nearly as welcoming to Bex as Robby had been. Maybe it was because she didn't get the introductory vouching phone call from Toni. Or maybe it was because she was a . . . what was it . . . they actually had a specific word for it in skating . . . . Oh, yes: Maybe it was because she was a bitch.

Now, granted, Bex supposed that a total stranger calling you from out of the blue asking you to speak, on camera, about your failed athletic career, abusive marriage, jailbird ex-husband, and the mysterious disappearance of a perky, blonde rival you couldn't have possibly liked very much might be reason for a bit of initial, frosty hostility. But, Felicia had apparently decided to take crankiness to a whole other level.

"I have nothing to say to you, Ms. Levy," Felicia announced.

That is, she announced it after she'd left Bex cooling her heels in the lobby of her apartment building for forty-seven (yes, she started counting after she'd completed her tally of the number of gold buttons on the doorman's coat and lovely matching cap) minutes. The only reason Bex even finally managed to make it up to Felicia's sprawling two-bedroom co-op with the river views to knock on the door and receive her rebuff was because the jauntily dressed doorman went out to hail a cab for a teenage boy and his dog (was the kid taking his pet for a walk or a ride?) and Bex, taking advantage of the fact that he'd forgotten all about her by now, simply rode the elevator upstairs while no one was looking.

The woman who answered the door ("Felicia Tufts, I presume," Bex never got the chance to utter) was, predictably, twenty years older than the photo of Robby's Nationals-winning Junior Pairs partner that Bex had found in his old file. The blonde ballerina bun had been replaced with a trendy, short haircut, complete with recent salon streaks, and the tasteful gold studs in her ears with equally tasteful silver hoops. She was still barely an inch over five feet tall, still practically breastless. The only thing missing was the Miss America smile. In fact, there wasn't even a Miss Congeniality smile to be seen for miles as the former U.S. Junior Pairs Champion told Bex, "Please, go. I have nothing to say to you, Miss Levy."

"I saw Robby earlier," Bex blurted out, wishing she could stick her foot in the door like the traveling salesman of old. Alas, those traveling salesmen were canvassing dirt-floor shanties, not trying to maneuver atop a luxury-building carpet so lush, deep, and slick, it was all Bex could do to keep from sinking into it.

"How perfectly wonderful for you."

"He gave me an interview."

"More pure bliss."

"We talked about Rachel Rose."

Felicia Tufts hesitated for the briefest fraction of a second, apparently temporarily without a sarcastic quip. Bex knew the feeling. She even sympathized. She also knew that this might be her only chance to chip at a chink in the armor, and she couldn't risk wasting it with empathy.

Before Felicia had a chance to regain her equilibrium, Bex pressed on. "I'm doing a story about what may have happened to her. Do you have any ideas?"

"Why?" Felicia blinked. It was the first time she'd blinked since Bex had snuck up on her. Surely, that had to mean something. "Why should I know anything?"

"She was Robby's partner. You were Robby's wife."

"And George Bush Sr. was president at the time, so what?" But, even as she snapped her albeit clever rejoinder, Felicia blinked again.

"May I come in?" Bex finally managed to glide her foot where she'd initially meant to all along. She must have caught Felicia mid-blink. The woman moved aside ever so slightly. Bex took it as an engraved invitation.

It's a shame she wasn't here to gawk. Residing as she did in a one-room studio in Hell's Kitchen, Bex often felt the urge to gawk upon encountering how the other half (oh, who was she kidding, the other one-sixteenth) lived. Alas, now was not the time nor place. She did, however, note that it seemed the other half actually had a room designated for the preparation and ingestion of food, rather than the area that, at Bex's place, was known as the two feet between her fold-out couch and TV stand. She also noted that none of the furniture had chips in it. This was probably what they meant by noblesse oblige.

Very briefly, Bex glanced at Felicia's cream-colored walls. Skaters and ex-skaters, she'd noted, had a tendency to plaster their walls (and coffee tables) with ribbons, medals, and trophies, alongside enlarged (to poster size) color photos of themselves winning and wearing said ribbons, medals, and trophies. Felicia's walls, however, were surprisingly bare of any such mementos. She only had art. It hung in antique frames. It wasn't stuck along each of the four edges by squares of rolled scotch tape. Bex made another mental decorating note.

"I really don't know what I can tell you, Ms. Levy." Felicia remained standing, lest Bex get too comfortable and feel an urge to plop herself down into a Louis-the-Something chair.

Bex pretended she didn't get the hint, and so plopped. She reached for her camera and said, "But aren't you curious about what happened to Rachel? Were you curious back then?"

"Back then, Ms. Levy, I was mad as hell. Rachel's running away ruined Robby's career. Now, I honestly could not care less." Felicia looked down at Bex, sitting so comfortably that even a San Francisco-scale earthquake wouldn't have dislodged her at that point. Felicia sighed deeply and, giving in, took the seat opposite. "You have to understand something. There was a time when Robby Sharpton was my whole life. We started skating together when I was fourteen. I thought he was the most amazing human specimen ever. It wasn't just his talent on the ice, although that was considerable—don't get me wrong, that man's flaws never included an inability to land jumps. I didn't merely think he hung the moon, I thought he created it. There are old tapes of us where my crush is so painfully visible, I'm amazed we didn't lose artistic impression points for my having the exact same look on my face no matter what music we were skating to. When he dumped me to skate with Rachel—"

Aha! Bex knew it! All that "Rachel was the better skater. It was Felicia's idea," was pure bunk. There were no Mother Theresas in skating.

"—I didn't mind."

Say what, now?

"That's how in love I was. I didn't mind. Robby and I were dating by that point, and I didn't care what he did on the ice, as long as I was the one who he loved off it."

"And were you?" It seemed an obvious question.

Except that it drove Felicia to a smirk. "He said I was. And five minutes later he asked me to marry him. And five minutes after that, he told me my parents would have to keep paying a share of his bills, even though we weren't skating together anymore, because the Roses were refusing to foot the whole bill until they saw some results from the new pair."

"Oh," Bex said.

"Yes," Felicia said.

"But, you did marry him. And you stayed married to him. Even after—"

"Rachel?"

"No. I was going to say, even after he . . . hit you."

"Oh. That. Your chronology is off. Robby started hitting me long before Rachel entered the picture. He was a perfectionist. He'd get frustrated. He never made mistakes on the ice. That was my domain. So he hit me."

"You didn't tell anyone?"

"Who was there to tell? My parents were in the stands. Our coach was standing two feet away. It was hardly a secret. Who was I supposed to tell?"

"Nobody did anything?"

"Why should they? He'd hit and I'd get in line. I skated better with him than I ever had with anyone else."

"You were scared of him."

"I didn't want to let him down. There is a difference."

"And then, after you stopped skating together . . . he kept hitting you?"

"Not as often. Not right away. And it was different then. I can't explain it, but it was."

Bex had the feeling they were about to enter one of those female bonding moments that would change both of their lives forever. But, she really didn't have time for that.

So, rather than following up, she nimbly jumped to, "If Robby hit you, he must have been hitting Rachel, too."

"No. He didn't. She was a much better skater. Much better in competition."

"So Robby never hit her?"

"Never."

"That must have freaked you out."

"No. I wanted them to win. I knew how important it was to Robby."

"So, he never laid a hand on her?"

"Never."

"Then why did she run away?"

"I told you, I don't know."

"Do you think she did, though?"

"Did what?"

"Do you think she actually ran away? Maybe it was something else."

"Like what, for instance?"

"Well . . ." Bex wondered how to tactfully phrase, "Your husband killed her and buried her next to Jimmy Hoffa."

"Rachel Rose may have been a wonderful skater, but she was . . . fragile. Emotionally. Not in competition. In competition, you couldn't knock her down with a two-by-four. In the air, she could look so crooked you'd think there was no way in hell she was coming down on one foot, and then, at the last minute, there she'd be, perfect as always. But, off the ice . . . she was very shy. I don't think she liked the attention and she certainly didn't like the way her parents obsessed over her career. Robby actually had to run interference with her folks, sometimes. Tell them to lay off and leave her alone. Let Rachel breathe, give her some space. He was very protective of her. You know how Pairs coaches are always saying that the man is the stem, and the woman is the flower that he presents to the audience? Well, I think Robby took it a little too seriously. He saw Rachel as this perfect, delicate flower that was his responsibility to shelter from the big bad world."

"Felicia?" Bex wasn't sure how to ask this. Somehow, it seemed even more personal than the question about Robby whacking Rachel. "Was your husband in love with his partner?"

"No." Felicia's answer came so quickly, she could only have been waiting for it. And if she was waiting for it, then she too must have known what a natural question it was. "I said he was protective of her. She was his partner. She was half of his ticket to the top. Of course, he wanted to protect her and make sure she was at her best when they skated."

Bex wondered if now would be the time to point out that, when he skated with Felicia, protection had been the last thing on Robby's mind.

Felicia insisted, "Rachel Rose was great on ice and a mess off of it. She couldn't handle all the crap her parents heaped on her, and she bailed out. It happens all the time in skating."

"So you never thought that she and Robby . . ."

"No." Again, with the quick answer. "Look, Ms. Levy, I know this is hard to believe, but Robby and I really did love each other. Skating crap aside, we loved each other. I loved him so much that I stayed with him even after he began hitting me again, after Rachel left him, because I knew that he didn't mean it. I knew he loved me. He just had a hard time managing his temper sometimes. It's not even really his fault. He had a horrible childhood. Neither one of his parents gave a damn about him. They were drunks and drug addicts and who knows what else. They'd lock him out and he'd have to sleep on the street when he was maybe four years old. Skating saved his life. I don't know what would have happened to him otherwise. He practically lived at the rink from first grade on. We all hoped he would forget his past. But, you don't forget something like that. It flared up. He'd get frustrated on the ice and he'd start to worry that he was about to lose everything he'd worked so hard for and he would get angry. Too angry. He couldn't help it. And he was always so sorry afterwards. He loved me. I know he did. Rachel Rose . . . Rachel was nothing to him. She really was nothing to any of us, in the end. Just a three-year blip in both our lives. She didn't matter. She was nothing."

Bex nodded her head fervently. She kept nodding even as she thanked Felicia for her time, and even as she got the hell out of her apartment as fast as skidding on the plush carpet could carry her. Because now, thanks to Felicia's oh, what should she call it—fervent? intense? just a teensy bit over the top?—tone, Bex had a new suspect in Rachel Rose's possible murder.

And it wasn't Robby Sharpton, at all.

She called Lucian Pryce as soon as she got back to her office at 24/7. She asked, "Did Felicia Tufts know that her husband was in love with Rachel Rose?"

"Well, let's see, the girl had two working eyes and a pair of working ears and it was all anyone at the rink ever talked about, so, just taking a wild guess, I would have to say, yes."

"How did she feel about that?"

"Now it's your turn to take a guess, Bex. How do you think she felt about it?"

"I just talked to her, Mr. Pryce. Felicia Tufts denied that Rachel was anything but Robby's partner. She said Rachel meant nothing to either one of them."

"Well, then Felicia Tufts lied. You put yourself in her position: First, she lost Robby as a partner, which had to sting, even though he and Rachel were obviously the better match, and if it wasn't Rachel, eventually it would have been someone else—he and Felicia weren't Senior champ material. And then she married the guy, supported him with her own money, only to have to watch him and Rachel hanging all over each other—"

"Wait a minute, wait!" Bex piped up. "I thought you told me Rachel couldn't stand Robby. That she wrinkled her nose or whatever whenever he touched her, that she treated him like garbage. How do you get from that to their hanging all over each other?"

"Rachel did treat Robby like garbage. She certainly looked down on him like she was a princess and he was some kind of peasant. But, she also knew that she needed him. There was no way in hell, even with all her money, that Rachel would ever find herself a better partner than Robby. You can buy a lot, but you can't buy talent. Or perfection. So Rachel knew she had to keep Robby under control. Her parents did it with money. But Rachel did it the same way girls have been keeping boys under control since the beginning of time. I saw the faces she made when she thought he wasn't looking. But she seduced him just the same."

"How would you know something like that?"

"I was their coach," Lucian replied, almost insulted. "I knew everything about them. We used to practice late at night. It was the best time to get private ice all to ourselves before a big competition. It was just the three of us in the rink and, after the practice, it was just the two of them in the changing rooms. Those rooms have very thin walls."

Ewwww . . . Bex thought. *Helpful, but, ewwww . . . .*

"So Robby cheated on Felicia with Rachel? He wasn't just in love from afar, they actually had a full-fledged affair?"

"How many pictures do you need me to draw for you, Bex?"

"And what was Felicia's reaction?"

"What could her reaction have been? She didn't dare interfere. Robby and Rachel breaking up off-ice might have led to their breaking up on-ice. And no one wanted that. Robby's success was more important to Felicia—to all of us—than any personal problems they may have been having. Which is how it should be, of course. Felicia understood what really mattered."

"So she bit her tongue, and then Rachel ended up betraying her and Robby, anyway."

"Yes. Selfish little bitch. Yes."

"So, in a way, Felicia had more of a reason to hate Rachel than Robby did?"

"Women are always more catty about such things, certainly."

"Well, what I actually meant was," Bex tried to defend her own sex while also furthering her latest burgeoning theory. "Rachel only cost Robby his career. But she humiliated Felicia, had an affair with her husband, which the whole world apparently knew about, and, in the end, ended up running out on Robby and their career, anyway."

"She ran out on all of us. We all suffered. Do you know that, after Rachel disappeared, I didn't have a championship pair to take to the Olympics? First time in over twenty years I didn't have a student at the Games. I actually ended up staying home, watching it on television like some . . . like some . . . outsider! Like some . . . regular person. You can't imagine the humiliation. I poured my heart and soul into that team. I put all my eggs into one basket. Well, I never did that again, I can assure you!"

"But, didn't Robby continue skating Singles? Weren't you his coach?"

"No!" Lucian barked. "That was another thing. After Rachel left and Robby decided to skate Singles, Felicia convinced him he needed better coaching. Better coaching! I was the number one ranked trainer in the country, then. Won the Professional Skater's Coach of the Year Award five times in a row. Five times! No one had done it before and no one's done it since, either. I think Felicia poisoned Robby's mind against me. He said he didn't blame me for Rachel's leaving, but I'll bet you death spirals to doughnuts, Felicia managed to convince him it was all my fault. She'd always hated me."

"For pairing up Robby with Rachel instead of her?"

"Oh, who knows why. That girl always overreacted to everything, that's what made her so high-strung in competition. Sure, I bet she blamed me for Rachel and Robby. Like I had any say over what my skaters did in their private lives. And she wanted to stick it to me after Rachel left. So she convinced Robby he needed a better coach. A Russian one, no less. She convinced him the Russians were better than we were, that only a Russian could put him on top in Singles. Right after Rachel left, Felicia used her parents' money, pulled some strings, paid off some bribes, you know how they do business over there; got Robby a spot with some fancy Russian coach in Leningrad—that was before they changed the name, you know. I think he ended up spending maybe two years over there. And what did it get him? Sure, he made the Olympic team. But no medals. He and Rachel would have been champions. Alone . . . it was too late. Too late to change disciplines. If he'd given me a chance, I could have found Robby another partner. Not as good as Rachel, sure, but we'd have had a fighting chance. Felicia's way, everybody lost. Her, too."

Bex felt like she had a pretty good picture of what Felicia had lost. And whom she might have blamed for it. But, she also had one more question for Lucian. "Mr. Pryce?"

"What?"

"Mr. Pryce, you do know what happened to Robby and Felicia after he finished skating, right? I mean, his going to jail and—"

"Of course I know. How could I not know? Day the news broke, practically every person I'd ever met in skating felt obligated to call me to ask what I knew about it. I didn't know a damn thing. Hadn't talked to either one of them in years."

"But," Bex's tongue tiptoed tentatively. "You did know something. In a way. I mean, Robby didn't just start beating Felicia after he stopped being your student. Felicia says . . . Felicia says he was hitting her while they were skating together. And that you knew all about it."

A pause on the other end.

The pause turned into a caesura.

And the caesura into a gap worthy of a "We interrupt this programming . . . ."

Bex wanted to say something. She really, really did. Alas, she also knew that saying something would blow whatever advantage she'd acquired by catching him off-guard like this. And so she struggled to suppress her basic instinct to shoot off her own foot, then stick it jauntily in her mouth, 1940s, Dorothy-Parker-cigarette style.

Finally, Lucian Pryce told her, "Like I've said before,

Bex, Felicia always had a problem with overreacting to things. She had no sense of proportion, everything was a major tragedy to her. The girl spent more lesson time crying and making up excuses for why she'd made a mistake, than actually trying to fix them. She was, and probably still is, a hysteric of the first order. She doesn't see the world the way it is, she sees the world the way she *thinks* it is—which, by the way, is convinced that everyone is out to get her. You can't believe a word she says. She changes stories the way some girls changed hair ribbons. It was excruciating coaching her. I never knew how that child would react to the exact same feedback—stand up straighter, check your arms out faster, that sort of thing, run-of-the-mill training—from one day to the next. Frankly, she's such a piece of work, I wouldn't put any vindictive accusation or action past her."

"So you're saying you didn't know that Robby was hitting Felicia while they were both your students? You're saying Felicia lied about that?"

"I'm saying that the World According to Felicia is not a happy place. And God help anyone who finds themselves trapped between what really is and what she thinks it should be."

Bex didn't even bother hanging up the phone after saying good-bye to Lucian. She simply kept the receiver tucked between her right shoulder and her ear, pushed the twin buttons in the cradle to disconnect, and promptly redialed Toni. Her ear felt red and swollen from being pressed against hard plastic for so long, but Bex didn't even care (well, she cared, but not enough to do anything about it; even shifting ears would somehow dilute the purity of the moment). She was so excited, she was amazed

Toni could even make out what she was saying—Bex certainly couldn't.

"I've got it," she babbled. "I've got it, Toni. Robby would never have killed Rachel. She was too important to him as a partner and, besides, he was in love with her. It was Felicia. She was jealous of Robby's feelings for Rachel. It all makes sense, Toni. Felicia killed Rachel!"

There was a pause on the other end. A very, very long pause. Even longer that Lucian's. It was so long, it gave Bex time to wonder what the two had been like as Pairs partners, if both took a lifetime to articulate a thought. She imagined practice sessions where they did nothing more than stare at each other mutely, both pondering their next utterances. The pause was so long that Bex figured Toni hadn't understood her after all, and was about to repeat her babble, exclamation points and all. Except that was when Toni, speaking very, very, very slowly, as if Bex were one of those foreign skaters who came for the summer intensive program with a vocabulary no broader than "Axel," "Lutz," and "Beer, please," gingerly asked her, "Bex, what in the world made you think that Rachel Rose is dead?"

Ten

Bex said, "Um . . ." And then she said, "She's . . . um . . . not?"

"Goodness, no, honey! Whatever gave you that idea?"

"Well, I—you said she disappeared, and I assumed . . ."

"I said she disappeared from skating, I never said she was dead. After she first left, no one heard from her for about a year or two. But, she eventually got in touch with her parents and some other folks. She didn't want them to worry. She's not that kind of young lady. But, believe me, Rachel is perfectly fine. She's doing rather well, as a matter of fact, from what I understand."

"You've talked to her?" Bex could feel her face getting redder and redder. She imagined if she had a handy bowl of water to duck her head in, she could generate enough steam for a sauna.

"Not recently, no. But we spoke several years ago on the phone. I believe she runs a high-end travel agency in one of those fancy vacation towns. It's her own business, she started it herself and she's very proud of what she's accomplished. She doesn't miss skating or competing at all, she told me. She's very happy doing what she's doing."

"Oh," Bex said. "Toni, I'm sorry, but why didn't you tell me all this when I first asked you about Rachel?"

"You didn't ask me about Rachel," Toni reminded gently. "You asked me about Robby."

She had a point. Bex had been so eager to unmask a murderer, she'd kind of skipped that crucial, first step—the one where you figure out if a murder ever actually happened.

"Yeah," Bex sighed. And wished that she weren't sitting, so that she might kick herself in the manner she obviously deserved. But, then again, there was still hope . . . . "Toni, do you think you could give me Rachel's number? I'd still like to talk to her for my piece about skaters like her and Jeremy Hunt, who dropped out with seemingly no reason."

"No," Toni said.

Okay, Bex hadn't seen that one coming. "But I—you gave me Robby's number."

"That was different. Robby isn't trying to keep a low profile and, besides, I called him first to ask if it was okay. Rachel is a different story. She doesn't want any publicity, she doesn't want to talk about the past. Rachel wants her privacy and I have to respect that. I'm sorry, Bex."

Bex considered whining. She considered pleading and begging and basically throwing herself on the mercy of the ice in order to wheedle out the necessary information.

But, in the end, all she said was, "That's all right, Toni, I understand."

Because, in the end, Bex also suspected that Toni had already told her everything she needed to know.

Her second day working as a professional researcher, Bex had been blown away by how truly easy it was to track down most people and facts—as long as you knew where to look. No, that wasn't quite correct. It was as long as you know *how* to look. The Internet, she'd long ago realized, was God's own gift to the researcher—or just to the perennially nosy. It would tell you anything, as long as you asked it the right question. And, most often, the right question was simply a matter of the right combination of words.

Immediately after hanging up with Toni, Bex got on her computer, pulled up her favorite search engine, and typed in two words: *"Rachel Rose."* She received about 26,000 results. Good. First part of the test passed.

Next, Bex typed in *"Rachel Rose" & "travel agency."* Her results were instantly cut down to twelve. God, but Bex did love it when a plan came together.

Two of the listings proved to be obituaries for an eighty-four-year-old woman who'd also been named Rachel Rose and apparently loved to travel. One was an agency in England. And eight were posts on various travel-oriented message boards, all praising the great time they'd had on trips arranged by one Miss Rachel Rose, who operated a one-woman agency from her home in the Pocono Mountains in Pennsylvania.

The final listing was a simple, promotional Web page for the agency, apparently called The Smooth Journey. And an address.

In the end, it took Bex two hours to drive from New York City to the Poconos, and another two hours to make heads or tails of the winding roads that seemed to loop around each other rather than lead to what one presumed should be their logical conclusion. At least the path was pretty—even in early December, the unseasonably mild weather they'd been having ensured that there were still remnants everywhere of summer greenery and fall flora and wholesome, farm-fresh country living. Bex expected to see Andy Griffith and the Oscar-winning Opie to come ambling past at any moment. Unless, they too, got lost on these roads, trying to find the fishing hole.

According to the address on the Web site, The Smooth Journey operated from a two-story cottage covered in creeping ivy and tucked discreetly into the corner of a cul-de-sac that, from the front, looked like any modest, middle-class vacation lane. From the rear though, it became clear that every house built into this mountainside had for its backyard a personal lake in the summer, a ski slope in the winter, plus a sturdy deck large enough to qualify as a second home.

Working from the "Whistle a Happy Tune" premise ("Make believe you're brave/And the trick will take you far/You can be as brave/As you make believe you are,"), Bex hurried out of the car before she had a chance to, perhaps most wisely, change her mind. Furiously whistling all the while, she marched herself up the steps to Rachel Rose's home.

Unlike at Felicia's, Bex was greeted here with a smile.

Of course, to be fair, Rachel had no idea who Bex was or what she wanted.

This was the right Rachel Rose, though, there was no doubt about that. Like Felicia, she too had given up the ballerina bun. Only, in Rachel's case, it was to allow her hair (clearly not streaked and possibly not even salon cut) to fall down the length of her back. Only a seashell clip at the base of her neck kept it from falling into her makeup-free face. She was dressed in blue denim jeans and a white tailored shirt with a narrow collar and the top button undone. The tasteful, gold hoops she'd worn in her ears for the publicity photos with Robby were gone. In fact, she wore no jewelry of any kind, except for a simple silver watch.

"May I help you?" Rachel asked pleasantly.

Bex said, "My name is Bex Levy. Well, it's Rebecca, actually, Bex is just a nickname."

Rachel continued to listen politely. Although a frown was beginning to creep into the tiny crevasse between her eyes. She probably thought Bex was an Avon lady. Or a babbling nut.

"I work for 24/7 Sports, and I'm doing a story on skaters who suddenly quit skating and—"

The tiny crevasse turned into a pit of distaste. Her green eyes darkened, changing from teal to a murky, swampish color. Her shoulders stiffened and she reached for the door. "I'm sorry, Rebecca. I don't do interviews. Ever."

"It's Bex. My name is Bex," she insisted, figuring if she and Rachel could just agree on that, they'd be halfway to lifelong bonding.

"I don't do interviews, Bex. And I don't appreciate being ambushed in my own home."

"I'm sorry," Bex said. And she really was, too. Despite outward appearances, Bex did have a clichéd, pathological need to be liked, and she suspected that barging into private people's homes and asking them questions about things they didn't want to talk about was probably not the way to do it. "But, this is important. See, I kind of told my boss that I would have this story for him, and when I couldn't find you at first, I thought maybe I could make it about Robby Sharpton, but—"

"Robby?" Rachel's voice dropped to what Bex might have guessed was a scared whisper, but, at the same time, she stood up straighter, stronger, not at all cowering, but rather confronting head-on. "You've interviewed Robby?"

"Yes," Bex said. And then added, in a moment of inspiration, as she fumbled in her purse, "Would you like to see the tape?"

Rachel hesitated. And then, very tentatively, she nodded yes.

Unwilling to risk losing whatever advantage she'd accidentally stumbled into, Bex hurried to pop the tape into her camera and flick it on play. She sat down on Rachel's couch and turned the viewfinder toward her. The former U.S. Pairs Champion watched the first part of the video silently, only flinching the slightest bit when Robby first appeared on camera.

When they got to the part where Bex asked Robby, "You've admitted that you had a bit of problem with women and with hitting and everything, and, you know, with Rachel disappearing so suddenly, I was wondering if, possibly, did you, when you were skating together, did you . . . did you . . . hit . . . Rachel? Maybe? Once or twice?" Rachel leaned forward, apparently as eager to hear his answer as Bex had been.

"Hitting your partner is stupid," on-camera Robby said.

Rachel burst out laughing. She instantly realized what she'd done and quickly clamped a hand over her mouth, looking at Bex guiltily. "I'm sorry," she said. "That wasn't funny, was it?"

"Did Robby hit you, Rachel?"

"Not as much as he did Felicia. I was a better skater, you know." Rachel laughed again. Then added, "I guess that wasn't funny, either."

"Is that why you quit? Because your partner was hitting you?"

"Have you ever been to a competition press conference, Rebecca—er, sorry, Bex?"

Okay, she'd asked one question and gotten another in return, but Bex was willing to play along in case this managed to lead her somewhere. "Actually, yeah. I'm the 24/7 researcher. I go to every press conference, both the before and after, at every event we do."

"Then you know. What is the one thing every skater says is their goal at any given event?"

"I just want to skate well and stay focused and have fun out there," Bex answered with utmost confidence. She could recite the programmed mantra in her sleep.

"Hitting and fun don't exactly go, excuse the Pairs skating pun, hand in hand. Do you understand what I'm saying?"

"I understand," Bex said. "And, really, that's all I want you to say on-camera. That you quit skating because you weren't having fun anymore, due to your partner's abuse. Just think of how your speaking up could help girls in similar situations." Bex figured if she couldn't appeal to Rachel's vanity—Bex's regular tool for getting people on-camera—she could try the Do Gooder approach. "I'm sure a lot of skaters today are going through the same—"

"No," Rachel said.

"It would be very quick. We'll air Robby's admitting to hitting Felicia, and then the part where he claims he didn't hit you, and then we'll have you telling your side of the story."

"If I wanted to tell my side of the story, I could have done it fourteen years ago. I made a choice, then. I chose to leave rather than confront Robby."

"Was it because you were scared of him?"

"I had my reasons."

"Did he threaten you? Were you afraid for your life?

Was there something else going on besides the abuse that you thought—"

"Please leave, Rebecca. Now. And, I warn you. If you mention a word about me, my life, what I do, or where I live in this feature of yours, I will sue you, and 24/7, for trespassing, invasion of privacy, and anything else my lawyers can think up. Am I making myself clear?"

Bex nodded. And gulped.

On the drive back into the city (over roads that somehow didn't look nearly as wholesome and picturesque now that Bex knew showing even a second of video footage about them might lead her and 24/7 into the heart of a lawsuit), Bex reasoned that, if she assumed Rachel was just bluffing—and really, she had to be; why would a person obsessed with her privacy risk launching what could turn into a very public lawsuit?—then Bex still had enough information to put together a piece more or less like the one she'd promised Gil in the first place.

She had Robby's interview, which was great television, especially with him going from Jekyll to Hyde like that. She could recap his and Felicia's story using vintage newspaper reports, old footage of them skating, and then the new interview. She might even take another crack at getting Felicia in front of the camera. After all, Bex did possess Robby's apology to his ex-wife. How fabulous would it be if Bex could screen the tape for Felicia and then get her reaction?

And then, after she reunited Robby and Felicia live on 24/7—a girl could dream, couldn't she?—Bex would segue into the Rachel part of Robby's life. Over photos and clips of their National and World triumphs, Bex could record a voice-over telling Rachel's side of the story. It wasn't nearly as effective as having Rachel telling it herself would have been, but, as the account was certainly dramatic enough, it just might work. Of course, Bex still had to run the idea by Gil. And she really should do it as soon as she got back to the office.

Bex decided to give it a couple of days.

She figured he was busy. She didn't want to bother him. Besides, Bex sucked at making oral presentations and Gil was even worse at listening to them. He had a tendency to literally get up in the middle of a pitch and start doing things like running documents through his shredder or playing with his window blinds. It was very disconcerting.

Gil was much better at staying focused if you came to him with at least some sort of visual guideline for what you were hoping to do. So, rather than speaking to him immediately upon her return from the Poconos, Bex retired to her office to compile a rough cut of what she already had and what she hoped the final product would look like.

She dug up all the archived footage she could get her hands on, plus some nice, glossy stills of Robby with both of his partners. She logged Robby's interview, picking the best (i.e., most psycho) bites and arranging them in an order that worked best for her, if not necessarily him. She wrote a tentative script and recorded her own voice on the scratch track to indicate where the announcer's narration would go. And then she got ready to present the whole thing to Gil.

Except that, on the morning of their scheduled appointment, just as Bex was adding some last minute touches and graphics to her demo, she got on-line to check her E-mail. And saw the latest digital news headline running on the sports ticker:

Ex-U.S. skating champ, Rachel Rose, mysteriously beaten to death . . .

Eleven

Bex thought, "Oops."

It was probably not the most appropriate response ever to a death, nor the most respectful, nor the most profound. And yet, it was the one that felt most right at the moment. "Oops."

Now, as a rule, Bex thought she had a pretty healthy ego. And while she had a rather high opinion of her abilities, especially in certain areas like writing, research, and witty repartee, she did not belong to the category of people who managed to believe that all things that occurred anywhere in the world were somehow connected to them. Bex wanted to make that point very clear.

Before she leapt to the obvious conclusion that what had happened to Rachel Rose was somehow connected to her.

This wasn't ego talking. It was duh-proof logic. The woman had stayed below radar for fourteen years, and three days ago, she was still alive. Then Bex decided to look her up, and, ipso presto, suddenly she's dead? Was Bex supposed to think it was a coincidence?

She really would like to think it was a coincidence. Honestly, the fact of her feature suddenly getting a lot more interesting aside, Bex would really, really like to think it was a coincidence.

She called Gil and cancelled their meeting. He sounded surprised to be reminded that they'd had one planned, so Bex doubted he would be shedding any tears over it. That done, Bex went back on-line, clicking on the link about Rachel Rose's death.

EX-U.S. SKATING CHAMP MYSTERIOUSLY BEATEN TO DEATH

> Rachel Rose, the 1987, 1988, and 1989 U.S. Figure Skating Pairs Champion with Robert Sharpton, was found by passing joggers at dawn this morning in a public park several blocks from her Clear Lake, Pennsylvania, home. She had been beaten to death by a blunt object of indeterminate origin. Local police report no suspects at this time.

Well, Bex thought, that was a singularly unhelpful experience. There was practically no more information in the text than there'd been in the headline. What was American journalism coming to these days? Didn't people take pride in their work anymore? Where were the diligent reporters rolling up their ink-stained sleeves *His Girl Friday*-style and digging up stories, chasing down leads, cross-examining sources . . . getting people killed?

Oh, God. Bex buried her face in her hands. Had she gotten Rachel Rose killed?

She had to know for sure. Because this just wasn't funny anymore.

This time around, Bex didn't even notice the picturesque trees or think about Andy Griffith as she swerved down the road to the Poconos. Her only focus was on finding the police station. And hearing them tell her that Rachel's death was the work of a well-known serial killer who'd long been stalking the area. It wouldn't bring Rachel back to life. But, it sure as hell would make it possible for Bex to breathe again.

Less than a year ago, like probably a majority of the law-abiding population, Bex could have honestly asserted that she'd never set foot in a police station before. But that all changed last March when, as part of her researcher duties at the World Figure Skating Championships, Bex found herself in the middle of an investigation into who killed the Italian judge who placed the Russian girl ahead of the American one and cost adorable little Erin Simpson the gold medal in Ladies' Singles. To be honest, Bex was the only one actually investigating the murder. Heck, Bex was the only one who thought a murder had been committed. She fervently hoped that wouldn't be the case this time around. After all, while a judge could have, by some stretch of the imagination, had a reason for walking into a refrigeration room, stepping into a puddle, pulling on the lighting cord, and electrocuting herself, Bex thought it would take quite a considerable suspension of disbelief to buy that Rachel Rose had beaten herself to death in a public park.

The Poconos police station proved as rustic as the rest of the area. If it weren't for two black-and-whites parked outside, it might have been just another tourist's summer cottage. But, when Bex got inside, she learned that, unlike the San Francisco police station she'd spent her time in last spring, this one actually had a professional liaison specifically to deal with questions from snoopy people like her.

The liaison's name was Gretchen. She looked to be about forty years old and, before Bex even had the chance to mention what she wanted, Gretchen took one look at Bex's 24/7 credential and launched into a tale (really more of a miniseries) about how she, too, used to live in New York City, doing big-time Public Relations for some major, major firms, but how, when she passed her thirty-seventh birthday and was still unmarried and without children (really, who had time, working those twenty-hour, hustle/bustle days?), she decided to chuck it all for a life of rustic splendor, and now she had a new husband, a local man, and they were trying to get pregnant and not being very successful at it but they weren't quite at the assisted reproduction stage yet, and Bex should really take care to make sure that never happened to her because the years really did pass quickly and you wanted something to show for them, you really did, take it from Gretchen.

"Uh-huh," Bex said.

"Now," Gretchen smiled brightly and took a seat behind her desk, atop of which was a picture of, Bex presumed, Mr. Local Husband Guy. To be fair, he looked very nice and Bex could probably do worse than to find one just like him. "What can I do for you, Rebecca?"

"It's Bex. And I wanted to talk to you about the Rachel Rose murder."

"Oh, yes, we've received a few calls about that. Mostly the wire services working on an obituary. I guess she was quite a famous skater in her day."

"Do you have ideas yet what exactly happened?"

"Well . . ." Gretchen shuffled though some papers until she'd found the one she was looking for. She squinted, tried to read, then put on her glasses and gave it another shot. "It's so awful," Gretchen laughed. "You wake up one morning and you're forty years old and suddenly you can't see a thing without your reading glasses."

"About Rachel . . ." Bex prompted.

"Yes, yes. Here it is. Let me see . . . . Oh, yes. It appears she was beaten to death in a public park earlier this morning, probably by a blunt object of indeterminate origin. The police report no suspects at this time." Gretchen set down her glasses and looked up, most satisfied with herself.

Bex, on the other hand, wanted to scream. And/or beat Gretchen to death with a blunt object of indeterminate origin and wait to see how long it took the police to report a suspect.

"That all was on the Internet this morning," Bex said calmly. Well, at least, she hoped she sounded calm. It was hard to hear over the frustrated howling in her head. "I was hoping for some new information."

"I really don't know what to tell you. I won't claim that our crime rate here is low, we actually get quite a rash of muggings and robberies, drunk and disorderly, that sort of thing—we get a lot of tourists, you understand, both summer and winter. They're mostly from the cities and they don't really respect our quiet, local community, if you know what I mean. But murder! We so rarely get a murder around here. Especially where the cause isn't immediately obvious, like a bar fight or a very public lovers' quarrel. This actually looks premeditated. I mean, Ms. Rose was presumably lured to the park so early in the morning."

"Was she dressed to go jogging? Shorts? Running shoes?" Bex took a guess. Having been a skater, Rachel might have been hard-wired to do her exercising early in the morning, even if there was no ice-time involved.

Gretchen checked her notes again. Since there was obviously no pertinent information on the press release she'd just read Bex, she excused herself and went to another room, returning with a disappointingly thin folder titled, "Rachel Rose." Heck, the file Bex had on her back at 24/7 was bigger than this sliver of manila.

Gretchen re-donned her glasses and read from another sketchily filled out piece of paper. "The victim," she said, "was wearing blue jeans, a green fleece jacket, and cowboy boots." She looked up at Bex. "Doesn't sound like Ms. Rose was jogging."

"No," Bex agreed. And then she asked, "Do you know what she was hit with?"

"A blunt object of in—"

"Of indeterminate origin, yes, I know. But, let's see if maybe we can't determinate it down a little bit, shall we? Where were her wounds, anyway?"

Gretchen shuffled more papers. "Primarily about the head. It appears there were multiple blows that got harder and harder as the assailant went on."

Well, Bex thought, that part was at least interesting. And even quasi-helpful. After all, a psychopath merely interested in the kill wouldn't start slowly and work his way up now, would he? (This was the part where Bex felt the need to remind herself that she really had no idea what she was talking about, dealing with, or even asking. Something to keep in mind before she leapt to her next, inevitably wrong conclusion).

"Did that mean that Rachel's injuries occurred in the

middle of a fight that got progressively more violent as it went on?" Bex leapt to a conclusion.

"That's one of the working theories, yes. It might have been a mugging gone wrong. The perpetrator asked Rachel for her money and hit her to make his point. When she didn't give it to him, he continued to hit her. He may have never meant to kill her at all, it just got out of hand."

Bex asked Gretchen, "Could the weapon used have been a stick? Or a rock? Something the killer could have just picked up in the park and didn't necessarily have to have brought with him?"

"That's certainly possible."

"Did you find anything in the vicinity?"

"Like what?"

"Like oh, let's say, a bloody stick?" Bex asked patiently. "Or a bloody rock?"

"No. Nothing."

"Could the killer have used his hands?"

"That's certainly possible, too."

And now, Bex had reached the end of her forensic knowledge. She clearly needed to brush up on her *C.S.I.* watching.

"About the suspects . . ." Bex figured this was an area she was stronger in. Asking about forensic evidence actually required knowing something about physiology and how things worked. Asking about suspects only required the ability to draw instant conclusions about the motivations of people she'd never met. Bex could definitely do that. "Even if you've got no physical clues, surely you've got a suspect theory or two? I mean, you must have questioned Rachel's friends—"

"She actually kept to herself quite a bit."

"Her neighbors . . ."

"They rarely saw her. She traveled a great deal. For her business, you know. It was a travel agency. She was constantly checking out new destinations and resorts."

"Well, then, her business clients."

"Most of them only spoke to her on the phone or online. And she wasn't the kind of person to share personal details. None of them even knew she'd been a champion figure skater! They were very surprised to read about it in the paper."

"How about a boyfriend."

"Oh, no, there wasn't one. We checked."

Great, the woman obviously left skating to become a nun. She didn't know anyone, she didn't see anyone, she never spoke to anyone. Heck, maybe she did kill herself by whacking herself over the head. To alleviate boredom.

Gretchen said, "Rachel definitely wasn't cheating on her husband."

Bex blinked. "Excuse me?"

"Our research shows that—"

"Rachel Rose was married?"

"Oh, yes. For almost fifteen years, I believe he told the police."

Almost fifteen years? Rachel Rose disappeared fourteen years ago . . . . Apparently, there was one person she'd kept in touch with.

"Is the husband a suspect in her death?"

Gretchen hesitated. She looked left. She looked right. She lowered her voice despite the fact that her office door was closed and seemingly soundproof. In all the time they'd been talking, Bex hadn't heard another conversation through the door, and she assumed that worked both ways.

Gretchen said, "It's not official. It's not even on the record. But, the fact is, whenever we're faced with a case like this, well, the husband is always the prime suspect. It's the only thing that really ever makes any sense."

Bex called Toni on her cell phone while hightailing it to Rachel's house. Taking care to cross her T's and I's and even a few H's while she was at it, she inquired, "Remember when I assumed that Rachel Rose was dead because I didn't bother to ask you whether she was or not?"

"Indeed I do, Bex."

"Did you also not tell me that Rachel was married because I forgot to ask?"

"Rachel was married?"

"That's what the police here told me."

Toni sighed. "The police. You have no idea how it breaks my heart to hear you say that. It's all anyone at the rink is talking about today. Rachel's death. She was such a lovely girl. So much potential. Bad enough to quit in her prime, but this . . ."

Only in skating, Bex thought, could murder be equated with basically giving up your hobby.

"So you didn't know if she was married or not?"

"I had no idea. But Bex, you must understand something: Rachel and Robby weren't my students. I only encountered them because they skated at the same rink. Naturally, I knew some private details about them because, well, people talk here, they gossip, and you can't help but hear, even if you're not listening."

"Did you happen to hear if Rachel at least had a boyfriend or someone in that last year before she took off?"

"I believe she did. We didn't see him much. Her parents . . . to be honest, they didn't like her being distracted from her skating. And they didn't like the boy, either. I don't remember much about it, except he had one of those Asian immigrant names, and I always thought . . . I thought . . ." Bex could hear Toni changing her mind and deciding not to finish the sentence. "I'm sure I could have been wrong. Like I said, they weren't my students. . . ."

"How did Robby feel about Rachel's boyfriend?"

"Robby didn't like her being distracted, either. Not that I think she was. I believe I may have seen the boyfriend a grand total of one time at the rink when they were practicing, and maybe another time at Nationals. As far as I could tell, he wasn't getting in Rachel's way. If anything, he made her happy. And it showed in her performance on the ice."

"So, Toni." Bex figured it had been minutes since her last conjecture. She had to be due. "Do you think Rachel quit skating and ran off because she wanted to get married and her parents and Robby were against it?"

"You don't have to quit skating to get married," Toni exclaimed. "This isn't a girls' school in the 1950s!"

"What if Rachel's parents threatened to cut off her money? What if they made her choose? Or what if she was afraid of what Robby would do to her?"

"Anything is possible, Bex." Toni hesitated. And then, quite logically, she asked, "But what does this have to do with her murder?"

Bex wished she knew. (She also wished Toni would stop asking her such logical questions, it made it hard to think.) As she pulled into the dark driveway of Rachel Rose's home, she tried to figure out how the heretofore unmentioned boyfriend/husband might fit into the "Robby was in love with Rachel, Felicia was a jealous wife, Robby had a temper, Felicia had a motive except that Rachel wasn't actually killed fourteen years ago but earlier this week" scenario.

All the lights were off in Rachel's house. Bex knew this because, after ringing the doorbell in the most annoying manner that she knew and getting no answer, she'd crunched through the late fall leaves and snuck around to peek into all the tightly closed windows she was tall enough to reach. She also considered climbing a tree to cross the second floor windows off her list. In the end, though, Bex decided that it wasn't worth the neighbors seeing her and raising the alarm. The last thing she wanted to do was spend the evening explaining to the local police why she was lurking around a recently murdered woman's home.

And so Bex chose to try a tactic utterly unfamiliar to her. She chose to sit down quietly on Rachel's front stoop, and wait. She figured the husband had to come home eventually.

Although, a half hour into her vigil, Bex was starting to seriously reconsider her hypothesis. For one thing, it was after eight P.M. and thus pitch-dark now. For another, it was December, and, while mild for the season, it was still rather cold. Most importantly though, Bex was starting to get very, very bored. There was just so much drama one could coax out of repeatedly blowing on one's hands for warmth, clapping them together when that failed, and, finally, sitting on them. It was equally dull to stomp her feet against the wooden porch to keep them from freezing and/or falling asleep. Even trying to make a little dance out of it failed to keep Bex's attention for long. Alas, when Bex got bored, Bex went looking to relieve that boredom.

By any means (sorry, Malcolm X) necessary.

Despite her vow to be a good girl and just stay put, Bex got up. She told herself it was just so she could jump around in place and get warm. But, it wouldn't be the first time she'd let herself down. (Herself could really be very gullible about things like this sometimes.)

Casually, still telling herself that it was all in the interest of precious warmth, Bex mozied over to Rachel's front door. She got down on her knees. She peeked through the mail slot.

Which was when she heard the car pulling into the driveway.

Bex leapt to her feet. Smacking the bridge of her nose along the way.

"Ow," Bex yelled out, covering her aching nose with one hand as she turned around in the direction of the car. And got hit by two blinding headlights blaring straight into her eyes as a result.

"Ow," Bex yelled out again, shielding her eyes with her other hand and wincing.

She looked like a little kid, trying to get out of trouble by covering her face and insisting, "You can't see me!"

She realized it was not the most mature or respectable of stances with which to introduce herself to Rachel Rose's husband.

But, as it turned out, introductions didn't prove to be necessary.

Because, when the headlights were turned off and the passengers exited their blue Toyota, Bex found herself standing angry face to bruised nose with Jeremy and Craig Hunt.

Twelve

Resolved: All the previous times in her life when Bex had been really, really speechless did not hold a candle to the dumbness with which she was struck now. Bex didn't just not know what to say on this given occasion, she'd also managed to forget what it was one said on any occasion. If asked that instant, she probably would not know the correct greeting for someone celebrating a birthday or even how to ask, say, a taxi driver to please back up off her foot. All she could do was stand there, looking deer-eyed from Craig to Jeremy, and pitifully clutch her nose. At the moment, even an encore "ow" seemed beyond her capabilities.

Her slightest consolation was that Craig Hunt seemed to be in the same boat. He'd rushed up the stairs, two at a time, to get a better look at his intruder. But, once he realized who it was, he stopped dead in his tracks, mutely wrapping his fingers around a porch pillar. Whether he intended to smack her with it, or just needed support, Bex couldn't be sure. Neither, apparently, could he.

Finally, it was Jeremy who broke through their Marcel Marceau imitations. He'd come up the stairs behind his dad. He, too, stood for a moment looking at them both. And then he said, "Ms. Levy? What are you doing here?"

"Yes, Ms. Levy." When Craig Hunt spoke, it wasn't with the cool, confident demeanor he'd exhibited back at the rink. His voice sounded raspy, as if he'd been screaming for days. Or crying. And yet, the trademark sarcasm was unmistakable. "What the hell are you doing here?"

"Rachel," she managed to croak out. It wasn't an explanation or even a verb, and yet it was truly the only honest answer.

"She's none of your business. Just like Jeremy was none of your business." Craig grabbed his son by the arm and moved to unlock their front door.

"You and Rachel are married," Bex stated the obvious. Perhaps it was for the benefit of those viewers who tuned in late to their regularly scheduled programming.

"What do you want?" Craig led Jeremy into the house and whipped around, stunning Bex with both his ferocity and his visible, utter despair. "What the hell do you want from us? Haven't you done enough?"

"I—I only—I was doing this piece—"

"Your precious piece!" Bex thought he might lunge for her then, but Craig only slashed his hands angrily through the air, then brought them to his head, running his shaking fingers through his hair and pulling so hard that Bex saw him rip out several follicles. "I don't want to fucking hear about your precious piece. Your piece, Ms. Levy, is what got my wife killed!"

He calmed down after that. Not because of anything Bex did, but because Craig realized that Jeremy was still standing right behind him. He took a deep breath, and, with a final if-looks-could-disembowel glare at Bex, turned around to face his son, forcing his voice to return to normal.

Jeremy stood half-hidden behind the front door, turning the knob this way and that with one hand. He didn't look up to face Craig or Bex. He just turned the knob. Back and forth. Back and forth. His shoulders were shaking, but the knob kept turning.

Craig knelt down, his knees cracking a bit, so he could look up into his son's face. Jeremy still avoided looking at him. Craig said, "I seriously suck, Jer. I'm sorry."

"Don't yell at her."

Craig looked over his shoulder at Bex, and sighed. "I won't."

That was a nice thing to know. Bex did notice, however, that Craig didn't promise not to pulverize or otherwise disassemble her.

"Can I go upstairs?" Jeremy asked. "I'm tired."

"You don't want dinner?"

"No."

"Not even a sandwich?"

"No." Jeremy finally looked up. "Can I just go upstairs? Please?"

Craig stood. He put his hand on the boy's shoulder. "I really am sorry."

Jeremy turned around and walked upstairs without another word.

Leaving Bex and Craig alone. Him inside the house, her on the porch. The way Bex saw it, she had two choices: She could turn tail and scamper away, not unlike Jeremy. Or she could force her way inside the house and ask Craig Hunt a few questions only he knew the answer to.

Bex knew what the professional and brave thing to do would be. But she stepped inside the house, anyway.

She waited for him to snatch her up bodily and toss her onto the welcome mat. When he didn't, Bex guessed that Craig was either too exhausted to do much more than shut the door behind her, or he was planning something much more insidious and didn't want the neighbors to see.

"Jeremy has barely eaten these last three days," Craig accused. "You have no idea how upset he is."

"I didn't mean to upset him."

"What did you mean to do? What are you, stalking us? Is this the new 24/7 thing? Stalk skaters until they crack?"

"I wanted to do a piece on Rachel."

"I know. She told me."

"I don't understand," Bex said. "Why were you all living like this? Why all the secrecy?"

"It's none of your business."

He had a point. But, if 24/7 let trivialities like that stop them, they'd never put anything on the air outside of name, rank, and USFSA number.

"Were you dating Rachel back when she was skating with Robby?" Bex asked. "Was she cheating on the Asian guy with you, and that's why you two had to run off and get married?"

Craig stared at her blankly. "What Asian guy? What are you talking about?"

"Toni Wright said Rachel Rose was dating some Asian guy that her parents and Robby didn't like her seeing, because he was distracting her from her skating."

Craig began to laugh. He laughed so hard that it turned into a cough and he had to sit down on the couch to compose himself. The cough went on and on until he practically gagged. Bex was afraid he was going to choke. Before he told her what was so damn funny.

Finally, he managed to croak out, "For your information, Ms. Bex Levy, crack researcher, *I* happen to be the Asian guy."

Bex gulped. One of the goals of her life was to be as politically correct as possible. She always referred to African-Americans and Hispanics in her notes and insisted the announcers do likewise on-air. She always made sure they knew which ethnic republics all of the former Soviet-bloc skaters were from so that they didn't accidentally call a Latvian a Russian. And she insisted her announcers use "he or she" when making general, nongender specific statements. Bex worked so hard. And here she'd messed up so badly.

"I—I'm sorry. I guess I assumed . . . I have no right to assume, I know that, it's wrong of me. All people don't look the same, of course, and I really should be more sensitive to—"

Craig asked, "Did Toni say Rachel was dating an Asian guy—"

"Asian-American. I know I should have said Asian-American."

"Or did she say Rachel was dating a guy with an Asian name?"

Bex hesitated. And she wondered when she would get into the habit of hearing what people actually said, instead of just what she wanted to hear. She said, "I think Toni said, 'Asian name.' "

"Hiroshi," Craig offered helpfully. "Was it Craig Hiroshi?"

"Maybe. She actually didn't say what it was." Bex heard a distant bell go off in the back of her head and sincerely hoped it wasn't the start of a concussion from her smacking her face against the door. She put two and two together enough to ask, "That place where you worked . . ."

"My mom and dad."

"Really?" The un-PC question slipped out before Bex could properly censor herself. She was immediately sorry. But, clearly not so sorry that she didn't add insult to blurt by adding, "You look nothing like either of them!"

For a moment, she was afraid Craig would go off on another *Camille*-worthy laughing jag. "I'm adopted," he explained. "Jenny and Michael Hiroshi adopted me when I was eight."

"Oh. I see."

"So you can relax. I'm not really Asian. Or Asian-American. So no offense taken."

"But, why did they say all those horrible things about you when I came to their store, then?"

"To throw you off track. Make you think I was a major loser who took off all the time for no reason, so there was nothing to be suspicious about."

"Oh," she repeated. "They did a nice job. I really thought you were pretty lame."

"Yeah, they're great. Not a lot of people would take a risk adopting a kid as old as I was. And I was in foster care before that, which made it even riskier. But, hey, it all turned out for the best. That's why I have all sorts of legal documents in two names. Craig Hiroshi, and Craig Hunt. Convenient, no? Especially for a life on the run."

"But, why are you on the run, that's what I don't understand. Was it because of Rachel's parents? Were you afraid they wouldn't approve of your getting married?"

"Rachel's parents' idea of disapproval was to frown in unison and maybe cross their arms. I think we could have handled that without too much lifelong trauma."

"Then it was Robby. It had to be Robby. I saw the way

she was looking at that tape I made of him. Robby beat Rachel just like he did Felicia, and she couldn't take it anymore. Her parents wouldn't let her quit skating and so you two had to run away to protect her."

"He raped her," Craig said.

"What?" Bex froze in her tracks. For someone who saw as many *Lifetime* TV movies as she did, it still embarrassed Bex how easily she got flustered by the brutality of the real world.

"Robby never hit Rachel. Isn't that funny? Not only because she was a better skater than Felicia, but because he had her on this pedestal. He thought she was some perfect princess put on earth for him to stare at and obsess over. He would have left Felicia and their marriage in a finger-snap if Rachel ever even suggested she might be interested. He never laid a finger on her. Until he got tired of waiting for her to dump me and fall into his arms. So he raped her. After a midnight practice session, in the dressing room at the rink. Rachel always suspected that their coach heard her screaming. But he didn't do a thing about it. In a way, that's actually what soured her on skating more than the actual attack. She could have gotten a new partner. Lots of women go on with their lives after being raped, and Rachel was the strongest person I ever knew. She could have survived the assault. But to know that her coach heard and didn't do anything to help. That's what killed her spirit."

"And Jeremy . . ." Bex prompted. It was obvious, but she still needed to hear Craig say it.

"What about Jeremy?"

"Jeremy," Bex couldn't quite bring herself to say the incriminating words. So she settled for something obvious. "He's thirteen years old. And a great skater. And he's blonde, Craig. I mean, he's really, really blonde."

Craig sighed. He looked up at a standing Bex from where he was sitting on the couch, his shoulders slumped, one hand covering his mouth to control the coughs that periodically recurred.

"Yeah," Craig said softly. "Jeremy is really, really blonde."

"Does he know?"

"No. And he doesn't need to."

"Does Robby know?"

"Are you insane?" Craig leapt off the couch and all but flung himself into Bex's face. The man wasn't just invading her personal space, he was sucking up all the air in it, too. "Why do you think Rachel and I did all this? You think we like living like fugitives? You think we enjoy lying to our kid and moving all the time and not being able to tell him why?"

"But, it's not like Robby could take Jeremy away from you." Bex had to take a step back. She knew it put her in a weaker position, but bargaining strength wasn't her primary concern at the moment. "The man is a criminal. No court would give him custody of a little boy."

"And, of course, Robby Sharpton is so law-abiding, a court order would just do the trick, no sweat." Craig turned away from Bex in disgust. "Get real."

"But how do you know Robby would even be interested in Jeremy? Or in finding Rachel? When I interviewed him, he didn't even mention her name until I brought it up. He was a lot more interested in talking about Felicia and that part of his life."

"How do I know?" Craig asked. "Well, let's see, how about this? How about the fact that, the week he got out of prison—the first week—Robby started calling around, looking for Rachel. Not Felicia—who he'd actually been married to and who he'd gone to prison over, but Rachel.

He was so not interested in Rachel that he called our house, asking to see her. That's when Jeremy and I moved away. Before that, we were living a more or less normal life. Not exactly publishing birth announcements in *Skating Magazine,* but more or less normal. After Robby called, though . . . we couldn't let him know about Jeremy. Rachel and I thought it would be better if I kept him with me because Robby knew what Rachel looked like, and if he ever saw her with a child, he'd make the connection right away. But, he barely knew me, so it wasn't as risky. We moved to Connecticut. My parents helped us out a lot. And the three of us could still see each other. We'd come up here once in a while, especially in the summer, when Jeremy was out of school. And then there were all the trips we could take, thanks to Rachel's agency. Not very likely we'd run into Robby or anyone he knew on an African safari. It was the perfect plan," Craig said, "if Jeremy's kindergarten class hadn't taken that damn trip to the ice rink."

Oh, yes. The ice rink. Bex had almost forgotten that's where this all began. Was it only a few days ago that Toni called to say that Jeremy was the most talented young skater in America? And that Bex would never get the chance to see him?

She said, "That's why you didn't want Jeremy going to Nationals. Too many people who could recognize him. Or at least recognize that he reminded them of someone they once knew."

"That would be a big 'duh,' Ms. Levy. But, actually, there was only one person I was afraid would recognize him. Especially if 24/7 insisted on putting Jeremy on television."

"So why let him skate then at all? Why take such a huge risk?"

"Because he loved it. Because being on the ice made him happier than I'd ever seen him anywhere. And because I loved my son. I wanted to see him happy. It was selfish of me, I know. I should have been stronger, I should have said no earlier. But, I didn't. I caved. Because I liked seeing him smile. And because I'd already screwed up his life in plenty of ways and, just once, I wanted to do something that really, truly made him happy. One day, when you have children, Ms. Levy, maybe you'll understand."

"But, you did build one safeguard into the system, didn't you?" Bex guessed. "You hired Toni to be his coach. Because you knew Toni didn't produce champions."

"That would be another 'duh,' Ms. Levy," Craig said. But, this time, there was definite respect in his voice. And then he shrugged. "Not that it worked anyway. Turned out Toni was a great coach. She's just never been given the chance because the good kids would usually leave her. Well, Jeremy stuck around, and I'll be damned if she didn't coach the hell out of him. Even you said he could medal at Nationals this year, didn't you?"

"Yes, I think he could."

"Great. Terrific. That's really great to hear. I'm sure Toni was glad to hear it, too. She definitely got her money's worth, calling you down to offer an opinion, didn't she? And I really hope you're pleased with yourself, too. Because you know, Ms. Levy—may I call you Bex?"

"Um, sure . . . ." Why was Craig suddenly being so friendly? And why was he advancing on her again, eyes flashing an anger that a more poetically inclined researcher might have described as an almost uninhibited madness?

"Because, Bex, you do know that my wife's murder is utterly, thoroughly, totally, and one hundred percent your fault."

Thirteen

"My fault?" Bex croaked, hoping mightily that her strangled query was managing to sound like an indignant question, rather than a guilty repetition of the fear that had been sloshing around her brain since she'd first read about Rachel on the sports ticker.

"What do you think prompted Robby to go after Rachel?" Craig demanded. "Why now? It's been eight years since he last tried to contact us. Do you really think he would have, all of a sudden, remembered his grudge against Rachel if you hadn't stirred all of this up last week?"

"Wait a minute, wait a minute, hold on." Bex may have lacked the ability to stop herself from leaping to conclusions based on minimum evidence, but she certainly could recognize the syndrome in others. "Where are you getting your information? Why are you so sure that Robby killed Rachel?"

"Who else could it have been? Do you think my wife had enemies lurking in the shadows? That this was some sort of, what, travel agency revenge killing? It's obvious, Bex. You reminded Robby Sharpton of Rachel's existence, and he tracked her down and killed her."

"Why?" Bex asked the obvious. "You said it yourself, it's been years since Robby's tried to contact Rachel. He's built a life for himself. He has a home; he's stayed out of trouble. Why would he suddenly want to go after Rachel now? You said he didn't know about Jeremy, so what could Rachel have possibly had that he wanted? And, more to the point, why would he ever want to go after Rachel? It's not like she pressed rape charges against him. It's not like she even told anyone what he did. What threat did she pose to him, that he'd need to kill her?"

"Well, to start with, he's a nut," Craig snapped. "How's that for a motive? The guy likes to hurt women. That's a fact. He beat Felicia so badly, she ended up in the hospital. That is also a fact. What motive did he have for that, Bex?"

"I—I don't know," she admitted. Then, as was her wont when facing a question to which she didn't know the answer, Bex changed the subject. "But you can't compare Felicia's situation to Rachel's. They were married, after all. Married people . . . get on each other's nerves."

"To the point of broken bones and jail terms?"

"Sometimes," Bex stubbornly insisted. Confident in the knowledge that, on this point, at least, her *Lifetime* movies squarely backed her up. "But Robby hadn't seen Rachel in years, right?" A thought occurred to Bex. "Or had he?"

"What's that supposed to mean?"

"Had Robby and Rachel been in touch?"

"Of course not!"

"How do you know?" Bex was making it all up as she went along, but it made a heck of a lot of sense in her head. She hoped the theory would carry over when words met sound. "I mean, you and Rachel lived apart. You didn't know everyone she spoke to or had contact with."

"Are you out of your mind, Bex? I just told you, the reason my wife and I lived apart, the reason we taught our son to lie about pretty much his entire life, was because we were trying to stay away from Robby Sharpton."

"That's what you say," Bex pointed out.

"Excuse me?"

"You told me your side of the story. About Rachel and Robby and how you two ran away to keep him from Jeremy. But how do I know it's true? What proof do you have?"

Craig stared at Bex, dumbfounded. "You expect me to prove my life to you?"

That would be very nice, actually. It would save Bex a lot of legwork.

"Well . . ."

"My God, you have a lot of nerve!"

"Thank you," Bex blurted out, before she had the chance to censor herself. Frankly, one of her biggest problems since taking this job had proven to be Bex's seeming lack of nerve. After all, she could barely stand up to Gil, or even Toni, most of the time.

"Just get out of my house." Craig marched over to the door and flung it open. "Get out and leave us alone. I think you've done enough damage."

Bex took a step toward the door. It was instinctive. Someone told her to get out, she got out. She liked to think of it less as cowardice and more as good manners. But, on the other hand, she'd just been accused of possessing an excess of nerve. Shouldn't she live up to the moniker?

Bex said, "I have a few more questions."

"Get out before, God help me, I throw you out."

"You promised Jeremy—"

"Not to yell at you anymore. I don't remember any pledges about physical violence."

"And Robby was the one with the problem?"

As soon as the words were out of her mouth, Bex knew she'd gone too far. It was one thing to bait and quarrel with a man on the edge. It was probably another to accuse him of being capable of the sort of violence that he claimed had just been visited on his wife.

She expected him to come at her. To lunge physically, or at least to explode into a barrage of words one couldn't say on television or probably around someone who worked on it.

But Craig did neither. He simply squeezed both his fists until Bex could see the blue veins on the backs of his hands pulse with such fervor, she feared they'd pop and hemorrhage all over the rug. He stared at her without moving, seemingly without breathing. Bex stared back, rooted to the spot in a combination of terror and curiosity. She'd obviously hit a raw nerve. The question was: Would it lead to an informational gusher?

Craig took a deep breath. No, that wasn't right. Craig *forced* himself to take a deep breath. Even as his entire body stretched taut to reject it.

His voice shaking despite the rest of him remaining deathly still, Craig demanded, "What do you want from me? What do you want me to say? My wife is dead, Bex. Do you understand that? She's gone. Fourteen years ago, she and I gave up the lives we had—now, granted, hers was a lot more glamorous than mine, but I was doing okay; I was going to college, I had plans for the future, I was going to be an electrical engineer, believe it or not, make my parents proud. But, none of that mattered ultimately. When it came down to making a choice, we both gave up our respective lives without a second thought, because the life we wanted to live together, as a family with Jeremy, was so much more important than any life we could ever live apart. That kind of attachment probably isn't a healthy way to live, is it? I'm sure there are all sorts of books being written now, on the subject of having your own life and your own space and not getting lost in being part of a couple or a family. Well, we never read those books. Our lives may have been strange, but we were happy. We were happy, Bex. That's also a fact and, frankly, I don't give a damn if you believe me or not. Rachel and I were together, and we were happy. And now, Rachel is gone. She is gone and she is never, ever coming back. And you know what? I have no idea what to do with myself now. If it weren't for Jeremy, I couldn't think of a single reason to even get up in the morning."

Bex didn't know what to say.

But, then again, when had that ever stopped her from speaking? She asked, "And you're sure Robby Sharpton killed your wife?"

"Of course I'm sure. Hell, Bex, you've been stalking—"

"Researching. I've been researching."

"Fine. Researching. You've been researching us and this whole sorry tale for days now. You tell me: Who else could have possibly had a motive for killing my wife?"

"Well," Bex hesitated, wondering if the question was meant to be rhetorical, but realizing that her need to show off what she'd learned would eventually supersede any other instinct or doubt, and so she might as well cut to the chase and give in to it. "There's Felicia, for one."

"Why would Felicia kill Rachel?"

"Because she was jealous of Robby's obsession with her. Have you ever talked to Felicia? I mean, talk about obsession—her feelings for Robby weren't exactly cool and detached. She told me she was so crazy about him, she didn't even mind his leaving her to skate with Rachel, as long as she was the one he married."

"So? How's that obsessive? You just said she didn't mind him going to Rachel."

"She didn't mind him *skating* with Rachel. Obsessing over her was another story."

"Wouldn't it make more sense for her to kill Robby, then?"

"Obsessives aren't known for their sterling logic, Craig."

"Rachel never gave Robby a second glance. She was no threat to Felicia. And besides, this all happened over fourteen years ago. Why would Felicia go after Rachel now?"

Bex hated to say it, since it didn't exactly shove her into the best light. But, it was the most obvious answer. She said, "For the same reason that you think Robby came after Rachel. Because I reminded her of it."

Craig shook his head. "No. No, it doesn't make any sense. Rachel was as much Robby's victim as Felicia was."

"Maybe that's not how Felicia sees it." It was time to tread delicately again. Bex sure did wish she knew how one did that. "I mean, you say that Rachel insisted that Robby raped her. But, what if Felicia didn't see it that way? What if she thought it was consensual? What if she thought her husband and your wife were having an affair?"

"Then she's an idiot. Rachel would have never in a million years . . . . Besides, logically, how would Felicia have even known about it? You think Robby went bragging to her afterward?"

"Well, people at the rink, they do talk amongst themselves, don't they? And didn't you say Rachel thought her coach knew about it? That he'd heard? Maybe he told someone and they told someone and before anyone knew it, it was all over the rink. That's certainly possible, isn't it?"

"And you think Felicia blamed Rachel? Blamed her enough to kill her?"

Bex was about to nod ardently when another conjecture gripped her chin and froze it mid-bob. "Craig? All these years you and Rachel were working so hard to keep Robby from finding out about Jeremy, did you ever think about Felicia finding out about him?"

"What do you mean?"

"Maybe it wasn't rink gossip that clued Felicia in about Robby and Rachel."

"For God's sake, there was never any Robby and Rachel except in Robby's sick, twisted, half-frozen mind, how many times do I have to tell you that?"

"Fine, fine." There would be time to debate those specifics later. "But, what I mean is, what if it wasn't the coach, or anyone else for that matter, who gossiped? What if Felicia found out about Jeremy being Rachel's son? Be honest, Craig. I know you love him and you raised him and you consider him yours. But, really, all Felicia would have to do is look at him, and she'd know he was Robby's, wouldn't she?"

Her question made Craig visibly uncomfortable. He shifted his weight from foot to foot and looked out the window. But, he did concede. "There's a strong resemblance. Only on the outside, though. Jeremy is nothing like Robby on the inside. He's a good kid."

"I know," Bex said softly. "You and Rachel did a good job with him. I'm really impressed. I mean, especially because it couldn't have been easy for you, raising Robby Sharpton's son. . . ."

"I never thought of him that way." Craig shrugged. "It sounds like a platitude but, I really never thought of him like that. Genetics are so stupid and unimportant. My own parents taught me that much, and I barely knew either of them. I consider Michael Hiroshi my father, and I consider Jeremy my son. It's pretty simple, actually. You probably don't believe me, but Robby Sharpton never really entered the equation."

"I believe you," Bex said honestly. "I do. But, do you think that would have mattered to Felicia Tufts? All she'd have seen is that her husband had a child with another woman. And not just any other woman. Felicia's rival."

"And so she killed Rachel? Fourteen years after the fact?"

"Jealousy is pretty powerful. And, honestly, Felicia wasn't too nice to me when I tried to talk to her about Robby and Rachel. I think she may still be pretty bitter."

"And you don't think any of that bitterness possibly had to do with your unaggressive and nonconfrontational interviewing style, do you?"

Bex valiantly fought the urge to stick her tongue out at him. She didn't think it was in the handbook for how to behave around the recently bereaved.

"Fine, so I put her in a bad mood. But, I still think my theory has validity."

"What's in this for you, Bex?" Craig suddenly asked. She wasn't sure if it was a clever plan to throw her off balance now that she was dangerously close to the truth, or if he was just tired of listening to her and so desperate to change the subject that he instinctively did so by focusing on the one topic he knew most folks found infinitely fascinating—themselves. "Why are you so doggone determined to get to the bottom of this?"

"It's my job."

"And that's all?"

"And . . . I like to know the truth. I don't like being lied to."

"You think I am? Lying to you? Why would I do that, Bex?"

"Because," and this was the part where, in retrospect, it really, really would have helped if Bex possessed the ability to think at least a second before she spoke. "Because maybe you actually killed Rachel and are using Robby Sharpton to cover it up."

Yes. In retrospect, the ability to think before she spoke and—here came the really key part—maybe, possibly censor herself, would have come in very handy, indeed.

Needless to say, following the articulation of her latest theory, Bex found her welcome in the Hunt home—not particularly warm to begin with—definitely wearing thin. Oh, who was she kidding? She hightailed it out of there as soon as she saw Craig's face start to resemble the Nazi from *Raiders of the Lost Ark* seconds before he melted. Only Craig somehow managed to look worse. She figured the time for talk was now over. It was time to duck and cover.

If it weren't for needing to use at least one foot to work the gas and brakes, Bex would have been kicking herself the entire drive home. What in the world had possessed her to say that?

And then she remembered: The notion had come to into her head at a time when she was not unconscious or chewing. Obviously that was enough reason to blurt it out without forethought.

Bex was still kicking herself when she returned to the office the next morning and, with a heavy sigh, plopped herself down in her chair, ready to listen to the dozens of phone messages that had accumulated in her absence.

The first two were from Gil, asking if they didn't have a meeting scheduled? He seemed to remember their having a meeting scheduled. Something about a feature she wanted to show him, and where the hell was she, anyway?

Another handful were from elite skaters returning her calls of God only knew how long ago, providing answers to holes she needed to plug in their official bios.

At least, Bex sincerely hoped that's what the calls were about. One message simply said, "This is Kerry Ryder. I'm gonna get you, sucka."

As Bex had called Kerry a week earlier to find out what music she'd be skating to for her Nationals short program, she preferred to think that she'd been given her answer via the title of a movie soundtrack, rather than issued a threat.

The last message in the rotation had been left the night before, about an hour after she'd left Craig's. And it was whispered. "Ms. Levy, this is Jeremy Hunt. I really need to talk to you. It's about my dad killing my mom."

Fourteen

Bex's first impulse upon hearing Jeremy's whispered message was to immediately hit the redial button. And who was she not to follow an impulse? Bex punched *69. The phone on the other end rang once. Twice. Three times. Bex waited for a machine to click on. It didn't. She waited for someone to pick up. No one did. Wanting to make sure she was calling the right place, and not simply redialing someone who'd called her after Jeremy and just didn't leave a message, Bex checked the number she'd found for Rachel Rose on the Internet and dialed again by hand. The ringing phone on the other end sounded exactly, she thought, like the one she'd just heard. It also rang seven times without either an answer or a machine.

Obviously, Bex needed to do something now. What they had here was a situation. A situation only she knew about and thus was responsible for. (There was also the minor detail that Bex, very possibly, might have set the whole thing into motion in the first place.) All the more reason for her to act. But, act how?

Well, that part was obvious, wasn't it?

She had to get to Jeremy. Before Craig did.

Bex wondered what Jeremy's message meant. On the one hand, "It's about my dad killing my mom," didn't seem to avail itself to various interpretations. Jeremy was telling her that Craig killed Rachel. Or maybe he was telling her that he suspected Craig of killing Rachel. Or maybe he was telling her that he had proof that Craig killed Rachel. In any case, Bex really needed to speak to Jeremy. The sooner the better.

She dialed the phone again.

This time, on the fifth ring, she got an answer.

"Hello?" The voice sounded as if it belonged to Craig Hunt.

Bex gulped. And wondered how, back when she'd been following her first instinct, she'd intended to respond when faced with Jeremy's father instead of Jeremy. Because the odds were good that's whom she'd get.

"Excuse me, Craig, could I please speak to Jeremy? I believe he had something to tell me about you killing your wife," she most definitely did not say.

Instead, Bex panicked and hung up the phone.

Very professional. Very mature. Very . . . what had Craig called her? Nervy.

She wished she could say she hung up because she'd suddenly come up with a much better, more efficient plan. But mostly it was because she was shaking so badly, Bex doubted she could have gotten the clever words out of her throat even if she had managed to think of some.

Under the circumstances, Bex decided to put clever on the back burner, and try something more in the cowardly and/or obvious category. She called up her new friend and life-advisor, Gretchen, to ask if there was any news on the Rachel Rose murder.

Like, "Did you get the autopsy report back?"

"Yes," Gretchen said brightly. "We did."

"And?"

"And there seemed to be nothing out of the ordinary. The only interesting result was that, due to some wooden splinters found tangled up in Ms. Rose's hair and embedded in her skull, we now believe that she wasn't so much battered by an—"

"You determined the indeterminate object?"

"May I finish, please, Bex?"

"I'm sorry." Nice going, Bex. Your first piece of tangible information in days, and you have to slip into eager-beaver mode and possibly piss off the only person still speaking to you.

"We now believe that rather than being battered by an indeterminate object, Ms. Rose's head was actually smashed against a tree, causing her death."

"So it could have been an accident then?"

"What do you mean?"

"I mean, maybe her assailant didn't mean to kill Rachel. Maybe he just pushed harder than he intended, and she fell and hit her head against the tree and died?"

Bex had never previously considered the possibility of an accident. But, it made a good amount of sense, especially if she accepted Craig Hunt to be the culprit. Because, to Bex, the biggest difficulty with moving him to the head of the suspect list was the fact that the man had appeared genuinely broken up about Rachel's death. Now, granted, he could be a fabulous actor, or a psychopath on par with Robby Sharpton (heck, maybe psychopath was Rachel Rose's type, who knew?). Or, more likely, he could really be distraught and broken up because he'd killed his wife by accident in the middle of an argument. An accident also made it a lot more likely that Jeremy had been a witness to the whole thing.

"So, is that a possibility? That Rachel fell and hit her head?" Bex asked Gretchen.

"Four times?"

Well, there went that theory. And it was such a nice one too, complete with tied up loose ends and a diminished capacity plea.

Bex sighed. "So somebody smashed her head against a tree. Charming." She perked up a bit. "Can you tell from maybe the height or the angle or something, if it was a man or a woman?" Might as well see if science allowed for Felicia Tufts to stay on the list.

"Not really." Gretchen shuffled some papers in the background.

Bex waited for Gretchen to follow up. When she didn't, Bex wondered why she had to do all the work around here. She then asked what, to her, seemed the obvious next question. "Well, was there anything you could tell from the autopsy that you didn't know before?"

"Cause of death," Gretchen reminded. "That's a pretty big one."

"Not if it doesn't help you find the killer," Bex—oh, here was a surprise—blurted out the correction without thinking, then desperately wished she could take the point back. Bex didn't mind being sarcastic or blunt on occasion. (It was part of her charming personality, and if anyone said otherwise, they were wrong.) But, she did try to draw the line at outright obnoxious. Alas, she seemed to have forgotten her drawing pen that morning.

Bex was about to apologize, when Gretchen stiffly told her, "I can assure you the Poconos Police Department is working on it. They're working on it awfully hard. Some of them have even given up vacation days to see if they can crack the case before it gets cold, and they were planning that vacation for months."

Bex bit her lip (also very hard) to keep from asking if maybe, possibly, just by random chance, the dedicated officer in charge of the case might not also be the perfect local guy with whom Gretchen was hoping to start a family despite them both being over forty and a host of other personal details Bex had done her best to forget since their last conversation.

Instead, she settled for, "I'm sorry. Really, I am. It's just that I have this boss, and he really needs me to bring back a story or else I have to pay all my expenses and—"

She never got the chance to finish. Her words triggered another avalanche of empathy and relating from Gretchen, along the lines of aren't bosses the worst, especially New York bosses who live and die by whether you got their client on Page Six, like that's the most important thing in the world and people will actually die if the box office gross doesn't break records its first weekend and don't they know there are more important things in the world like marriage and family life and boy, was she glad to be out of that rat race; Bex should really think of doing the same, she sounded really stressed, did she know that? Maybe some yoga classes would help.

Bex took a deep breath. It was the only thing she actually remembered from the one yoga class she ever took (there was a coupon and the words *free trial* involved) except for how much doing something called a "Down Doggie" hurt, and how, despite the instructor's insisting that there was wisdom trying to get out of her body, Bex begged to differ—the only thing trying to get out of her body were her Achilles tendons, which were strained so tightly she expected them to pop right out of her skin. On the other hand, taking a deep breath did keep her from interrupting Gretchen's ode to family values, so she now deemed the class money well (not) spent.

Bex kept her own counsel while Gretchen pontificated on how much better it was to raise a child in the country rather than the city, and how much better the schools were, even better than the private ones in New York City, which were impossible to get into anyway and then, what did they really offer for their twenty thousand dollars a year except the chance for your kid to mingle with snobs, whereas here, everything was so wholesome, the children practically skipped everywhere while sipping milk fresh from the cow and singing show tunes. (Okay, so Bex paraphrased that last part, but it sure sounded like what Gretchen was implying; Bex wondered if, in addition to her P.R. work with the police department, the woman also sold real estate in her free time.)

Finally, Bex managed to get a word in edgewise and inquire, "Gretchen? Remember when we first talked, you told me that, in cases like this, it's usually the husband who's responsible. Do you have any evidence that Craig Hunt might have killed Rachel?"

Gretchen said, "When we interviewed him, he told us he was home with his son, Jeremy, I think is the name, the morning Rachel was killed. The boy backed him up."

"Did you believe him?"

"Who? Craig or Jeremy?"

"Well, either, actually. How did they seem during the interview?"

"Devastated. They both seemed just devastated. It was such a huge shock. Rachel went out in the morning, didn't tell either of them where she was going, and then, a few hours later, just when they're starting to worry, here come the police at their door to tell them she's been murdered. Can you imagine? That poor little boy! We sent a social worker with the notification unit; it's our standard policy up here. This department is very sensitive to the needs of the community."

"Did Craig tell you if Rachel often went out at dawn without telling her husband or child where she was going?" If she did, that would be most odd, considering how security-obsessed that family was.

"It's a little hard for him to know her routine. From what I understand, Mr. Hunt traveled quite a bit for business, and the boy was away at boarding school for most of the year." Ah, so that was their cover story. It was a pretty good one to explain to the neighbors (and to policemen) why the family was so rarely together. Gretchen added, "But, Mr. Hunt did say he had no idea why she was at the park."

"Was she meeting someone?"

"He didn't know."

"Well, did he have any theories?"

"Not that the officer wrote down."

"Did the officer have any theories?"

"In situations like this, it's usually the husband," Gretchen offered helpfully.

Bex hung up the phone.

Well, she actually said good-bye first and then listened to a story about the odds of in-vitro working on the first try. There was no need to be unnecessarily rude, especially since she might find herself needing Gretchen again in the near future. Minimal information was still better than no information, and even if she took the mountainous scenic route, Gretchen did eventually get around to telling Bex at least one thing that she didn't know.

So, to recap: One down, seventy-eight million details to go.

Bex needed confirmation. Of what didn't even particularly matter at this point. The fact was, over the last few days, she'd heard a lot of different stories from a lot of different people. And not a single one matched up exactly against another. If Bex could only get one person to agree with another's account, she would at least (she hoped) know what direction to continue digging in. As it was, she didn't know who to believe or where to turn.

She supposed she could call Toni again and get her take. But, how many times was Toni supposed to remind Bex that she really didn't know Robby, Rachel, and especially Craig? (Heck, Toni didn't even recognize the latter when he was right in front of her face every day for five years. Obviously, they weren't that close.) What Bex needed was a neutral, U.N.-type observer, who saw all fourteen years ago, yet was far enough removed from the situation to remain unbiased.

Bex looked back over her list of suspects. And, with a sigh, realized that, at this point, the person who seemed most likely not to be harboring a present day agenda was Felicia Tufts. After all, she appeared to have come out from the fracas the most unscathed (wife-battering aside). She wasn't living in hiding like Rachel and Craig. She hadn't served a prison term like Robby. Heck, she had the nicest apartment of them all. By New York real estate laws, obviously that meant she was the happiest. Plus, she really did have the weakest reason for killing Rachel. It was one thing to carry a grudge. But to act on it, out of the blue, fourteen years later was just weird. (And, yes, Bex was aware that it might not be "out of the blue" if one factored in Bex's recent opening of old wounds. But one did not care to do that sort of factoring right now, thank you.)

So, while waiting for brilliant inspiration to strike re: what she should do about Jeremy, Bex decided to bite the bullet of rudeness and give Felicia another call. After all, she couldn't strike out any worse this time than she had initially.

Except that, this time, when Bex called, Felicia didn't seem to be home.

Would that, technically, be a strikeout, Bex wondered?

No, she decided, it was more of a draw.

Although it did make it clear to Bex that she was now officially out of stalling options. She picked up her purse, locked her office door and headed for the 24/7 parking garage. To gamble that her ancient car had one more trip up to the Poconos in it.

This time, Bex did not park in the Hunts' driveway. She wanted to be free to make a quick getaway. And she was too chicken to let Craig see her before she was ready.

And so, for about fifteen minutes, Bex sat in her car.

A most productive use of her time, to be sure. She passed it by doing some calculations: If 24/7 were paying her by the hour (which, God forbid, it would ever do; they liked their employees indentured . . . oops, sorry, salaried—Freudian slip), then how much money was her procrastination costing Gil? The thought of his losing even pennies due to her cowardice made Bex feel a smidge better about herself. But then she remembered that the said pennies (quickly turning into quarters as she sat) would be coming out of her own pocket unless Bex came up with a viable story for the Nationals broadcast.

It was amazing how quickly her self-esteem shrank in direct proportion with her bank account. And how immediately parsimony overruled fear.

Bex got out of the car. She walked up the stairs to Rachel and Craig's house. She rang the bell before her brain had time to, self-protectively, snatch away her finger. Her determination caused Bex to push the button so hard that she bent her nail back in the wrong direction. She yelped and stuck it in her mouth to soothe the pain.

Which was naturally what she was doing when Craig opened the door.

Someday, after this was all over and Bex was a legendary murder-solving hero, and she and Craig (assuming he wasn't the murderer whose killing spree made her legendary) had a chance to sit down for a nice, long chat, Bex would love to find out what he thought of her, considering that, every time they'd met up so far, she'd been either banging her nose on his mail slot or sucking her finger on his porch. Classy, no?

"Go to hell," Craig said immediately upon seeing her.

All right. So, at this juncture, Bex could extrapolate that his current opinion of her wasn't particularly high. And it probably didn't even have everything to do with the nose bumping and finger sucking.

"Please," she said, not sure what exactly might come out her mouth, but deciding civility was as good of a place to start as any.

"Please what?"

Oh, sure, put her on the spot, why don't you?

Bex hesitated. She hesitated for a number of reasons. Not the least of which was the fact that Craig Hunt most certainly didn't look good. And not in the way he hadn't looked good the day before. The day before, Craig had merely looked like he'd slept in his clothes, hadn't shaved for a while, and had been ripping hair out of his head more frequently than was probably recommended by the president-and-also-a-customer of The Hair Club for Men.

Which, under the my-wife-has-been-killed circumstances, was a perfectly reasonable state to be in.

Today, though, Craig looked like not only had his clothes served another night as de facto pajamas, but also as if he'd attempted to shave but somewhere along the way had lost the ability. Both cheeks, and a horizontal line right under his left cheekbone, were scraped and starting to scab. Dried blood caked his lower lip from where he'd dug in his teeth and opened two raw gashes. His hands didn't so much shake as twitch, the fists seemingly opening and closing of their own accord.

"What?" he asked, emphasizing every letter of every word as if doing anything less would cause him to lose his grip on the sentence. And on anything else currently dangling by a slender thread. "Do you want?"

Nothing. Now more than ever, Bex thought, would be a good time to say nothing, turn tail and flee. And maybe whip out her pepper spray for good measure.

But then she took a second look at Craig's battered face. And she wondered if the slashes across his skin were really caused by a shaving razor. Or by a pair of hands clawing desperately to defend themselves?

"Where's Jeremy?" Bex demanded, drawing melodrama-type courage from the fact that she was finally acting in someone else's best interests for a change, instead of her own.

"It's none of your business."

"He called me last night," Bex said.

"He what? Last night? What did he say?" Craig took a step toward her, as if he needed the answer so quickly, only shaking it out of Bex could get it to him fast enough.

"He said he needed to talk to me."

"About what?"

"About you."

"Me?" Craig appeared so genuinely stunned by her reply that Bex had to wonder what he'd been expecting her to say.

"Yes." She looked around the living room, which, unlike Craig, actually looked relatively tidy. Either father and son hadn't been spending much time there, or else he'd recently cleaned up. To cover up an activity that could only be described as nefarious. "So, may I see him, please?"

"He isn't here."

"Where is he?"

"I—It's none of your business."

"I just told you, Jeremy called me last night. That makes it my business."

"Prove it," Craig said.

Bex considered suggesting they call into her voicemail so Craig and she could listen to Jeremy's desperate message together. But then she realized that standing next to a ready-to-snap Craig Hunt as he heard his son whisper, "Ms. Levy, this is Jeremy Hunt. I really need to talk to you. It's about my dad killing my mom," just might fall under the category of activities that could prove dangerous to children and other living things.

"I need to speak to Jeremy, Mr. Hunt," Bex heard herself getting all official, and decided it must be to cover up her fear. She hoped her self-preservation instincts knew what they were doing, because she certainly no longer did. "I'm afraid that if you keep hindering me, I'll be forced to—"

"You'll be forced to what? What? Stalk me, again? Try to break into my house, nose first—again? Turn my life upside down? Get my wife murdered? Kidnap my son? Because you know what? About that last one? Sorry, but I've got you there, Bex. You're too late. Jeremy's already gone!"

Fifteen

"Gone?" Bex repeated. It was a trick she picked up from zoning out in high school. If you repeated the last word you'd just heard, it might give your wandering brain opportunity to run after and capture the previously missed sentence in its entirety. This, in turn, would buy you enough time to come up with a clever answer before the asker even realized you were stalling. At least, that was the theory, anyway. "What do you mean Jeremy is gone?"

"It means, Bex, that I have no idea, at this moment, where my thirteen-year-old son might be, who he's with, or what's happening to him. Are you happy now? You tried so desperately to turn him into a missing person and, voila! You got your wish!" Under the circumstances, Craig's taunting of her might have seemed grossly inappropriate or callous. If it weren't for the fact that it also looked like, any minute now, the grown man might sit down on his living room floor, cover his face with his hands, and burst into tears.

"What happened?" Bex asked softly, realizing that

Craig Hunt was at the end of his rope. That fourteen years of impeccable control had just shattered in the space of three unbelievably unbearable days. And that she, if not solely responsible for the breakdown, was also in way too deep to pretend that her involvement could even be limited to the Supporting Actress category.

"I don't know," he said. "I have no idea. I went out this morning . . . . I knew I should have taken Jeremy with me, but he was sleeping and he's been so . . . I wanted him to get some rest."

"Where did you go?" Bex couldn't help it. Who, what, where, when, why, and how was tattooed on her consciousness like some people knew their ABCs and multiplication tables.

Craig looked at Bex as if he wished he could strangle her. For most people, this would have probably been disconcerting. Luckily, Bex worked in television. People looked like they wanted to strangle her rather often. It was one of those fringe benefits of working with Gil Cahill. Ergo, she barely flinched.

"I went to the morgue." Craig snapped his words, rather than Bex's neck. This was a good thing. "Is that okay with you? They released Rachel's body this morning and I had some papers to sign. I didn't really think Jeremy needed to be a part of that."

Bex nodded sympathetically. And made a mental note to check out his story.

"When I got home, Jeremy was gone."

"Just gone? Just like that?"

"You know another definition of *gone* that I'm not aware of?"

"Did he take anything with him? Like his clothes or . . . his skates?"

"You think Jeremy ran away to join an ice show?"

Actually, the thought hadn't crossed Bex's mind. She was just trying to be thorough. But, Craig did have a good point. Whether he'd initially meant it sarcastically or not. Bex asked, "Do you think Jeremy might have run away from home?"

"Why would he do that?"

Because his mother was dead and he'd called a more-or-less total stranger to implicate his father in the crime? That sure did sound like a good enough reason to Bex. Of course, once again, this wasn't really info she thought might be prudent to share with Craig at this particular time. So she improvised. "Maybe . . . maybe . . . maybe he did it because he really wanted to go to Nationals!"

Oh, boy, that was a good one! And so thematic, too. Almost like a *Lifetime* movie! After all, hadn't this all started because Jeremy wanted to go to Nationals, and Craig wouldn't let him?

"Are you out of your mind?" Craig asked. And this time, it didn't even sound like an insult. It sounded like he really and truly, once and for all, wanted to know. "You think, after everything, Jeremy is still thinking about Nationals?"

"He loves to skate," Bex said simply. "You said it yourself, skating makes him happier than anything in the world. Maybe, with everything that's been going on, he just needed something solid to hold on to. Something he could focus on that wasn't his mother." Or what you did to her.

Craig shook his head, either refusing to listen, or desperately trying to wrench her obvious logic out of his brain.

"Are his skates gone, too?" Bex asked.

"I don't . . ." He nervously rubbed the gash on the left side of his cheek, opening it up again and leaving a streak of blood on the back of his hand. "I don't know. I didn't check."

"Can I check?"

This time, the "Are you out of your mind?" was simply implied by the look in Craig's eyes.

"It might help us to figure out—"

"Us? When did any of this become a scavenger hunt for *us*? I know what you're after, Bex. Jeremy is just a story to you."

"I'm trying to help."

"I think you've been helpful enough already, thanks."

"Did Jeremy leave a note or anything?" Bex pressed on. Craig was the one out of his mind if he thought mere sarcasm would be enough to derail her. Once again, thank you, Gil Cahill.

"No," Craig said. "Nothing."

But he stuffed his hands in his pockets as he said it. And he wouldn't look Bex in the eye.

"No message of any kind?"

"I said, he didn't leave a note." This time, Craig raised his head and held Bex's gaze for an extra long time. Like a kid in a staring contest.

"Well, what do the police think?" Bex considered playing his game. She'd actually been pretty good at this back in grade school. The trick was to look not at the person, but at some fixed point in the distance. That way, you weren't tempted to blink at sudden movements. And you had to be really good at ignoring chaffed eyeballs, too.

"The police?" Craig was the first to blink. He also looked at Bex as if she'd uttered her latest question in Swahili.

"What did they say when you called? Are they treating this as a missing persons case, or as a runaway kid?"

"I haven't called the police."

"Why not? Jeremy is missing."

"And Rachel is dead. The police were so terribly helpful with that."

"They're doing their best."

"Yes, I know. Something about skipping vacations they'd promised their wives."

"You've met Gretchen."

"I try to keep our encounters to a minimum."

"I don't understand why you haven't called the police."

"Because this is none of their business. I repeat, America's finest haven't ever been exactly helpful when it came to Rachel and me."

"Did you try? Fourteen years ago, did you or Rachel even consider going to the police to press rape charges against Robby?"

"Oh, that would have gone over well. That's just what Rachel needed, to become the talk of the ever-supportive skating world. People whispering about her as she walked by, then shutting up as soon as she turned around. Skating mothers arguing over who did what to whom and who was telling the truth and who was just trying to get attention and who was secretly jealous and who, as long as they were at it, had finally proven herself to be the slut they always suspected she was. Yes, that would have been fun. And, once again, the police would have been so helpful."

"Fine. Maybe that would have happened. But, Jeremy is a totally different case. Your son is missing and you won't call the police? That's nuts." Bex was about to add, "What if the person who killed Rachel got Jeremy, too?" But then, she realized that that person might be standing right in front of her.

And that was when she got scared. Really, really scared.

This wasn't about getting a great story and/or outsmarting

Craig with her razor-sharp wit and keen insights anymore. Suddenly, this had stopped being a game.

She tried to keep her feelings to herself. She struggled to keep her face neutral, her stance relaxed, her tone light.

She failed miserably.

The instant she actually believed—not just academically tossed a theory around, but really and truly believed—that Craig might have not only accidentally killed Rachel, but also deliberately done something to hurt his own son, Bex felt herself shutting down. Her cheeks flushed. Her breath caught. Her shoulders sunk into each other as if trying to roll into a ball and duck for cover. If there was a cliché activity to indicate shock, fear, horror, et al. . . . she engaged in it. And Craig was no fool. He saw it all.

For a moment, he didn't say anything. He simply stared at Bex, as if trying to figure out what to do with her.

And then, wearily, he said, "Get out, Bex. Get out of my house, get out of my life. Leave me alone. Please, just leave me alone."

Bex had to do something. Because this had gotten so far out of hand, Bex couldn't even see her fingers from where she was standing. There were lives at stake now. Real, actual, people lives. Bex sometimes lost track of that. That was the problem with working in a job where real, actual, people's lives were referred to as "storylines."

As in, "What storyline should we play at this championship?"

"Well, So-and-So's mother was in a car accident a couple months ago. She's paralyzed."

"Oh, that's great. Fabulous stuff. Yeah, let's play that. What else have we got?"

When Bex's primary job consisted of ferreting out a good story and presenting it in a three-act manner—Introduction, Tragedy, followed preferably by big-time Comeback, it was hard to remember that these were real people they were talking about, and not just characters created for 24/7's benefit.

Sitting in her car, half a block away from Craig Hunt's home, Bex had to admit to herself that, up until this point, she'd still been looking at the entire situation as a great story to be told. Even Rachel's death hadn't felt real. It was more of a plot twist. To be totally honest, Bex had been more concerned about how she would get footage to support her story, than she was in how it might come out. As long as it was cinematic (and made Bex look good in front of Gil and, what the heck, the whole world), she really didn't care who actually done it.

But now, Jeremy was missing. It should have been just another great plot twist. But this was a kid, for Pete's sake. From the looks of it, a scared little kid. Who'd just lost his mother. And who wanted to tell Bex how his father was involved.

Had Craig really done something to Jeremy? Bex found it so hard to believe. The few times she'd seen them together, Craig looked every inch of the devoted dad. But, the man had also obviously snapped recently. If he'd made Bex fear for her own life, who knew what else he might have done?

She was in way over her head on this one. That fact might have been obvious to the casual, visually impaired observer on day one. But, for Bex, it came as a revelation. She couldn't handle this alone. She needed guidance. She needed, God help her, Gretchen.

"I don't know what you expect me to do, Bex," Gretchen's hands fluttered nervously in the air as if she were pushing her way through a wall of sixties-style beading. "The department can't just charge in and start searching Craig Hunt's home."

"Isn't he a suspect in the murder of his wife? Isn't that ample just cause, or whatever you call it, to search the premises?"

"Craig Hunt is not an official suspect."

"But, you told me it's usually the husband—"

"That was off the record."

"His son has disappeared!"

"We don't know that officially, or even for a fact."

"That's where searching the house would be helpful, wouldn't it?"

"Bex . . ."

"He's a little kid, Gretchen. A little, defenseless kid." Bex wondered if this chat was what, technically, would qualify as hitting below the belt—and right into the uterus. "It's not fair, is it, how some people are lucky enough to have kids, and then they can't even take care of them right? Craig Hunt was supposed to take care of Jeremy, he was supposed to protect him and nurture him and . . ." Bex was fast becoming in desperate danger of running out of synonyms.

But, as it turned out, she didn't need any more.

Gretchen reached for her phone. She said, "I'll call my husband and see what we can do."

Gretchen's husband, Travis, turned out to be a detective on the force and, in person, he also turned out to be as nice as he'd appeared in the photo on her desk. Though he towered over both Bex and Gretchen by at least a head and a half, his voice proved so mellifluous it was like he was always whispering. It forced Bex to lean in, focus, shut her own mouth for a change, and pay very careful attention to his every word. Which, she suspected, was the point. (She did wonder how he and Gretchen got along, she with her ongoing monologues about the evils of big city life, and he from the I-never-repeat-myself school.)

Bex soon got her answer.

Gretchen called Travis into her office and, in a flood of words, relayed the entire Craig and Jeremy saga as Bex had earlier conveyed it to her. She used lots of arm flourishes, lots of nodding her head emphatically, and several reiterations of the phrase, "poor little boy."

Travis listened without saying a word. He patiently waited for his wife to finish and, unlike Bex, wasn't fooled the few times she appeared to be done, but was really only taking a break to wind up for the next sequence. At the end of the command performance, Gretchen looked at Travis expectantly. Bex anticipated him asking a few pertinent, police-type follow-up questions, maybe even looking to Bex for clarification. But Travis simply turned toward the door and, in that I-could-not-be-ruffled-if-you-shot-a-grenade-through-my-hair-but-I-strongly-wouldn't-recommend-trying voice of his, said, "Let's go, ladies."

This time, when Craig opened the front door to find Bex on his porch—again—she didn't fear his slamming it shut in her face. Travis's police badge was very helpful in getting them inside with a minimum of fuss or protest. On the other hand, the Craig Hunt who took one look at Travis's badge, shrugged, and opened the door wider without a word of protest was also not the same man Bex had left just a few hours before. For one thing, he'd changed clothes. Out with the wrinkled, makeshift sleepwear, in with a clean pair of jeans and gray turtleneck sweater. He'd stopped ripping his hair out of his head long enough to comb it. And even the gashes on his face had been washed and cleaned out so as to look like a trio of wholesome, practically all-American scratches.

Although, to his credit, the first thing Travis did ask after introducing himself was, "What happened to your face, Mr. Hunt?"

"Cut myself shaving." Craig held out his hands, palms up. Both were visibly trembling. "I'm not exactly my steadiest these days."

It was a brilliant maneuver. Bex almost wanted to stand up and applaud. In one gesture, he'd managed to paint himself both as a grieving widower and as a nonviable murder suspect. After all, a man who can barely hold a razor steady enough to shave without bleeding could hardly be walking around perpetrating other forms of chaos, could he?

Travis said, "Hm."

"What can I do for you, Officer?" Craig asked. Bex noted that, since they'd come in, he had yet to so much as glance at her. Obviously, this performance was strictly for the man in blue, to hell with what Bex thought about his recent personality transplant.

"You know Ms. Levy here, don't you, Mr. Hunt?"

"Oh, yes." Craig still didn't look at her. "I know Ms. Levy very, very well."

"She tells us your son is missing."

"I beg your pardon?"

"Ms. Levy tells us that your thirteen-year-old son, Jeremy, is missing, and yet you refuse to call the police or act in any other, what might be considered appropriate, manner."

"Oh, no," Craig said. "Oh, no. I'm afraid there's been a terrible misunderstanding. Jeremy isn't missing."

"Then where is he?" Bex interrupted. She knew it was probably the wrong thing to do. Travis seemed to be handling this interrogation much better than she ever could. But, then again, why should she let a little thing like that stop her?

"Frankly," Craig finally deigned to address her, even if he did manage to do it without so much as turning his head or torso in her direction, "I don't see why that's any of your business."

"Mr. Hunt," Travis cleared his throat. "I'm afraid we have a bit of a problem, here. The Clear Lake Police Department has received a complaint. And, while I agree with you that Ms. Levy does not, in and of herself, have any business knowing where your son might be, we, the Department, that is, do have an obligation to act upon—"

"Stray gossip brought to you by muckrakers trying to destroy my life and reputation in the interest of a three-minute story for her network?"

Travis didn't blink. "Sometimes."

"That's really protecting and serving, isn't it, Officer?"

For the first time since they'd come in, Bex could visibly see Gretchen's hackles rising. No. Really. While Bex had never seen an actual hackle before, rising or otherwise, she had to assume that Gretchen's back arching, her shoulders narrowing and her tongue pressing against her back teeth in preparation for spitting, feline-style, had to be an honest-to-goodness hackle. And she also had to assume that it was in response to Craig's sarcasm. Gretchen could obviously manage to stand back and be out-of-character quiet while gazing adoringly, not unlike Nancy Reagan (and Felicia Tufts of fifteen years earlier), at her big, strong, non-New York husband doing his job. But, God forbid someone refuse to shower him with the adoration

Gretchen thought he deserved. In that case, it was damn the suburbia, full New York attitude ahead.

Travis, obviously, knew all about the situation, raised hackles and all. Because, even as he continued smiling pleasantly at Craig, he also put one arm out behind him, as if to keep Gretchen from charging.

"I understand your anger, Mr. Hunt. No one likes their privacy invaded. However, I feel that I must respectfully ask you to produce your son. I just want to get a look at the boy. Make sure everything is all right."

"He's not here."

"Aha!" Bex said. Sometimes smugness could be warmer than cashmere on a cold day.

"But, he isn't missing." Craig's smile looked more like a grimace to Bex. Or a dog baring its teeth. "I'm afraid Ms. Levy misunderstood me, earlier. When she asked to see Jeremy, I told her that he wasn't here. Ms. Levy took that to mean he was missing. She jumped to a conclusion. I'm afraid she's been doing that quite a bit, lately."

"You said he was missing!" Bex heard the whine in her voice. She might as well have been stamping her foot and trilling, "You did, you did, you so totally did."

"You misunderstood," Craig repeated.

"Well, that's just fine, Mr. Hunt. That's fine. Now, where did you say your boy was?"

"He's on a trip. With a family friend. I'm sure you understand why I didn't want him here. After everything that's happened, I just wanted Jeremy safe and away from it all."

"You sent him away before you even buried his mother?" Bex demanded.

"I don't happen to think a funeral is an appropriate place for a child. Is that all right with you, Ms. Levy, or should we call Dr. Spock to issue a final verdict?"

"It just seems pretty strange . . . ." Bex mumbled, no longer quite as afraid of being murdered on the spot, but definitely at risk of death by embarrassment.

Travis looked at them both as if the entire exchange hadn't happened. And then he picked up right where he'd left off. Bex had to hand it to him. The man had class.

"So, if I could just speak to Jeremy, Mr. Hunt, by telephone would be fine, I'm sure we could straighten this all out without any more fuss. Wouldn't want anyone to strain a sarcasm muscle now, would we?" To his credit, Travis's homespun, deadpan expression didn't change, even as he verbally smacked both Bex and Craig upside the head.

"Well . . ." Craig looked around nervously. Good. It was about time the bastard felt nervous. Where was the guy so racked by grief earlier that he could barely keep it together? Bex liked that guy a lot better. Not in a potentially homicidal way, of course, but in the way where he tended to blurt things out before thinking them through. An in-control Craig was really a lot less useful than the edgy one. "Jeremy is actually traveling right now, so I don't know if we could reach him . . . ."

"Aha!" Bex almost said again, but decided to let Travis take the lead on this one.

"Well, then, Mr. Hunt, I'm afraid I'm going to have to ask you to come down to the station with me. Maybe, if we put our heads together, we can figure out how to reach Jeremy without—"

"But, wait, here, I have an idea." Craig moved over to his telephone answering machine. "How about this? Will this do?"

He pushed the Messages button, and, after a beep, Bex clearly heard the same voice that was recorded back on her own voicemail at the 24/7 office. Only this time, the voice was saying, "Dad? Dad, are you there? Okay, well, anyway.

My skates. I totally forgot them. I really wanted to show Aunt Felicia my new long program and she says there'll be a rink next to the hotel, so could you do me a favor and put them in the mail for me? Oh, and my music tape, too? Overnight, please? Pretty please? She said you've got the address. Thanks. See you when I get back!"

Sixteen

Bex had to hop desperately down the porch steps two at a time to keep up with Gretchen and Travis as they, following a tight-lipped apology, stormed out of Craig's home.

"Wait," she called, only catching up with the couple once they'd reached their car. "Wait, I'm sorry. He told me Jeremy was missing, really he did. I was worried."

"Bex," Gretchen plopped her hands on her hips while Travis walked around to unlock the driver's side door. "You are not a police officer."

"I know that. Really."

"And, to be honest, your snooping around, without any authority, I might add, is really not appropriate or appreciated. I was willing to bend some of our established rules for you, because I understand what kind of merciless pressure you're under, working for a heartless New York media corporation and all. But, honestly, I thought I could trust you to be honest with me, and not just use Travis and me as a plot point to spice up this imaginary story of yours!"

"It's not imaginary!" Bex gave up and resorted to full-fledged whining. She figured if Gretchen was going to treat her like a child, then it was the same as offering her implicit permission to act like one. "I spoke to Craig earlier and he told me that Jeremy was missing."

"Telling you the boy isn't there isn't the same as saying he's missing, Bex."

"He told me he didn't know where Jeremy was."

"I'm sure he meant, at that particular moment. What I think we have here, Bex, if you're saying that it isn't deliberate subterfuge on your part—"

"It's not. Of course it's not. What would I have to gain from lying to you?"

"Then, what I think we have here is a real deficit in productive listening skills on your part. I know that what sometimes happens with young, ambitious, pressured women who are as bright and articulate as we are, is that we tend to do a lot more talking than listening."

"But—"

"And then we jump to erroneous conclusions based on what we wanted to hear, rather than on what was actually said. It's a very dangerous habit, Bex. I suggest you work on it."

"Yes, I will. Okay, thanks. But, see, it wasn't just what Craig said. I got this message from Jeremy on my work phone last night." Bex fumbled in her canvas bag for her cell phone. All she had to do was dial into her messages, let Travis and Gretchen listen to Jeremy's cryptic plea, and they would have to realize that she wasn't making things up, that something very strange was, in fact, going on at the Hunt household. And then they both would be properly sorry for doubting her. Not that the latter was Bex's primary concern, of course.

"Bex," Travis had already leaned over to let Gretchen in

on the passenger side. He started his engine, so his words were tossed in Bex's direction through Gretchen's open window and over the hum of his warming-up car. "This isn't a game we're playing here. It's not a TV show. This is a real murder investigation with a real dead body and a real suspect. Now, whether or not Craig Hunt is a suspect is none of your business. But, I can tell you this. Stunts like this make it harder and harder for the department to turn in a clean, uncorrupted case to the District Attorney. It also clues in various people who have no need to be clued in, about what we're thinking and planning. And it makes us look like idiots. That last one, Bex? That last one was really unnecessary."

And then he pulled away from the curb. Leaving Bex standing there, a doughnut of "but . . . but . . . buts" stuck in her throat, her cell phone dangling from one outstretched arm, it's message playing impotently into the empty street. Bex closed it and severed the connection. And then she thought of something even more horrible.

She'd come to Craig's in the backseat of Travis and Gretchen's car. Her own vehicle was still parked back at the police station. She was now officially alone and abandoned in the middle of nowhere in particular. It was getting cold again. And dark.

Oh, yes, and one more thing.

Craig Hunt was coming her way.

Bex froze.

She watched him open his front door, clearly waiting to step outside until after Gretchen and Travis pulled away from the curb. And then she watched him amble down the steps, heading in her direction.

Bex looked around. Every house on the block had its doors tightly shut. The few windows that reflected lights, also reflected no people in them. In a community this affluent, Bex bet they all had fancy soundproof windows. In a neighborhood where the annual income was more than a hundred thousand dollars, could anyone hear you scream? And, even if they did, would they give a damn?

Bex supposed that, with half a block still between her and an approaching Craig, she could always run. The question, of course, was, where could she run to? Down the cul-de-sac? That seemed less than productive. Bex had a mental image of herself being whipped around like a pinball straight into Craig's waiting mania.

Could she run in the opposite direction? Wouldn't that just lead her to another cul-de-sac?

Should she try darting behind the houses and onto the currently snow-free ski slopes? Oh, yes, tumbling down a tree-and-other-obstacle-strewn hill just as it was getting too dark to see was definitely the way to go. If you were suicidal, that is. The plethora of options was why, in the end, Bex ruefully decided that the devil she did know was still safer than the one she didn't. And so she stayed rooted to the spot, letting Craig come to her.

In the twilight and half-shadow, she couldn't make out the expression on his face. He might have been smirking. He also might have been surrendering. Apparently there was now a rather fine line between the two. Who knew?

He said, "Looks like you've got a problem."

"Oh, I'll just add it to the list."

Craig sighed. "I have a problem, too."

"Yes. And I daresay, it's even bigger than mine."

"I was thinking." He turned toward his house, the front door still open in what, under other circumstances, might even have seemed a warm and inviting manner. "Maybe we could help each other out?"

Bex instinctively asked a most familiar question most politely. "Are you insane?"

"Truth?" He rubbed the gash on the right side of his face. "I'm not so sure anymore."

"Well, that's a ringing endorsement."

"Do you want to hear what I have to say, or not?"

And here, ladies and gentlemen, was her problem. Bex did not want to die. She did not want to be beaten or strangled or bludgeoned to death and left outside in the park for the Clear Lake Police to find and puzzle over. The above had already happened to the last woman in Craig Hunt's orbit. And he had even claimed to love that woman. Bex was pretty certain his feelings for her were not quite in the same league. That being said, Bex's most logical course of action, at this point, was clearly to stay away from Craig Hunt—with screaming hysterically a close second.

Except they had a problem. Because Bex really did want to hear what he had to say. By this point, she figured she deserved it.

Bex asked, "You want my help?"

"Yes."

"Why?"

"Because you're smart."

"I was smart this morning. You didn't want my help then."

"Actually, this morning you were more of a smart-ass. Not unlike now."

"So why are you talking to me now?"

"Because. You know things. You've been snooping around and asking questions and getting information that, quite frankly, I believe could help me. I think you know more than you think you do. And I think you can help me find Jeremy."

"So he is missing!"

"Will you help me?"

"Why didn't you tell the police that? What was up with

that message? Was that really Jeremy? What are you trying to hide?"

In lieu of an answer, Craig, once again, indicated his open front door. "Would you like to come in and talk about this?"

Bex bit her lower lip. And slowly nodded.

Craig didn't say another word until they were in his living room, door closed firmly behind them, a plethora of objects that Bex imagined could be used to bash her brains in without anyone being the wiser within easy reach. This time, she was the one who chose to stand, even after Craig took a seat on his couch and gestured for her to settle in the easy-chair perpendicular to it.

Bex said, "I'd rather remain poised to flee at any moment."

"I don't blame you."

"Was that a confession?" Bex asked, sincerely hoping the answer would be no. After all, what would she do with one, except be pondering it in the last few, precious moments of her life.

"No," Craig said.

Bex hoped he didn't see her sigh of relief. She cleverly disguised it as a cough. And then she asked, "So what was that with the police? If Jeremy is really missing and you're as worried as you claim, I'd think you'd want their help."

"No. Not the police. Not now. It's all too . . . complicated now. I have to figure out what's really going on first."

"What a coincidence! So do I!"

"I'm trying to tell you."

"Cool. Let's start with Jeremy's message on the answering machine. His Aunt Felicia. That would be Felicia

Tufts Sharpton, right? Because, you know, I read a lot of mysteries when I'm not living in the middle of one, and, in my experience, two characters never have the same name unless there's some obfuscation point to be made, and that doesn't seem to be the case here. Besides, it's all a little too convenient."

"Aunt Felicia is Felicia Tufts, yes."

"What's Robby's ex-wife doing with Jeremy?"

Craig linked his hands together and looked down at his fingers. He rubbed the inside of his left palm with his right thumb until his nail awkwardly bent back from the pressure, not unlike Bex's had earlier from his doorbell. He said, "Rachel and Felicia were friends. Best friends. I mean, long before Robby. They used to skate together as little kids, compete against each other. I think we've maybe got some pictures around here of the two of them, from back when they were these cute little Preliminary Girls, both of them with their hair in pigtails. It was cute . . . really cute. Jeremy used to love looking at those old pictures when he was younger. I think he had a hard time imagining his mother was ever that small. Rachel didn't keep any of the memorabilia from her later years around. I think it hurt her too much. Or maybe she just didn't care. I was always of two minds about that. I thought: She earned those medals, she ought to hold on to them. But anyway, those early pictures, they weren't really about skating for her. They were about her and Felicia. Rachel is the one who encouraged Felicia to take up Pairs."

"With Robby?"

"No, just in general, I think. Rachel knew Felicia didn't have what it takes to be a Single skater. She didn't have the jumps, her nerves always got the best of her. But, she was small and she was quick . . . and her parents had the money to afford a pretty good partner. Rachel encouraged Felicia to skate with Robby when the opportunity came up. Hilarious, isn't it? In a way, Rachel brought Robby into all our lives. Not that she knew what she was doing. And I think she realized pretty fast that it wasn't the best match. Felicia and Robby had only been skating together for maybe a year before Lucian Pryce suggested Robby dump her and pair up with Rachel. Rachel was the one who said no, then. She didn't want to do that to Felicia. The only reason she eventually agreed to do it was because Felicia practically begged her to. Felicia realized Robby would do better skating with Rachel than he would with her. And, Felicia, well, she was so crazy about him . . . ."

"I know. She told me. She cared more about his career than she did about her own. I think it's the only positive thing Lucian Pryce can say, in retrospect, about her."

"You've spoken to Lucian?"

"Yes."

"What did he say? About how Robby treated Rachel?"

"In his version, Rachel is the bad guy and Robby the innocent, put-upon victim."

"Yeah. I figured. Lucian thought Robby smacking Felicia around was good for her. Well, good for her skating, anyway. I'm sure he didn't give a damn about her as a person. He probably would have encouraged him to do the same to Rachel, except Rachel, she doesn't really put up with a lot of crap. I mean . . . I mean, she didn't . . . ." Craig trailed off.

Bex felt sorry for him, she really did. She was even beginning to come around to the idea that maybe Craig didn't kill Rachel, after all.

But, on the other hand, she wasn't getting any younger.

"Rachel and Felicia . . ." Bex prompted.

Craig nodded. "Right." He cleared his throat, cracked

his knuckles and started nervously rubbing his palms one against the other. "Right. Rachel and Felicia. Anyway. Rachel and Felicia had been friends forever. After Rachel took off fourteen years ago, Felicia was the only one from the rink who she kept in touch with."

"Felicia?" Bex couldn't believe it. "The only person Rachel kept in touch with from the rink was Robby Sharpton's wife?"

"Yes. They've been in touch all these years, from even before Jeremy was born. She's Aunt Felicia to him."

"Okay, that's really weird, Craig. Really, really weird."

"Actually, Bex, it gets weirder."

She took a beat. And then she decided to sit down. When Craig Hunt—he of the very, very interesting past and even more interesting present—claimed that something was about to get even weirder, she felt it best to believe him.

Bex settled in the armchair he'd previously indicated. It was brown leather and recently polished. Bex's thighs squeaked as she sat.

She leaned forward, mirroring Craig's posture. She rested her elbows on her knees, and set her chin on her fist. She said, "Hit me, Craig."

He smiled ruefully. He turned his head, looking Bex in the eye.

Then, sounding almost as if he couldn't believe he was actually doing this, Craig told Bex, "Felicia Tufts isn't Jeremy's aunt. She's his biological mother."

Seventeen

As a professional reporter—well, all right, a lowly researcher; but they both started with "r" and ended with "er" and required notebooks and stuff—Bex knew that she would probably never encounter a better occasion upon which to let loose with a stream of "who, what, where, when, why, and how?" Alas, while her brain understood the above quite well, her tongue chose that particular moment to strike like a Teamster deprived of his coffee break.

So, while her mind snapped to attention with a whole host of questions, all brilliant, pithy, and probing, her mouth settled for a combination of the "four Ws and an H," and what actually came out in response to Craig's declaration was, "Wwwwhhhh . . ."

"Rachel and I are Jeremy's parents," Craig clarified for the vowel and verbally impaired. "But Felicia Tufts gave birth to him."

"You adopted Jeremy?" Bex pushed the question out past her lips during a brief novocain break for her tongue. It was like giving birth to a coherent thought.

"Not exactly."

"You kidnapped him?" Bex yelped.

Craig looked at Bex strangely. "You watch a lot of *Lifetime* movies, don't you?"

"Well, at least if you don't know what's going on there, you can look up the synopsis in *TV Guide*. You got one of those for me, Craig? Maybe a *Cliffs Notes* or something?"

"I'm sorry. No, really, I am. It's just, this is a little bit complicated."

"Oh, you don't say?"

Craig leaned back into the couch and momentarily studied the ceiling. His chest heaved, seemingly exhausted, with every breath. The poetic (it was nicer sounding than "peculiar") part of Bex imagined that the truth was like the monster from *Alien,* desperately trying to claw and throb its way out of Craig's chest in a mess of blood and goo. The more practical (it was nicer sounding than "boring") side could only imagine how exhausted he must be, both from the horrific events of the past few days and all of the long-repressed secrets of the last fourteen years. Anyone with a brain and a heart would obviously know that it just would not be right to rush a person in such obvious physical and psychic pain. But . . .

Bex said, "So, what's the deal, Craig? What's going on here?"

He took a deep breath. He stopped studying the ceiling. He resumed rubbing his palms one against the other. The rhythmic scrape of dry skin against dry skin slowly began to drive Bex mad, but it seemed to soothe Craig somewhat. He exhaled. "Okay. So, like I said, Rachel and Felicia were friends from the time they were kids. And they stayed friends while Rachel and Robby skated together. After Robby raped Rachel—"

"Lucian Pryce said he didn't." Bex wasn't sure if,

sensitivity-speaking, now was the best time to bring this up. But, she figured if Craig was going for full disclosure, so should she. "He says he was there and he heard them—"

"Rachel always knew he heard them, he was practically outside the door."

"He says Rachel and Robby had an affair. That there was no rape."

"Son of a bitch." Craig shook his head as if the memory were a screeching siren he was trying to shake out of his ears. "Goddamn son of a bitch. You know, I'm not big on the whole pop psychology thing. I don't care how many Twinkies you ate as a kid, in the end, you're still the one responsible for your actions, nobody else. But, to be fair the other way, Robby Sharpton may have stumbled into that rink with all the raw material just ripe for a psychopath, but Lucian Pryce didn't exactly put up any barriers in his way. I mean, you've got a seventeen-year-old kid who can't keep his fists to himself, even with a girl half his size; do you maybe suggest that his behavior isn't the most appropriate ever, or do you reward him with gold medals and pats on the head and tell him to "just keep doing what you're doing, son, and we're headed straight for the top." It's bad enough boys who take up Pairs skating or Ice Dance get treated like royalty. The girls and their parents are so terrified of losing them to a better offer that they practically genuflect. There's a kid at the rink, ice-dancer, I think, the girl's parents bought him a car and a condo just so he wouldn't take off and skate with someone else. But, at least they're not encouraging him to beat their daughter. Lucian didn't have that problem. Robby may not have known right from wrong when he got there, but, to be fair, Lucian wasn't exactly role model of the year."

A fascinating digression, to be sure. And, considering that Robby's psychology was still of interest to Bex, seeing as how Craig was adamant that his wife's ex-partner was also her murderer, it wasn't even too irrelevant of one. But, it was off-point for the topic at hand.

"What does this have to do with Felicia being Jeremy's mother, Craig?"

"Everything," he said pointedly. "Considering Lucian's attitude of putting Robby on a pedestal, and Rachel's parents' tendency to sweep any problems she and Robby were having under the rug so as not to rock the partnership, the only person Rachel could turn to after Robby raped her was Felicia."

"Robby's wife?"

"Rachel's best friend."

"You're telling me Robby's coach didn't believe he was a rapist, but his own wife did?"

"Yes. Because Felicia knew Rachel. And she knew Robby. She loved him, but she knew him, too. In a way, I think she was almost happy to hear it."

"Do you have any idea how sick this all sounds?"

"She wasn't happy to hear that Rachel had been hurt, but . . . Look at it from Felicia's point of view. When she skated with Robby, he used to hit her. Only everyone around her told her to stop being so melodramatic and blowing things out of proportion. How was she supposed to trust her own judgment when everybody was telling her that what she thought was happening, wasn't happening at all? Then, when Robby started skating with Rachel, he didn't hit her. Do you blame Felicia for suspecting that maybe all the previous abuse had been in her head? Add to that the fact that Robby was still hitting her off the ice, then telling her it was because he loved her so much, and that it wasn't abuse, at all. Do you see how it drove her crazy? At least when Rachel came to her and said that Robby raped her, Felicia finally had proof that she wasn't making it all up. Robby really was violent and abusive. That's what I meant by she was happy to hear it. Well, maybe not happy, but relieved. She wasn't crazy."

Bex nodded numbly. The whole situation was so outside her sphere of comprehension, they might as well have been discussing some obscure kinship ritual among the Maori people of New Zealand. (Not that Bex wished, at this or any other point, to infer any sort of wife-abusing tendencies about the Maori, all of whom, she was sure, were good and noble people; she was just using them as a metaphor for her lack of knowledge about many, many, many things.) Bex simply could not wrap her brain around the notion that a woman would not know if she were actually being abused.

"Having Rachel tell her about Robby finally gave Felicia permission to admit—to herself—heck, the rest of us already knew, right?—what kind of man she was married to. The night Rachel told her she'd been raped was the night Felicia decided to leave her husband."

"But . . ." Bex said slowly. "She didn't. Felicia stayed with Robby for almost another four years, I think. What changed her mind?"

"Jeremy."

"I don't understand."

"The same night that Rachel told Felicia she'd been raped by Robby, Felicia told Rachel that she was pregnant. Also, coincidentally, by Robby."

"A big evening."

"Oh, you don't know the half of it."

"Yes, it certainly looks that way."

"Most women spend their girls' night out watching videos and eating ice cream, or even throwing back shots and picking up men at the local cowboy bar. Not Rachel and Felicia. Their idea of girl bonding was to come up with a plan where Rachel dropped out of sight and she and I raised Felicia and Robby's baby, with him never being the wiser."

"Excuse me?"

"Amazing." Craig came close to cracking a smile for the first time since Bex had met him. "That's exactly what I said when they presented their little plan to me."

"I don't understand." It was a phrase Bex rarely used, and here she'd had occasion to whip it out twice in the span of one evening. This truly was a monumental day.

"See if you can follow this logic. Felicia wanted to leave Robby, but if he knew that she was pregnant, he'd have never, ever let her go. He was obsessive like that. Now, granted, Felicia could have tried to go underground herself, but if Robby ever found out she had a child, he'd put two and two together. He's not the sharpest blade on the ice, but this, he would have figured out. Meanwhile, Rachel didn't ever want to see Robby again. She didn't want to take him to court, she didn't want to talk it out on *Oprah*. She just wanted to leave and forget about the whole thing."

"That's not a very healthy reaction." Bex had done a piece on post-traumatic stress in rape victims, so that made her practically an expert on the subject.

"That's not how Rachel felt. She told me once, 'If I'd been hit by a car, no one would expect me to spend the next twenty years obsessing about it and analyzing my feelings. They'd expect me to physically recover and move on. Well, Robby is no more important to me than a car. I refuse to give him that honor. He's not a person, he's a thing. I don't want to confront him and I don't want to understand him. I just want to forget him.'"

Bex understood the sentiment, truly she did. It sounded

perfectly logical. And yet all of her research indicated, "That's not really the best way to deal with it."

Craig looked up at Bex and asked, not unpleasantly, just sadly, "What difference does that really make now?"

He had a point. Rachel was dead. Her mental health was no longer an issue. On the other hand, who knew whether or not it had contributed to her murder. Still, considering Craig's fragile state, Bex decided to keep that observation to herself for the time being.

She said, "I guess you're right," and hoped he couldn't tell she didn't mean it.

Craig said, "So Rachel came to me and asked how I would feel about us raising Felicia and Robby's baby."

"And you said?"

Craig smiled ruefully. "Not for mixed company."

"I don't blame you."

"I mean, at that point, I wasn't even old enough to drink yet, and Rachel wanted me to drop everything and play daddy?"

"Oh," Bex said, realizing she'd misunderstood his initial point. "I thought it was because of who Jeremy's father was."

"Nah." Craig shrugged. "That was actually the least of it. Sure, Robby was a bastard, but so—I can only presume—was my own old man. I mean, I never met him, but you rarely end up in foster care because Mommy and Daddy are Parents of the Year. Imagine if Michael and Jenny had decided not to adopt me because of who my parents were. No, Robby being Jeremy's father never really bothered me. In fact, the one thing I agreed with Felicia and Rachel on right away was that he should never know he had a kid, much less be allowed anywhere around him. What I couldn't understand though was why Felicia couldn't just disappear and do whatever she wanted. Her folks had money, it's not like she'd have been destitute. But, Felicia said Robby would want to know why she left him."

"Felicia's bruises wouldn't have clued him in?"

"To be honest with you, Bex, I don't think he saw them."

It was a very odd thing to say. And yet, under the circumstances, Bex actually thought she could grasp what he meant by that.

"Felicia said he would go after her," Craig continued. "Robby hated to lose and he certainly hated to be made a fool of."

"Plus, if both Felicia and Rachel abandoned him at the same time, wouldn't he be out of money to continue skating?"

Craig nodded, visibly impressed by Bex's quick uptake on his bizarre non-nuclear family dynamics. Little did he know she'd been doing nothing but pondering those bizarre dynamics for the past few days. "That was part of it, too. If Robby lost Felicia and skating at the same time, he'd probably go crazy trying to get one or the other back. Felicia couldn't risk that being her."

"But how did she figure she'd be able to hide her pregnancy? It was one thing to ask you and Rachel to raise the baby, but weren't there nine months in between to take care of first?"

"She sent Robby away. After Rachel took off, Felicia convinced Robby that he shouldn't even try looking for another partner and risk another last-minute betrayal. I gather it was an awful scene. Lucian Pryce practically choked her with his bare hands, he was so angry about losing his prize pupil. I gather it meant he'd be forced to sit out his first Olympics at home or something."

"Yes." Bex invoked her earlier conversation with the coach. "Like a regular person."

"Anyway, Lucian was livid, but Felicia held her ground. She convinced Robby that singles skating was where it was at for him. And she managed to get him a spot and funding to train with a top Soviet coach. For two years. In Russia."

"And away from a quickly ballooning her."

"Exactly."

"So Felicia had the baby somewhere in secret, and you and Rachel adopted him?"

"Not technically. Felicia just checked into the hospital using Rachel's ID. They looked alike enough so no one was ever the wiser. Jeremy's legal birth certificate lists Rachel Rose as his mother and Craig Hiroshi as his father. So there wouldn't even be a paper trail that could link him to Felicia, must less Robby."

"I don't think that's legal," Bex felt obligated to point out.

"Want to call a cop?"

"I tried that already." Bex sighed. "Didn't work too well."

Craig smiled rather triumphantly.

"By the way," she added, somewhat grudgingly. "Congratulations on your performance. You even had me convinced everything was fine and dandy."

"The minute I told you Jeremy was missing, I knew I'd made a major mistake. I was just so tired and so frustrated, and you were being such a pain in the ass. . . ."

"One man's pain in the ass is another girl's brilliant research strategy, but go on."

"I knew I'd said too much, and I knew it was only a matter of time before you were back—and this time with the fellows in blue. I realized I had to pull myself together;

not give you or them any ammunition to bring me in for questioning."

"You did a nice job. But, the fact is, I don't understand why you're so adamant against the police helping you. I mean, Jeremy may be with Felicia, but he is technically missing. She didn't ask you if she could take him anywhere, did she?"

"No," Craig reluctantly admitted.

"And you have no idea where they are, do you?"

"You know I don't."

"So Jeremy asking on the answering machine for you to send him his skates because you know what hotel they're going to—"

"I have no idea. Felicia must have lied to him. I think she'd have had to, to get him to go with her. She'd have had to tell him it was okay with me. Jeremy wouldn't have gone otherwise. He's a good kid. But he trusts Felicia, so if she told him it was okay with me . . ."

"Craig, that sounds to me like your son's been kidnapped. By someone you and he both know, sure, but kidnapped just the same."

"You don't understand. That word, kidnapped, it suggests . . . it suggests . . ." Craig insisted, "You don't know what kind of sacrifices Felicia has made to keep Jeremy safe. After he was born, she went back to Robby. Even though things between them weren't any better, she went back to him to make sure that he stayed focused on his skating and never got suspicious enough to ask any questions that might lead him to Jeremy. She kept him going until the Olympics. Afterward, she stayed with him even though he was just this loose cannon waiting to go off on someone, anyone. And who do you think that usually was? Who do you think bore the brunt of his rage after his skating career fell apart? I think Felicia would have stayed with Robby indefinitely to keep Jeremy safe. The only reason they even ended up in court was that one time, he beat her up so badly that the she ended up falling unconscious in the hallway, and a neighbor called an ambulance. Once she was in the hospital, it all became a matter of public record, and the District Attorney decided to press charges. He convinced Felicia that Robby would be convicted and she finally went along, figuring Jeremy would be even safer if Robby was in jail. But, if that had never happened, they might still be together today. That's why I can't wrap my brain around Felicia kidnapping Jeremy. I don't understand why she would do that. I know she would never hurt him. So there must be a good reason for this. I can't just go running half-cocked to the police, Bex. I have to figure out what's going on here, first. I have to figure out why Felicia did this."

"Well," Bex said, because now they were at her favorite part of the game—coming up with theories based on what they already knew. "How about this for a possibility? Now, granted, I'm just talking out loud here, but, Craig, have you considered the fact that maybe Felicia killed Rachel so that she could get her son back?"

Eighteen

"You're insane," Craig said calmly.

"Why?"

"Because Felicia has no reason to. . . . She's been a part of Jeremy's life since the beginning. She sees him all the time. They talk on the phone. She takes him on trips, for God's sake."

"What did Jeremy call Rachel?"

"I beg your pardon?"

"What did Jeremy call Rachel? What did he call her?"

Craig shrugged. "Mom. He called her Mom. What was he supposed to call her?"

"And how did Aunt Felicia feel about that, day in and day out for thirteen years?"

Craig hesitated. He obviously saw her point. And he was just as obviously determined to dismiss it. "No. Felicia wasn't jealous of Rachel. She wasn't. You're wrong."

"Craig. Look at the facts. Rachel took Felicia's skating partner. She enchanted Felicia's husband. And she played Mommy to her son. You don't think that could make someone a little unstable? Especially someone who you say was as messed up as Felicia to begin with?"

"But all of those were Felicia's ideas! Rachel never took anything from her. Felicia begged us to raise Jeremy!"

"So where is Jeremy now, Craig?"

He leapt to his feet, starting to pace, the calm discussion of a few minutes earlier replaced by the desperately on-edge man Bex had dealt with all the days before. She couldn't help thinking, "And speaking of unstable people who had a reason to kill Rachel . . ." but temporarily shelved the impulse. The fact was, no matter who killed Rachel, Jeremy was in fact missing. And there was no hard and fast proof that killer and kidnapper were, in fact, the same person.

Craig snapped, "I asked you to help me find Jeremy. Rachel's killer had nothing to do with this."

"Okay, then," Bex snapped back, unhappy to have her tidy solutions questioned. "Then how about we try this theory on for size? You killed Rachel and Felicia knew it. So she kidnapped Jeremy to protect him from you, and now you're using me to track them both down?"

"Oh, God, are we back to that again?"

"You didn't like my other Felicia theory. Is this one more accurate?"

"Robby," Craig said, every last ounce of effort he had left seemingly going to pronouncing each syllable without screaming. "Robby Sharpton. How many times do I have to tell you that it was Robby who killed Rachel? There was no one else it could be."

"And how does Felicia taking Jeremy fit in?"

"It doesn't. It's probably not connected at all. It's probably . . ."

"What? What, Craig? Tell me, because I'm doing my

best here based on what I know. You know more about this than I do. Fill me in. What?"

"I don't know," he said, quietly. "I don't know. I just want to find my son."

"Fine. Then stand back and watch a pro work." Bex rolled up her sleeves. Though she really wasn't sure why. It's not like she was about to shovel coal. Or finger-paint. Still, it felt like the right thing to do under the circumstances. She crossed over to Craig's answering machine and asked, "Has anyone called you since Jeremy left that message about needing his skates?"

"Not that I know of," Craig said. "I mean, they could have, but no one left a message."

"So, we'll take a chance." Bex picked up the receiver and told Craig, "I am now going to show you the one research trick I always have up my sleeve." Ah! So, that's why she'd rolled up her sleeves! Boy, Bex's subconscious was metaphorically clever. How depressing to realize that it was more clever than she was.

"The *69 button," Bex said. "It should connect you to the last number called from."

"Oh," Craig said. Then sheepishly added, "I knew that. I've seen the commercials. I guess it just never occurred to me . . . ."

"That's okay. I'm a professional." Bex was really enjoying this part. She liked playing the all-knowing, all-powerful researcher. It sure beat confused and defensive busybody. Though she knew she had to play it quickly since, any minute now, her brilliant, one-trick pony of a plan might prove itself an utter dud.

Bex hit the appropriate keys, and waited. The phone rang. That was a good sign. At least it wasn't a blocked or international number.

One ring. Two rings. Three rings.

And then the sound of gunfire.

"Hello!" A voice shouted over the din.

"Uh . . . hi," Bex shouted back.

Immediately, Craig was hovering over her shoulder, practically snatching the receiver away from her ear. "Is that Jeremy? Did you reach Jeremy? Who are you talking to?"

Bex waved him away and furiously shook her head. She asked, "Who's this?" just as another round of AK-47s seemed to go off in her ear. *Where the hell had she called?*

"This is Drew." Drew sounded like a teenage boy. Bex could practically hear the pimples pulsating against his skin.

"And where are you, Drew?"

"Tuffy's."

"Tuffy's, what, gun shop and bowling alley?"

"Arcade."

Ah. That explained it. Now that Drew mentioned it, the AK-47s did kind of sound more like space lasers. Bex asked Craig, "Is there an arcade around here called Tuffy's that you know about? Maybe someplace Jeremy used to hang out?"

Craig shook his head. "The only arcade in town is just called the Video Arcade."

"Catchy," Bex noted. She turned back to the phone. "Where's this arcade located, Drew?"

"Hilton Springs."

"Hilton Springs?" Bex looked at Craig, quizzical, but he just shrugged, as geographically clueless as she was.

"We're right over the state line," Drew offered. "If you're coming from Pennsylvania into New York past Highpoint State Park. Part of the Hilton Springs Mall. You can't miss it when you pass. Got signs all over the interstate."

Bex said, "Listen, Drew, I'm wondering if you could help me out. We received a phone call earlier this morning from the machine you're using now."

"Well, it's a pay phone. People are always using it. You know, to call and stuff."

"Do you remember if, earlier this morning, the person using the phone was a blonde boy, about thirteen years old, but looks younger?"

"I don't know. We get a lot of kids in here. All times of the day. We're part of a major rest stop, so people are always dropping by for a bit, and the kids head straight for the video games. It's a great location we've got, you should come check it out."

"Thanks," Bex said. "I just might do that."

And she hung up the phone. Between the time that it clicked in the cradle and the sound's echo bounced off the wall, Craig was at the door, pulling on his jacket.

"Tuffy's Arcade," he said, "Hilton Springs Mall, just over the state line. I've seen the signs. I know where that is."

"Craig, Jeremy's call came hours ago. You don't think they're still there, do you? What do you think, Felicia kidnapped your son, then took him for a day of mall shopping? They must have just stopped there to get breakfast or something. The trail is long cold."

"It's the only trail we've got. I'm going out there."

"No," Bex called. "Wait. Wait, Craig. I told you I was a professional. Will you at least let me try one more thing before you run off half-cocked? Just trust me. For five minutes?"

Craig hesitated. His right arm was already inside his jacket sleeve while he rifled around for his car keys with his left hand.

"I got you this far," Bex reminded.

He fished out the keys. He looked at them for a moment. Then he put the keys back in his pocket. But he did finish putting on his jacket. "Five minutes," Craig said.

Bex said, "What's the phone number for Felicia's doorman back in New York?"

"How the hell should I know? And why the hell should I know?"

"It's a very handy number to have. New York doormen know everything. Who's coming, who's going, were they with anyone, how long since they were in their apartment, who's come to visit them every day for the past seven years? They're like a public library crossed with the KGB."

"I have no idea what the guy's number is."

"That's okay. I have her address, that should be enough." Bex plopped down at Craig's computer. "May I?"

"Knock yourself out."

Bex tapped the space bar with her thumb to bring the previously quietly humming machine to life, then typed in Google. A little side trip to www.WhitePages.com, and within minutes, Bex had the phone number for not only Felicia's doorman, but her building's super, as well. If the first didn't pan out, she fully intended to check out the second.

She dialed with confidence, despite Craig's suspicious hovering. The fact was, she was kind of enjoying the attention. It was about time he got a chance to see her in her element for a change, rather than with her nose stuck in his mail slot.

"Fitzroy East, this is Vlad speaking. How may I help you?"

"Hello, Vlad!" Bex said brightly. After a year of working with Russians, Bex thought she could detect an Eastern

European accent. Not pure Russian exactly, but perhaps one of their former invasion spots. Poland, maybe, or Lithuania. "My name is Bex Levy. I'm a friend of Ms. Felicia Tufts. I stopped by to see her a few days ago, do you remember? I waited for quite a while before she let me in. I complimented you on your finely polished uniform buttons?"

At that last one, Craig stared at Bex as if she'd finally and definitely lost whatever he'd believed there was left of her mind to begin with. Bex just smiled and waved her hand, indicating she had the situation utterly under control.

"Ms. Tufts is not to be at home," Vlad barked. His tone indicated that yes, he definitely did remember Bex. And her praising his buttons didn't even begin to make up for the position she'd put him in when she snuck upstairs to see Felicia without permission.

"Oh, really?" Bex made a sincerely surprised face, even though Vlad obviously couldn't see her through the phone. She liked to think of it as method acting. "Where is she?"

"I do not know this. Good-bye."

"Wait! Wait!" Bex cajoled. "Come on, Vlad. You're a doorman. You're the man. You know everything!"

"I do not know where Ms. Tufts to go."

"Well, can you tell me when she left?"

"This morning. She leave early this morning. Still dark."

"Were you already on duty, then?"

"Yes."

"So you know where she went!" Bex deduced triumphantly. "Come on, Vlad. I know how things work. You hailed Felicia her cab, so you have to know where she went."

"No."

"Yes."

"No."

"Yes."

Craig couldn't take it anymore. He turned around and threw his hands up in the air. Bex wished he would just chill out. Everything was going according to plan. Bex was being extremely clever. He just didn't realize it, yet. What with her acting so stupid and all.

"No!" Vlad's frustration hit its peak. Which is exactly where Bex wanted him. "No. I tell you. I did not hail Ms. Tufts her cab. Ms. Tufts tells me she rents a car."

"Really?" Bex said, pleased as proverbial punch. "Where did she rent the car from, then?"

"I do not have to speak to you about this," Vlad remembered.

"Yes, you do."

"No, I do not."

"Yes, you—" But Vlad had already hung up the phone by then. Which was fine with Bex. She already had all the information she needed.

Bex told Craig, "Felicia rented a car early this morning."

"To go where?"

"I don't know."

"Oh, you are good at this, aren't you?"

"I don't know. Yet," Bex said. She turned back to the computer. She punched a few more keys. She told Craig to take a breath and relax. He told her to get on with it. After their previously acerbic exchanges, they were practically bonding now. Bex said, "There's an Ignel car rental place a block and half from Felicia's apartment."

"So? A car rental agency doesn't know where their vehicles get driven, even if you could get them to part with customer information, which is probably confidential."

Bex sighed. "You're so naïve, Craig."

She dialed the number listed. When someone at Ignel

picked up, Bex asked to speak to the manager. After a few minutes spent listening to snippets from Tracy Chapman's "Fast Car" and The Cars' "Drive," Bex was transferred to a woman who sounded as if she were doing seven things at the same time, and Bex was about to become the eighth straw that broke the manager's back.

As a result, Bex matched her tone for harried tone, and announced, "This is Felicia Tufts, and I want an immediate explanation for this latest cacophony of incompetence."

Bex figured the harried tone and big words would make her sound more East Side-y. Or at least less like a twenty-four-year-old busybody making it up as she went along.

"What can I do for you? Ms. Tufts, is it? I'm sorry, we're very short-handed today, and—"

"I rented a car from you this morning, and now I'm trying to return it, and the idiot at the desk is telling me it's already been returned! If this is your way of sending me home, then charging me for an extra week, I won't stand for it. I know how you charlatans operate. Finding imaginary scratches or claiming the tank wasn't returned filled. I won't have it, I tell you!"

"That's very strange, Ms. Tufts. I don't know why our computers would show that you've already returned the vehicle. Why don't I speak to the attendant and—"

"I don't need you to speak to the attendant. I've already spoken to the attendant. Despite her assurance that she was born in Akron, Ohio, to fine, all-American stock, I'm still not convinced that English isn't her second, or possibly third, language. So how about we leave the attendant to struggle through the latest chapter of "See Jane run," and you talk to me, instead. What say you tap a few keys on that fancy computer I'm sure you've got in front of you, and tell me what's going on, in English, this time."

Gil Cahill may have been a rotten person to work for.

But, he was the *only* one to imitate when you wanted to alienate friends and intimidate people.

A pause on the other end. And then, "Yes, ma'am. I guess I could do that for you."

"That's Tufts." Bex refused to let up on her hectoring tone. "T-U-F-T-S. Felicia. I rented the car in New York City this morning."

"Yes. Yes, ma'am, Felicia Tufts, New York City. I see your records, right here."

"And?"

"And . . . well, it looks like the information you were given was correct. According to our records, your car was turned in at the Highpoint New York Airport about an hour ago. Now, I'm not certain how that happened, but, if you connect me to your attendant—"

"That's all right," Bex said. "I think I've got it now. Thank you for your help."

She hung up the phone. She turned to Craig. With impeccable politeness, he inquired, "Does that obnoxious act always work so well for you?"

"Go with your strengths, that's my motto," Bex told him. And then she dropped the piece de resistance. "Felicia Tufts turned in her car about an hour ago at the Ignel hub of the Highpoint Airport. Highpoint Airport . . . the Mall at Highpoint . . . *now* I think we've got a trail to follow."

Craig stared at her in disbelief.

"This is the part where you shower me with compliments vis-à-vis my research skills and all-around general brilliance," Bex prompted.

He just kept staring. Bex guessed he wasn't in the mood for showering.

Craig blinked. He seemed to be processing her

information. And then he said, "What are we waiting for? Let's go."

This time, he had the keys out and was already on the front porch before Bex caught up with him. "No," she said. "You can't go."

"Why the hell not? She dropped her car off at the airport, Bex. She could be taking Jeremy anywhere on the planet. They could already be gone. I've got to get over there!"

"No." Bex grabbed his arm. "For one thing, Highpoint Airport isn't JFK or La Guardia. I bet it's just a tiny little commuter place. So it's not like they've got flights leaving every couple of minutes. They can't be going too far, definitely not overseas, and it should be easy to find someone who remembers them, so we've caught a break there."

"They could still be out of state, by now!"

"You're right. Someone should go up there immediately. But, it shouldn't be you."

"He's my son!"

"And if he were going to call anyone again, who do you think that would be?"

Craig hesitated.

Bex said, "He might call again, Craig. Do you really want to risk missing it?"

She could practically see the tug-of-war going on in his head. Craig's eyebrows were so furrowed, they looked like one was poised to swallow the other. Finally, he relaxed his stance just a little and stopped trying to pull away from her. He asked, "You'll go to the airport?"

"I'll leave as soon as you give me your car keys."

"And you'll call me. You'll call me as soon as you get there? Tell me what's going on?"

"I've got my cell phone, right here."

Craig still looked not thoroughly convinced.

"I've gotten you this far," Bex gently reminded. "Let's see if my patented obnoxious act can bring Jeremy all the way home?"

Craig swallowed hard. And handed Bex his car keys.

She drove as fast as was humanly possible, without breaking the speed limit—well, okay, without doubling it—to the Highpoint Airport. As expected, it was one of those tiny, we've-only-got-three-planes deals rarely seen by world travelers like Bex outside of *Wings* reruns. The road ninety-nine percent of the way there was utterly straightforward. Highway after highway, complete with colorful signs touting the Hilton Springs Mall at Highpoint on each side. The last half a mile, though, was up a mountain (hence the "high" and the "point," Bex figured out), along a winding, ostensibly two-lane but more like one-and-a-half lane road. With no guardrail.

Driving an unfamiliar car—albeit, a nicer one than her own—where, half the time, her attempts to shift gears resulted in turning on the windshield wipers, did not exactly fill Bex with confidence. Neither did the rocky drop that seemed to loom like a demented, open-mouthed jack-in-the-box and pull her by the elbow every time Bex made a turn. By the time she'd made it to the parking lot, Bex was nauseous, not to mention stressed. As she sat in the car, trying to catch her breath, settle her stomach, and formulate a tentative plan prior to her traditional barging into the airport act, Bex heard the whoosh of a small plane taking off overhead. She sighed. With her luck, Felicia and Jeremy were probably on it. Looking down at her. Chortling.

Bex got out of the car, and, already expecting to fail, entered the airport's main terminal. And by main, she meant only. The entire place was only six counters and four airlines. The staff practically outnumbered the passengers.

Six blue benches, one in front of each counter, were the only other furnishings of note. They were the double-sided kind, where you could face either the clerks, or the big, open window to watch the planes take off.

Jeremy and Felicia had chosen to face the window.

Bex spotted them as soon as she came in. In a place that size, it was hardly a major feat of detective work. Jeremy sat on the leftmost seat, both his legs tucked underneath him, Indian-style, reading a brightly illustrated (was there ever any other kind?) issue of "Fangoria" that still had its white price sticker on the front. His denim jacket lay in a ball on the floor, beside his duffle bag. Next to him, Felicia, wearing jeans and a black turtleneck sweater so subtle it could only have cost several hundreds of dollars in an Upper East Side boutique (where they specialized in expensive clothes that were practically imperceptible, that's how you knew they were expensive), had a magazine open on her lap, but she was staring straight ahead. Not so much at the planes, as past them.

For a moment, Bex was so relieved to have found them, not to mention so darn proud of her own cleverness and key contributions to the endeavor, that she didn't pay any attention to the third person sharing Jeremy and Felicia's bench.

Bex was, in fact, in the process of heading over to confront Felicia and Jeremy when her incontrovertibly brighter subconscious suddenly rang a bell loud enough to frighten away every pigeon in the tri-state area. The third person sharing Jeremy and Felicia's bench had blonde hair. He wore black sneakers, a dark green, V-necked sweater, and wrinkled khaki pants strained to the hems from the muscles in his thighs and calves. He was fingering his airline ticket, ripping tiny, even ridges in the envelope without seeming to notice that he was doing it. His head was down. Bex could only make out his profile. Even with the picture window in front of him, he'd chosen, instead, to study the tiles on the floor. And yet, even from that awkward angle, his identity was unmistakable.

The third person sharing Jeremy's and Felicia's bench was Robby Sharpton.

Nineteen

Bex's first instinct was to hide.

It was not an instinct born of many years of investigative experience and the knowledge that the last thing you want to do in a fragile situation is tip your hand and reveal your presence before formulating a game plan. It was more like the instinct of a toddler who, upon seeing something she hadn't expected, covers her eyes with her chubby palms in the erroneous belief that if you can't see the scary man, the scary man can't see you.

A split second after spotting Robby sitting next to Felicia and Jeremy, Bex found herself trapped somewhere in between the two states. While she did very much want to cover her eyes with her hands and hide, she also had just enough mature life-experience to realize that it most likely wouldn't get the job done. So, while she still intended to hide, Bex suspected that a slightly less diaphanous surface might be required.

Easier ruefully thought than done, though. The airport was basically a football-field-sized open room. There were no luggage carousels, no other passengers, or even a handy shrub to duck behind. Bex's selection of hiding spaces came down to One: behind the reservation counters—and wouldn't the women working there have something to say about that?—or Two: the big white pillar at the entrance. So, really, what she was saying was that Bex had no choices. She ducked behind the pillar.

Subtly, of course.

Once behind the pillar, Bex evaluated her choices. She could step out, approach the happy and unconventional Sharpton/Tufts/Hunt family and politely ask something along the lines of, "So, what are you all doing here, lounging about in a nonchalant manner while Craig believes Jeremy has been kidnapped? Oh, and by the way, did any of you recently bash in Rachel Rose's brains?"

Or, she could always not.

Of the three, Bex eventually decided that she would probably get the most honest answers from Jeremy. Unless, of course, he was some sort of child-genius psychopath (which, with his iffy DNA, was not exactly out the question, if you bought into that whole nature over nurture thing). On the other hand, Bex thought Felicia was more likely to have a better grasp of the whole, big picture, since, according to Craig, she was really at the center of this whole convoluted saga.

And there was one more detail to consider. The only way Bex could hope to get Jeremy alone was if the boy spontaneously decided to wander out of the airport and into some area where neither Felicia nor Robby could follow him (but Bex could). That didn't seem to be a very likely scenario. The kidnapped were rarely given free play time.

On the other hand, there was an area where Felicia and Bex could both go, with the full expectation that they would not be disturbed by either Jeremy or Robby. The Ladies' Room.

It was conveniently situated at exactly the midpoint between Felicia's bench and Bex's handy-dandy pillar. Now all Bex had to do was figure out how to get Felicia into said Ladies' Room, and her plan could be deemed a whopping success.

Her first instinct was to keep sending complimentary bottles of water over until nature could no longer be denied. Bex judged that plan about on par with her earlier, close-your-little-eyes-and-hide scenario.

Her second instinct was just to stare really hard at the back of Felicia's neck.

Yes, Bex knew how bizarre that sounded. What was even more bizarre, though, was that she knew it worked. When Bex was a child, she and her mother passed many an afternoon at the mall (neither had been born with a shopping gene, and so their idea of a good time was to go into the first store open, buy the first item they saw that was within the general parameters of what was currently desperately needed at home, and then retire to the food court), where they would amuse themselves by staring intently at the backs, shoulders, and necks of random passersby, until they quizzically turned around, or at least began uncomfortably scratching the suddenly unexplainably itchy, stared-at area. Bex didn't know how the process worked scientifically. All she knew was that it worked more often than it didn't. And that, at the moment, it was the only plan she had.

And so Bex stared. She picked a spot on Felicia's neck, right below where her expensive, Upper East Side haircut ended, and her equally expensive, Upper East Side sweater began. And she stared. Very intently. While thinking thoughts along the lines of, "Turn around, Felicia. Turn around now. Oh, and please do it in a subtle way, so Robby and Jeremy don't see you, okay?"

A minute passed.

Felicia began to shift uncomfortably in her seat. First she arched her back, and then she brought her shoulders inward, lowering her head until her chin touched her chest. This was good. The staring was obviously working.

Or she just needed to stretch after a combination of God knows how many hours behind the wheel and then sitting on an uncomfortable airport bench.

Felicia, chin still pointing toward her lap, turned her head, first right, then left. She ran a hand though her hair, shaking it a little. Jeremy noticed. This was less good.

He asked Felicia something Bex couldn't hear. His question caught Robby's attention, who also asked her something. Definitely less good.

Felicia answered them, patting Jeremy's hand for good measure, and then—oh, great, only then!—she looked around the airport, as though searching for something.

It could end up being Bex's only chance at getting Felicia's attention.

But it could also end up giving Robby and Jeremy the chance to see her, too.

Did she dare risk it?

Did she dare not risk it?

Bex didn't even know what flight the three of them were waiting for. They might be getting ready to board now. And then what was Bex supposed to do? Huff and puff after them down the runway, still trying to stare at Felicia through the little oval shaped window? Her plan had been kind of odd to begin with. No need to add totally crazy to the list.

And so, figuring this might be her only shot, Bex took a deep breath and stepped out from behind the pillar.

Felicia, of course, at that moment, wasn't even looking in her direction.

Great. Here Bex had gone all brave, and it wasn't even being appreciated.

She wondered if jumping up and down and waving her arms would help.

Probably not if Felicia was still sitting with her back to her.

And then a miracle happened. (Or, as Bex liked to think of it: The logical conclusion to her brilliant, scientific, and well-thought-out plan happened.) Felicia turned her head, and her eyes met Bex's. Her eyes also clearly recognized Bex, because they got very, very wide, and her head froze at an angle that could not have been comfortable or natural. She swallowed hard and, like Bex only a moment before, stared intently. She seemed frozen and unsure of what to do.

This is where Bex came in. They were fine, as long as one of them had a plan.

Making sure that Felicia was still watching, Bex used both her hands to point toward the Ladies' Room door. She even stuck out two of her fingers like arrows and animatedly shook them in the right direction several times, so there could be no misunderstanding.

Felicia continued staring, seemingly uncomprehending.

What, did Bex have to hold up a sign for her?

Instead, she decided to casually head toward the Ladies' Room, herself, and hope Felicia got the message and followed. Boy, did Bex really hope that Felicia got the message and followed.

Bex didn't dare turn around and see for herself. There was too much risk of coming face-to-face with Robby or Jeremy. Her ears strained to make out the sound of Felicia's shoes on the gray tile floor. But, at that moment, a plane chose to come in for a landing, and there went that idea.

Bex entered the Ladies' Room and closed the heavy, swinging door behind her. And she waited. And she wondered if Felicia wasn't taking advantage of her waiting to hustle Robby and Jeremy out of there. And she wondered if she were an idiot.

The jury was still annoyingly out on that last one, when the bathroom door swung open and Felicia appeared—sans escorts. Bex exhaled slightly. At least she wasn't a total idiot. Maybe merely a fool. After all, hadn't Bex just invited a potential murderer to trap her alone in a more-or-less soundproof room with plenty of opportunity to wash up afterward?

Perhaps it was that particular possibility that prompted Bex, with no preamble whatsoever, to blurt out, "Did you kill Rachel, Felicia?"

Felicia had obviously been ready for a variety of questions. Felicia had obviously not been expecting that one.

"No!" Felicia didn't just metaphorically spit out her emphatic denial. There was an actual spit bubble that shot from her lip and toward the bathroom mirror to the left of them. "Ms. Levy, what the hell are you doing here?"

"I'm looking for Jeremy," Bex said.

"Where are the police?"

Now it was Bex's turn to be dumbfounded. "The police? What police?"

"I don't know what police. The local police, the state, the FBI. This is a kidnapping. Why aren't the police here?"

"You *want* them here?" This conversation was most certainly not going the way Bex would have imagined it, had she had time to imagine it, between all the ducking behind pillars and frantic, pointy hand gestures.

"Where's Craig?"

"He's at home. In case Jeremy calls again." But, that wasn't the important part. What Bex really wanted to know was—

"Calls again? What do you mean, calls again? Did Jeremy call Craig? When?"

"This morning. From some video arcade. He said he'd forgotten his skates and you told him Craig could just mail them to the hotel where you were staying. Jeremy said Craig knew where the two of you were going. This came as a pretty big surprise to Craig. Or, at least, so he said to me."

"The arcade!" Felicia said. "I should have known. He kept asking me about the skates, so I had to make up that story about Craig—I never thought it would come to this. I thought it would all be over by now. Craig knew Jeremy was with me? Damn it! His skates, of all things! His goddamn skates! This has got to be some kind of joke, right? Why does every screw-up in my life come with a pair of goddamn skates attached?"

"Felicia," Bex said calmly. "You aren't making any sense. What is going on here? Why did you take Jeremy without telling Craig?"

"Because I needed him to call the police!"

"So they could arrest you?"

"Not me! Robby!"

"How would your kidnapping Jeremy—"

"You don't understand. There's more going on here than you know."

"I know that you and Robby are Jeremy's biological parents," Bex offered, figuring that one single statement would stem the "you don't know what's really going on here" tide.

And indeed it did. Felicia's mouth closed abruptly. And then it opened. And then it closed again. "Oh," she said.

"Craig told me."

"Good God, why?"

"Because. He needed my help to track down Jeremy, and I refused to move a muscle until he gave me all the facts."

"What the hell did Craig need you for? Why didn't he just call the police and report Jeremy missing, like I expected him to?"

"Because when Jeremy called and said he was with you, Craig had no idea what was going on. And he was afraid of getting you into trouble before you'd had the chance to explain yourself."

For a moment, Felicia looked like she was going to cry. She whipped her eyes away to avoid Bex's gaze, swallowed hard, looked up at the ceiling and shook her head. "Damn Rachel."

"I beg your pardon?"

Felicia smiled ruefully. "Damn her for getting the last nice guy on the planet."

"Why did you kidnap Jeremy, Felicia?" Bex figured they'd gone around in circles long enough. And there was also just so much time Felicia could spend in the bathroom before Robby became suspicious.

"Because Robby killed Rachel. And I had to make him pay."

"He confessed to you?"

"He didn't have to. As soon as I heard what happened—who else could it have been? She was beaten to death, Bex. Beaten to death!"

"Did you tell the police?"

"What for? I had no evidence. Neither did they. I knew they wouldn't be able to arrest him for Rachel's murder. But, they could arrest him for Jeremy's kidnapping." Felicia smiled, more to herself than for Bex's benefit, and Bex recognized that glint of pride in one's own plan. She'd certainly seen it enough times on her own face. "So, I called Robby. I called him, just out of the blue, and I told him the truth about Jeremy."

"I don't understand."

"I had to convince him. I had to convince him that what I was telling him was the truth."

"That what was the truth?"

"Oh, that I was still in love with him. That I wanted the three of us to run away together. I told him now that Rachel was dead, I didn't want Craig raising our son. That we could do it, be a real family. I made a really convincing case, Bex, you should have heard me. For a minute there, I almost believed it myself. But, then again, Robby was always good at that. Playing with my mind. Even when he didn't know he was doing it."

"What were you trying to accomplish, though? Were you trying to get him to confess to killing Rachel?"

"Oh, that would have been nice. But, I wasn't shooting for that. No, what I wanted was for Craig to call the police as soon as he came home and realized Jeremy was missing. I left clues all over the place about where we were going. As we were heading out of town, I stopped at that gas station right on the Interstate and had Robby get out to ask for directions to the Highpoint Airport. I made sure the attendant saw Jeremy, too. I figure that would be one of the first places the police would come looking for us. And then I insisted we pull over at the mall—it's right on the other side of the state line, and we'd taken a minor across it, so the felony charge was guaranteed. We stayed there for almost two hours; I kept hoping that would give the police enough time to catch up to us. And then, of course, the reason I picked Highpoint instead of one of the New York City major airports was so that, in case the cops didn't make it in time, we'd be easily remembered. I even had Robby buy the tickets under our rightful names. I thought I had it planned so perfectly. A trail of breadcrumbs that practically glowed in the dark. But, who knew Craig wouldn't go to the police? Who knew he'd turn to some researcher for help?"

And an idiot researcher at that, Bex thought. Here she'd believed herself so clever—calling Vlad, then the car rental agency, not to mention her patented *69 trick. And, all along, Felicia had been throwing clues right and left!

"Your plan was to tell the police that Robby kidnapped you and Jeremy both," Bex guessed. "He's still on parole, isn't he? This would have gotten him thrown right back in jail."

"Where he belongs," Felicia snapped. "For what he did to Rachel. Not to mention all the other havoc he managed to wreak along the way."

"You're certain Robby killed Rachel? It couldn't have been someone else?"

"Like whom?"

Well, you, for instance, Bex didn't say out loud. Instead, she went with the slightly less inflammatory, "Craig?"

"Don't be absurd."

"Felicia," Bex tread as delicately as she could, under the circumstances. "The morning before you took him, Jeremy called me at work. He told me wanted to talk about his dad's role in his mom's death."

"Is that what he said?"

"Well, maybe not exactly . . ." Bex conceded. So much had happened since that initial phone call that she'd forgotten the exact wording. She reached for her cell phone, meaning to call in and double-check her saved messages, when Felicia interrupted.

"Because Jeremy told me that he overheard you accusing Craig of killing Rachel, and he called you to let you know that could never, ever happen."

Oh. Now that Felicia mentioned it, Jeremy's exact words came back to Bex like an audio flashback. "Ms. Levy," he'd said, "This is Jeremy Hunt. I really need to talk to you. It's about my dad killing my mom." Bex supposed "about my dad killing my mom" could have meant, "I want to tell you that he didn't do it."

"Bex, please," Felicia put her hand on Bex's arm. The awkwardness and hesitation of the gesture suggested that Felicia Tufts was not particularly used to reaching out to people, much less asking them for help. She was stiff as a board and utterly devoid of warmth. And yet her sincerity was unmistakable. "Please, don't ruin this for me. Let me finish what I started. Let the three of us get on a plane, and then you contact Craig and tell him to call the police, ASAP. They should still be able to follow the clues I left them. We're going to California. With any luck, the cops will have it all figured out and a squad car standing by to arrest Robby even before we land. I'm doing this for Rachel, to avenge her, yes. But I'm also trying to protect Jeremy. He isn't safe as long as Robby is out walking the streets. Do you think Robby will ever let him go now that he knows that Jeremy is his son? He'll make Jeremy's life miserable. And God only knows what he might do to Craig. I am trying to protect them all. Please, please, Bex. Please don't interfere."

Bex hesitated. Felicia took it as consent.

Before Bex even had the chance to utter a definitive "yay" or "nay," Felicia whispered, "Thank you," and turned to hurry out of the bathroom.

Bex waited a moment. Unsure of whether she'd just done the right thing, or even if she'd done anything at all.

Was she really willing to let Felicia and Robby get on a plane to California? How in the world would Craig ever find them, then? And how did she know for sure that Felicia was telling the truth? What if Bex's initial instinct was right and Felicia had killed Rachel to get back her son—and his father? What if Jeremy really was being kidnapped by his natural parents (who may or may not also be murderers) and Bex was the only one with a chance to stop them?

She couldn't take that chance. She owed it to Jeremy, if to no one else, to get to the absolute bottom of things before she allowed them to go any farther.

Her mind made up, Bex boldly exited the bathroom.

Only to be greeted by a suddenly hysterical Felicia who, pointing to the now empty bench where Robby and Jeremy and their luggage had sat only a moment before, moaned, "They're gone. Robby took Jeremy. I can't find them anywhere. They're gone!"

Twenty

It was a terribly petty thought, especially under the circumstances, but Bex had to admit that it was nice, for a change, to not be the woman Craig Hunt looked like he wanted to strangle.

After scouring the airport for Robby and Jeremy and only eventually being told by someone at the reservations desk that they'd gotten on the shuttle bus heading into town, Bex drove a nearly catatonic Felicia to the shuttle's drop-off point where, of course, neither Robby nor Jeremy were to be found, and the driver could only recall that the blonde man and boy had walked off, "somewhere in that direction. Or maybe it was that one." With no more leads to follow (Bex did drop in on the local bus station, but no one there remembered the pair), Bex insisted that she and Felicia return to the Poconos and tell Craig what had happened. Bex figured it was about time he was let back into the loop—though she didn't look forward to the scene. Neither, obviously, did Felicia, as she spent the bulk of their drive staring out the window and taking deep calming breaths that, nine times out of ten, turned into barely suppressed sobs. Bex tried to engage her in conversation, but when that proved futile, decided to utilize her time more wisely and spent the remainder of the drive calling local car rental places on her cell phone to see if Robby might have rented a car there. Naturally, nobody had a record of any such thing. The man had, to all intents and purposes, fallen off the face of the earth. And taken Craig Hunt's son with him.

Which brought them back to her not being the woman Craig currently wanted to strangle.

Well, at least not the number one woman, anyway. . . .

He did take time, in the middle of his tirade against Felicia, to remind Bex, "You promised you would call me the minute you found Jeremy. The very minute that you found him. If you'd only kept your word, maybe we could have avoided all of this?"

What could Bex say? He had a valid point.

"What were you thinking, Felicia?" Oh, good. He was back to Felicia now. Bex exhaled and, just in case, took a step back so as to be even further outside his field of vision.

"I'm sorry, Craig. You don't know how sorry I am. I just wanted to help you and Jeremy."

"Did Robby give you any idea where he might go? Did he mention friends? Does he have family in the area? Think, Felicia, please! You were married to the man. You convinced him to run away with you, for Pete's sake. You must know something about how his mind works!"

"I—Robby doesn't have any family. Not anyone he's spoken to in—I don't know—over thirty years, anyway. And friends . . . he was never exactly the friend-making type."

"There's a surprise," Craig snapped.

"Craig," Bex chimed in, her entire body poised in case she had to spring back suddenly.

"What?" He spun around, glaring at her either for simply being there, or for his forgetting that she was there and now having to be reminded of her co-starring role in this whole adventure.

"I think," she chose her words with care. "I think it's time to call the police now."

It took a bit of cajoling and a lot of apologizing on both Bex and Craig's parts before they managed to convince Gretchen and Travis to return to the house, ASAP. In Bex's case, it also took listening to Gretchen's version of "The Little Researcher Who Cried Wolf." But, in the end, they did manage to convince the Poconos' finest that the story they were telling now was, in fact, the actual story. Not to be confused with the actual story they swore they were telling them earlier. And the time before that. And all the other stories Bex had just kind of postulated along the way.

Within fifteen minutes of becoming convinced that Jeremy really was missing (this time), and that he was with a man who, while they had no proof was also Rachel's killer, was definitely not the custodial (even if he was the biological) parent, and a convicted felon, to boot, the police put out an All Points Bulletin on Robby and Jeremy, as well as an Amber Alert for missing kids. They assured Craig that they were watching airports and bus stations and car rental places. They told him Robby wouldn't be able to take Jeremy out of state. Though they didn't appreciate Bex butting in to ask how they even knew what state Robby was in. Last they'd tracked, Robby was in New York. But he was also just a few miles away from the New Jersey and Pennsylvania borders. Robby could have taken

Jeremy in any direction and just kept going straight. Heck, they could be in Connecticut, or Washington D.C., or Vermont by now!

"You know what, Bex?" Gretchen said, "I think it's time for you to let the professionals do their job. I realize how, for bright and talented women like us, it can be awfully hard to let go of a project once we've committed to it. We're such professionals, aren't we? But really, sweetheart, you simply must believe me: It is very important to learn to relax, to confront those control issues, to go with the flow. Are you hearing me? It isn't healthy to obsess. That sort of thing is horrible for your natural body rhythms, and you certainly don't want to be messing with those, especially at this time in your life when you're coming up on choices and—"

Craig cut to the chase. He turned around from where he'd been standing next to Travis, shuffling through a handful of recent Jeremy photos to decide which ones to put out over the wire.

"Go home, Bex. Thanks for your help, but I think you've done quite enough here for now."

Which is how Bex ended up on the sidewalk outside of Rachel and Craig Hunt's house, still as carless as she'd been a few hours (and a lifetime) earlier, when Gretchen and Travis had peeled off and left her stranded. Her own car, Bex realized too late to beg for a ride, was still at the police station. So here she was, at nearly midnight, chilled, marooned, and definitely unappreciated. And after all she'd done for those people! They wouldn't even know that Jeremy was with Robby if it wasn't for her. Of course, Robby probably wouldn't have taken off with the boy, either. And then there was that whole, she-started-all-this-drama-in-the-first-place thing.

Bex sighed, using the warm, expelled air from her

mouth to defrost her rapidly stiffening fingers. And she considered the possibility that it might be time to hang up her researcher shingle and go home. She'd made a spectacular mess, that much was clear to anyone with rods and cones in their eyeballs, and even to a few blind people with excellent hearing. At best, she'd disrupted the life and career of—what had Toni called him back when all this began?—the best young skater in the United States. At worst, she'd gotten an innocent woman killed and left a defenseless boy at the mercy of a murderer. Maybe Craig was right. Maybe she really had done enough here for now.

Bex reached for her cell phone, fully expecting, the way her last few days had been going, to find the battery drained. Much to her surprise, it was merely low. She had enough juice to either call a cab to take her to her car at the police station, or to call New York and check her messages. Even though it may have seemed like Jeremy Hunt was her only story of the moment, she actually had a couple of other pressing things on her plate. There were bios to be finished and several last-minute interviews to set up. Bex had calls in to skaters in both Lithuania and China, and, because of the time difference, if any of them had called, she needed to respond within the next few hours, or miss another twenty-four hours of accessibility.

It was a simple decision to make, really. What with the motto at 24/7 being: "If you don't come into work on Saturday, don't bother coming in on Sunday," Bex didn't even hesitate before deciding to use her one remaining phone call to check her office messages.

There was nothing from either Lithuania or China. But Bex did have a message from Gil. She knew it was him even before he began talking because of the fun habit her executive producer had of prefacing any message with a vigorous throat clearing.

"Bex!" He exclaimed upon conquering his latest influenza attack. "Where the hell are you? Did I give you a vacation? I don't remember giving you any vacation! You better not be goofing around on the company dime. And where's that feature you promised? Some disappeared skater chick from the eighteenth century or whatever. I need that footage yesterday if you're planning to make it in the Nationals show. We've got a hole waiting for it and it's either your piece or the network going coast-to-coast black with a little Chyron sign reading, 'Bex Levy screwed up, that's why we don't have a piece.' I'm waiting, Bex. I'm waiting."

He didn't mean it, of course. Gil would never put the entire 24/7 network in black for five minutes just to teach Bex a lesson. He would have to be a total lunatic to do that.

Oh. Right.

Well, at least she had one thing to be grateful to Gil for. All those pesky thoughts she was having just a moment earlier about cutting her losses and going home? Not an option anymore!

It didn't matter how many more bodies piled up in her wake. Bex had to see this through to the bitter end. And preferably with captivating video footage, too. Which, to be honest, she'd been quite lax about up to this point. At the moment, she only had the earlier interviews with Robby and Felicia, neither of which was relevant anymore. A good researcher would have documented every moment of Craig's near breakdown, not to mention her and Felicia's exclusive Encounter in the Bathroom. She should, at the very least, have snuck a hidden camera into Rachel Rose's autopsy. And gotten some shots of the bloody tree she'd been smashed against. Bex figured now the only way she could get her proverbial ass out of the literal sling Gil was so gleefully stringing for her, was to . . . what? . . .

Let's see . . . single-handedly rescue Jeremy, capture Robby, and get him to confess to Rachel's murder? On camera?

Piece of cake.

Oh, and she also had to keep the police and other media from getting to Robby first. Gil was very particular about his exclusives. If every local TV station in the country had the same footage, it was useless to him.

Which was still a piece of cake. No problem. It was just more like the kind that you had to actually bake yourself and measure ingredients for and stuff, instead of the one you tossed in your shopping cart and ate straight out of the box.

Bex tried to think. In the cold and dark, it was kind of hard. She needed warmth and she needed a working cell phone and, most importantly, she needed a computer. Bex didn't know what for yet, but considering how limited her repertoire of research tricks was, she strongly suspected she would need one sooner or later. And she was not going to find any of those things standing in the street.

Her phone was officially dead now, so there went her cab option.

Good thing Bex still had Craig's car keys in her pocket, huh?

For the record, Bex hadn't deliberately not returned them to him. She just hadn't found the time in the middle of his yelling and accusing and looking like he wanted to strangle someone—anyone. Clearly, it was too late to return them now. Craig had made it very unambiguous that she wasn't wanted in his home, and any attempt to engage Travis and Gretchen could very well lead to another lecture about Bex's lifestyle choices. Nobody wanted that.

Bex wondered if it would be ethical for her to . . . uh . . . borrow Craig's car. She wondered if she could be charged with grand theft auto for it. She wondered if it counted as grand theft auto if she only took the car as far as the police station and then left it there while she got her own. And then she wondered why she was still wondering these things since, the next thing Bex realized, she was behind the wheel and pulling Craig's car into a spot directly in front of the police station, so it was obviously too late to change her mind now.

Bex walked into the police station, asked politely for an envelope, dropped the keys inside with a note of explanation, sealed it, and wrote Gretchen's name on the front. She left the missive with a clerk and asked if there was a phone she could use. She was directed to a pay one down the hall, next to a military-tidy arrangement of four blue plastic chairs, none of which was, fortunately, occupied by a criminal at the moment.

Bex took a seat closest to the phone, plugged her cell into a nearby jack for recharging, and tried to think. She tried to think like both a researcher with more experience than she actually had, and also like a cop. Not to mention a possibly psychopathic ex-skater. Because Bex didn't just have to get to Robby anymore. She had to get to Robby first.

Bex guessed the police would have already done the obvious and sent a car to his apartment in New Jersey to ask about friends, acquaintances, business associates—any place he might go when he felt cornered. Because, Bex had to figure, for Robby to take Jeremy and run like this, he had to feel cornered. And desperate. Bex also assumed that the police had called his job and his parole officer for information, so all of those avenues were closed to her. Not to mention that it was the middle of the night, and sources like bosses and parole officers were probably unavailable until morning. Bex forced herself to think harder. Who in the world would Robby Sharpton know who was available in the middle of the night? Available, and packing relevant information?

Bex smiled.

The answer was so obvious, it was amazing she hadn't thought of it hours ago. Of course! The middle of the night and packing relevant information, to boot! It was a goldmine. And one she doubted the police would ever think of.

It took her a single phone call to Jersey City information, and Bex had the number for the ice rink closest to Robby's apartment. She dialed the main office and waited stubbornly through eighteen shrill rings before a male voice, sounding equal parts pissed and out of breath, picked up and demanded, "Yeah, what?"

Bex asked, "Is this the New Jersey broomball league?"

"Yeah. What?"

"I'm calling from the Poconos Pennsylvania Police Station," Bex recited efficiently. She didn't even feel vaguely guilty about the lie. Was it or was it not a fact that, at the moment, she most certainly was calling from the Poconos Pennsylvania Police Station? She was standing smack in the middle of it, wasn't she?

"Yeah?" A little more cautious now. "What?"

"Robert Sharpton plays in your league, does he not?"

"Robby's not here right now. Hasn't been around for a couple of nights, actually."

Bingo! (And not only because she'd gotten him to stop repeating the same thing over and over; that was just an added bonus.) "I know he's not there right now. I'm afraid Mr. Sharpton's been in an accident. We're trying to locate his next of kin."

"We're just some guys he plays broomball with." The belligerence was gone, replaced mostly with confusion. "We've got no next of kin here."

"Oh, I realize that, I realize that, I certainly do. But, you see, we found a punch-card in his wallet from your ice rink, and we thought, certainly he must have filled out a release form when he signed up to play. That usually has a person to contact in case of emergency on it, doesn't it?"

Bex held her breath. Any minute now, she expected the guy to ask how she knew it was broomball that Robby played, or why she assumed the rink would be open in the middle of the night, not to mention questioning her credentials to even be asking this. But, apparently, the siren song of the ongoing game was too strong, and her new friend just wanted to get this over with and head back to the ice. "Hold on," he said. "I'll check that for you."

In a few minutes, during which Bex fed several more coins into the phone and prayed that her emergency stash wouldn't run out before her time did, he was back. "Yeah. Yeah, I got it right here. Person to contact in case of emergency. Hey, let me ask you: Robby going to be okay?"

"I don't know," Bex told him honestly.

"That's a fucking shame. Guy's really got something on the ice, you know? Said he never even played hockey before he got here, but it's like he's a natural. Probably could have gone pro or something, if things had been a little different."

"Yeah," Bex agreed. "If things had been a little different."

"So, anyway. The name he put down here. Emergency contact, you know? Looks like—let's see if I can read it; his handwriting's kind of wonky. Oh, yeah, here we go, name he put down for emergency contact, it says, Mrs. Antonia Wright."

Twenty-one

Bex made him repeat the name. And then she pretended to be writing it down just so he would repeat it one more time. Mrs. Antonia Wright? Antonia Wright? *Toni?*

This didn't make any sense. Toni told Bex she hadn't had any contact with Robby since he was a child. Sure, she'd given Bex his home telephone number, but Toni had everybody's number in skating. And, if she didn't, she knew whom to call to get it. But, she'd claimed to know nothing about Robby beyond the perfunctory basics.

Bex mumbled a hurried thank you to her broomball-playing source. It wasn't until after she'd hung up that she even realized she hadn't asked him for Toni's phone number—a definite screwup if she wanted him to believe her story about needing to contact the next of kin. But, Bex was too distracted to care at this point.

Toni, of all people.

Toni!

She should probably call her. Who cared that it was the middle of the night? Bex needed answers and she needed them now. But, on the other hand, this wasn't the sort of conversation Bex wanted to have over the phone. And not only because she was afraid of tipping her hand.

And so, even though it was coming up on two thirty A.M., Bex got a cup of bitter coffee from the vending machine next to the pay phone, using it to both wake up her mind and warm her hands. And then she got in her own car, and started driving to Connecticut.

Bex turned into the driveway of Toni's suburban two-story home (all the while singing the *My Fair Lady* standard, "On the Street Where You Live," at the top of her lungs, to keep from slumping over into ZZZ-land) at a few minutes before five A.M. She'd been up now for exactly twenty-four hours. Luckily, Bex had almost a year of skating television coverage under her belt. In the world of skating television coverage, twenty-four hours without sleep was also known as "the first half of the day." So, while Bex was giddy and sleep deprived and lightheaded, she'd operated in such a state so many times before that it felt almost comfortable. If comfortable could be stretched to include headache, cotton stuffed behind both eyeballs, and an inability to connect nouns to verbs in any sort of coherent manner.

Yup, Bex was ready to play detective.

She parked her car across the street, and dialed Toni's number from her newly recharged cell phone. Were it anyone else, Bex might have worried that a five A.M. phone call would draw undue suspicion to itself. But a skating coach was always getting calls at five A.M., either from students needing to cancel an early morning lesson, or to beg for one. If anything, Bex was afraid she might be too late, and Toni had already left for the rink.

Bex watched the house while she listened to the phone ring. All of the windows were dark. Toni's husband had died a few years earlier, and her two sons were grown and living on their own, so Toni should have been the only one inside. And yet, when the phone first rang, was it Bex's imagination, or did she, in fact, spot movement in what should have been an empty guest room?

"Hello?" Toni didn't even sound groggy or curious. Bex guessed that a lifetime of early morning phone calls had given her an algorithm for dealing.

"Toni? It's Bex Levy."

A pause. Bex got the feeling Toni was about to repeat her name, and so she rushed to intercept. "Don't say anything, please. Toni, I—" Bex took a deep breath. And then she took the biggest gamble of her career. Because, if her bluff failed, Bex would not only lose her last chance for an exclusive on the Robby Sharpton story. She would also lose her good friend.

"Toni," she said. "I know Robby Sharpton is there with you. And Jeremy Hunt, too."

Another pause. Bex wondered if her wild shot had hit its target, or whether Toni was just taking her edict to not say anything a little more seriously than Bex intended.

"Toni . . ."

"Yes." She could have meant, "Yes, this is Toni." She could have meant, "Yes, I'm still here." Or, she could have meant, "Yes, Robby and Jeremy are in my house as we speak."

Bex said, "I'm just outside, sitting in my car. Please come out and talk to me. Please."

Begging. It was Bex's other patented research trick.

This time, the pause seemed to stretch longer than the entire conversation that proceeded it.

Finally, Toni said, "Give me a few minutes. I'll be right there."

* * *

It took Toni almost ten minutes to exit out her front door. In that time, Bex entertained herself by desperately changing radio stations, looking for a ballad that didn't include the word *betrayal.* She opened the window, hoping the cool air would clear her head. And she wondered if Toni wasn't coming out because she was too busy tipping off Robby and Jeremy and hustling them out the back door. She also wondered if Toni's house had a back door. Bex was tempted to walk around and find out, but, in the end, she was too scared of missing Toni if/when she finally came out the front to budge.

At last, the older woman emerged. She wore baggy jeans and sneakers, a large, down-filled jacket with the OTC logo stitched over the breast pocket, and a gray, woolen hat pulled down low over her eyes and ears, her hair hastily tucked under the edges. Toni slid into the passenger seat next to Bex, studied her for a few minutes, and finally asked, "How?"

Bex said, "Robby listed you as his broomball league emergency contact. I called. I asked."

The shadows on Toni's face made her actual expression unreadable. "You're a bright girl, I always said that. Very, very bright."

"Why did you lie to me, Toni?"

"About what?"

"You said you hadn't had any contact with Robby since he was a little boy taking lessons from you. That's not exactly true, is it?"

Toni said, "I lied because it was none of your business."

"You were protecting him."

"Yes."

"Why?" Bex twisted uncomfortably, resting her left elbow on the steering wheel, wincing when she inadvertently brushed the horn and let a muffled bleat out onto the silent street. *Good going, Bex. Why don't you tell Robby you're here, in Morse code?* "I don't understand. I've seen you teach. You'd never let any of your students get away with the kind of abuse Robby heaped on his partners. How could you have wanted to protect someone like him?"

Toni looked out through the windshield. She rubbed the glove compartment with the tips of her fingers, brushing off dust Bex wished she could say was imaginary. She really didn't clean her car as often as she should. On the other hand, in this dusk, Toni couldn't possibly have been able to see it. Bex had to assume it was just a stalling tactic.

Toni said, "The first time I saw Robby, he was maybe six or seven years old. I was coming in to the rink to teach, and he was standing right in front of me, at the turnstile. He had to stand on the very tips of his toes just to get his nose over the counter, so he could see the girl selling tickets. I think I smelled him before I saw him. He smelled like neither he nor his clothes had been washed in weeks. He had an open scab on one knee and his nose was running. No, not running. There was just this crust above his upper lip. I think he ended up wiping it against the counter. He was telling the girl that he had been there the day before, with his first-grade class, and that he didn't have any money with him today for admission or skate rental, but, if she would just please, please, please let him in and let him skate again, he could maybe help out by cleaning up afterward or any other odd jobs we might have for him to do. He promised he wouldn't be any trouble."

There, Bex thought, *was a promise Robby Sharpton definitely hadn't kept.*

"And you know what the girl said to him? Do you know

what she told that child?" Toni looked straight at Bex now. "She told him, 'No. No trash allowed.'"

The echo was unmistakable.

"No niggers allowed," they'd told Toni.

"I put him on the ice that same day," Toni said. Nearly thirty years later, Bex could hear the pride in her voice. "Right away, he was trying to jump and to spin like he saw the other kids doing. He fell so many times that day, I was sure I'd never see him again. But, there he was, the next day and the next and the next. I finally gave him a little private lesson just so he'd stop hurting himself so badly."

"And was he good from the start?"

"He was determined. That made him good. And he loved it. That's what made him great. Finally, I realized I'd have to give him some serious training. I told Robby I was willing to do it for free, but we'd have to talk to his parents, get their permission. Frankly, I wondered where they thought their six-year-old son was all afternoon. He always came alone. I think he walked straight from school. Robby fought me on it, at first. He wouldn't give me his address—he wouldn't even tell me his last name!—until I threatened to stop teaching him. We went over to see his folks one afternoon. They lived in a trailer. And I don't mean one of the nice ones where everything is tidy and there are fresh flowers in the windows. Believe me, we saw plenty of those on the way, so it's not like there wasn't something to emulate. This place was a mess. It was, quite frankly, the trailer equivalent of what Robby looked like. Except that the aromas included cigarettes and booze and several less legal things. It was a cliché, that's what it was. Honestly, Bex, before I met the Sharptons, I truly didn't believe people actually lived like that. I thought it was something made up for the movies. These people didn't give a damn about Robby. They didn't care if he skated or if he sat in a ditch all day, as long as he didn't bother them. After that, I ended up taking him home with me most nights. Of course, when Lucian took over Robby's training, he got him a spot in one of the dorms—you know, the ones the foreign kids board in? My kids were rarely accepted there. Lucian had to pull some strings."

"Is that why you let Lucian take over teaching Robby? Because Lucian could do more for him?" In Bex's mind, she was already watching the skating version of *Stella Dallas*.

"I didn't *let* Lucian do anything. As soon as he saw how much potential Robby had, he swept in and took him. It was his center. It was his prerogative."

"And how old was Robby, then?"

"Oh, I don't know. Nine, maybe? Ten?"

"Did he want to go?"

Toni sighed. "I never knew what was going on in Robby's head. On the ice, he did exactly what he was told. He was incredible at following directions. You could make one suggestion, and he would implement it immediately. That's what made him so easy to teach. And he was the same off the ice. But off the ice, I don't know, it was kind of . . . odd. It was almost as if he had no idea how to behave, as if he had no instincts whatsoever. At least, none he was willing to follow. It was as if . . . sometimes I felt . . . sometimes I felt like he was learning how to . . . how to be . . . human. Or at least how to pass for one."

Okay . . . Cross *Stella Dallas* with *Invasion of the Body Snatchers*.

"He learned all the right things to say. He learned how to behave, so that he didn't draw undue attention to himself. But it never felt natural with him. It felt like it was all just another skill he had to perfect, like his triple Toe Loop."

"And the abuse? I know he hit Felicia Tufts when they were skating together. Was that something he learned, too? From Lucian, maybe?"

"No. No, Lucian isn't like that. He may have looked the other way when Robby hit Felicia, but he certainly never told Robby to do it. Robby's hitting Felicia . . . he just . . . it was so difficult for him . . . self-control. He was in such tight control of himself all the time, always afraid of doing or saying the wrong thing without knowing it, that every once in a while, he just blew up. We would all see it coming, but there was nothing we could do."

"Did you try?" Bex demanded. "Did you at least try to talk to him, get him help, maybe?"

Toni said, "He was Lucian's student now. I couldn't interfere."

"I thought you cared about him!"

"I couldn't get personally involved with every student, Bex. Do you know how many of the kids I see every day could use therapy? I'm a coach, not a social worker. Besides, I'd had my own children by then. They were my priority."

"So you just cut Robby loose?"

"He had Lucian. He had people to look out for him. I thought he was in good hands."

"Did you know that Robby raped Rachel Rose?"

"Lucian told me that—"

"I can guess what Lucian told you. Did *you* know?"

"No. Not until recently."

"How recently?"

"Last night," Toni said.

"Robby told you last night that he raped Rachel?"

"He . . . no . . . He just told me that he and Rachel . . . He told me everything. At least, I think it was everything. About Jeremy and Felicia and Craig and . . ."

"If you didn't have anything to do with him while he was skating with Rachel and Lucian, when did you two reconnect again?"

"It was after Robby went to prison. Maybe a year later. He sent me a letter. He told me he'd been doing a lot of thinking. He told me he needed to talk. He asked me for help."

"What kind of help?"

"He wanted to get his life in order. He knew he'd made a lot of mistakes and he wanted to start . . . fixing them. He just didn't know how."

"And you helped him?"

"I tried." Toni shrugged. "I visited him, I called him, I wrote him. I don't think anyone else ever did. He was all alone in the world."

"Did he ever talk to you about Felicia? Or Rachel?"

"Yes. He felt awful about what he'd done to Felicia. He wanted to apologize to her. He did love her, you know. Maybe you can't believe it, but I do. He really did love her. He just had no idea how to behave. I tried, several times, to call her on his behalf. But she wouldn't see him. I couldn't very well force her to, so, eventually, Robby had to let it go."

"And what about Rachel? Did he want to apologize to Rachel?"

"He wanted to talk to her. He never told me why or what for. I tried to find her for him, but I could only get her phone number, at first. I think Robby tried to reach her when he got out of prison, but she didn't want to see him. By the time I did have her address, Robby seemed to have gotten over it. I saw no point in stirring all of that unpleasantness up again. Robby was on parole. He had a job, he was trying to rebuild his life. I didn't see what good his reconnecting with Rachel would do. So, I kept quiet. Until you came along, that is."

"Me?" It wasn't so much of a question as a yelp on Bex's part. She'd kind of been hoping to avoid this chapter. And yet, she knew that she couldn't. "It was me?"

"After you interviewed Robby, it stirred up all of his old memories. He came to me, again, and asked if I knew where he could find Rachel. This time, I gave him her address."

"And a few days later, she was dead."

"Yes," Toni looked like she might cry. "Yes. She was."

"Did Robby kill Rachel?"

"He didn't mean to. He told me he honestly didn't mean to. He told me he just went up there to talk to her. And then he saw her with Jeremy."

Bex groaned. "Jeremy was with Rachel because I'd scared him and Craig away from the rink. He would have never been there, Robby would have never seen him, if it wasn't for me."

Toni patted Bex's leg reassuringly. "None of us knew. How could we know?"

"Robby knew Jeremy was his son the moment he saw him, didn't he?"

"The resemblance is striking." Toni indicated the still silent house. "I was looking at the two of them last night and wondering how in the world I could have missed it. They don't only look the same, they even skate the same, they move the same. I always knew Jeremy reminded me of Robby, but I never, even for a moment, made the connection."

"Robby did, though."

"Yes, Robby did. He called Rachel later and asked her to meet him in the park. All he wanted was for her to admit that Jeremy was his son. That's all he wanted."

"But she wouldn't."

"No."

"So he beat her to death."

Now, Toni really was crying. The tears rolled silently out of her eyes, down her cheeks, and dripped down her chin. She didn't even bother wiping them away.

"He told you this?"

"Yes," Toni whispered.

"And he told you how Felicia fit in?"

"Yes. He told me she called him later, told him that Jeremy was his son. But that he was also hers, not Rachel's. He believed her when she said she wanted them to be a family. It was like a dream come true for him. Finally! A chance for a normal life! A wife, a son. You don't know how badly he wanted that."

"Then why did he run from the airport?"

"Because he saw you, Bex. He was afraid you would turn them in."

"And so he ran to you."

"He has nowhere else to go."

Bex said, "You know we have to turn him in, Toni. Even if he didn't confess to you about killing Rachel, Jeremy belongs with his real father. He belongs with Craig, you know that."

"Robby didn't mean to kill her."

"But he did."

"He's not a bad person, Bex. He has problems. He needs help."

"Then get it for him. Help him plead temporary insanity or whatever you think will get him what he needs. I'll even testify to my part in riling him up or setting him off or whatever you and his lawyer want to call it. But help Jeremy, too. Send him back to his father."

Toni asked, "Are you going to call the police?"

"I have to."

"Okay," Toni said. She looked at her house, eyes settling on the still silent guest-room window. "Okay, Bex . . . ."

The police arrived within fifteen minutes. They had the APB on file and they took Robby into custody. He looked stunned. Walking from Toni's front door to the squad car, he looked exactly as shell-shocked as he had in his post-Olympic press conference photo years earlier. Like he didn't know how he'd gotten there, or what any of it meant. Toni held Robby's hand up until the moment they put the cuffs on. He didn't seem to notice.

At one point, Robby looked across the police car at Bex. He was a killer and a wife-beater and a kidnapper. And still, Bex wanted to apologize to him.

Jeremy came out at almost the same time as Robby did, walking silently a few feet behind his newfound father, staring at the ground and kicking imaginary pebbles out of his way. In the hustle and bustle of the arrest, he, the victim, was practically forgotten. He looked smaller than Bex remembered him. Smaller, and also older. He stood on the sidewalk, still dressed in the same clothes he'd been wearing at the airport, and watched Robby get loaded into the squad car. The strobe lights from its roof turned his face first red, then white, then red again. Jeremy watched Toni talking to Robby through the half-open window. And then he saw Bex across the street.

She walked over, taking the long way, making sure to stay out of the police's way. Jeremy looked as if nothing in the world could ever surprise him again. Of course, the 24/7 researcher he'd met just a few days earlier was there.

Why shouldn't she be? In an insane universe, this made as much sense as anything else he'd just been through.

Jeremy didn't even ask Bex, he just guessed. "You're the one who found me."

"Yeah. I guess. I mean . . ."

"Is my dad really worried?"

"Yeah."

Jeremy found another pebble to kick. He swore, "Aunt Felicia said he knew. She said I didn't have to leave a note, because my dad knew all about it and said it was okay. I'd have left a note, otherwise. I know how he gets worried."

"He doesn't blame you."

"Is he really mad at Aunt Felicia?"

"Yeah."

Jeremy raised his eyes enough to look at the police car, then looked away again. As if the lights—or something—was hurting his eyes. "Robby told me a lot of stuff. About him and her and my mom. Rachel, I mean. My mom, Rachel."

"Did you understand it?"

"Pretty much. You know my dad, Craig? My dad, Craig, he's adopted, too."

"I know. I've met Jenny and Michael."

"They're great, aren't they? And they love my dad a whole lot. They don't even care that he's not really their kid."

"No. I don't think they care at all."

Jeremy asked, "Are you going to take me home, now?"

"That's a great idea," Bex said.

Bex knew she should have called Craig the minute she had Jeremy safely in her car and headed for home. But, she couldn't help it. She wanted to see Craig's face the first time he set eyes on Jeremy, standing safe and sound on his front stoop.

And, in the end, it was everything she could have hoped for.

Craig's face, still covered with the scars he'd incurred practically ripping his own flesh off with worry, seemed to crack in two the moment he set eyes on Jeremy. For an instant, he looked as if he didn't believe his own eyes. And then he screamed.

No, he howled, really.

It was a sound so primal, it was beyond emotion. It was beyond expression. It was simply raw, unchecked, practically animalistic joy. He swept Jeremy up off the ground, hugging him so tightly, Bex was surprised he didn't break a rib or two along the way. He may have been laughing, he may have been crying.

It would be up to the 24/7 audience to sort it all out.

Because, this time, Bex had the entire joyous moment on tape.

And exclusive.

Turn the page for the next
Bex Levy Figure Skating mystery

Death Drop

by Alina Adams

Coming from Berkley Prime Crime
in October 2005

Prologue

Figure skating champion Igor Marchenko twice made the front page of *The New York Times.*

The first time, in 1977, he was fourteen years old, a skinny beanpole of a boy wearing an oversized down jacket and ill-fitting boots stained with gray Moscow slush, nervously running his hands through straw-fine blond hair that looked like it had been chopped by the same blind barber who once used to hack at Prince Valiant, three fingers shyly covering his forehead and eyes as though he were afraid to truly take in the full consequences of what he'd just done. But, at the same time, his lips were set in the firm determination of a man twice his age ready to take responsibility for his actions.

At the height of the U.S.–U.S.S.R. Cold War, the all-capital letter headline above his slightly out of focus, black and white, Associate Press wire photo triumphantly taunted: "Defecting!"

No one could blame them the big type. It was a superb story, thoroughly worthy of such braggadocio coverage, even by a newspaper as traditionally averse to headline-blaring yellow journalism as *The Times.* For, even as Moscow played host to the 1977 World Figure Skating Championships, the Russian Men's Bronze Medalist had ducked his assigned KGB guards and snuck out of the athelete's hotel, braving sub-zero temperatures to cross several blizzard-ravaged miles on foot in the middle of the night. He arrived at the American embassy hours before it opened and buried himself in the snow beneath a pair of bushes by the front gates to avoid being seen by passers-by. He huddled there, shivering until sun-up, when he was finally able to stumble inside the embassy, and, teeth chattering on top of a heavy Russian accent tempered by a cracking adolescent tenor, he managed to blurt out, "I defect."

The Soviet Skating Federation, naturally, put up an invasion-force-sized fuss, claiming that the boy had been coerced, bribed, kidnapped, and any other synonym they could coax out of their handy Russian/English dictionaries. But, Igor, with a poise and calm utterly unexpected of a one hundred and twenty-pound ninth-grader had remained firm in his convictions. The only time he came even close to wavering was when the president of the Skating Federation dragged Igor's mother, older sister, and brother-in-law to the sidewalk outside the U.S. embassy, where Igor could clearly see them from the window. The Federation Head handed the Ambassador a note to pass on to the boy, which read, "You will never, ever see them again."

Igor came to the window, and he stared at his family. His mother was crying. His sister was crying. Igor was crying. But, after a tense, hour-long stand-off, he simply turned around and walked away.

Eventually, the Soviets gave up. They had to. Young Igor certainly showed no signs of doing so. And, after nearly a month of high-pressure tactics, they allowed their top male skater to be taken to the United States.

There, he received a hero's welcome traditionally reserved for World Series Champions, astronauts, and Girl Scouts who have sold the most cookies. He met with the president. He chatted with Johnny Carson on *The Tonight Show.* (Well, technically, Johnny chatted with Ed McMahon about how wild and wacky it was that male skaters wore all those sequins on their costumes and did those jumps where they spun round and round, and how did they keep from feeling dizzy or getting a sequin in their eye? while Igor sort of nodded politely, smiled and waved at the camera, and looked desperate to defect again, this time from Burbank.)

Donations pored in from well-wishers eager to help the young hero continue his skating career in the U.S.A. The United States Figure Skating Association (USFSA) gave him free room and board at their Olympic Training Center in Hartford, Connecticut, and pressured their Congressman to rush through Igor's citizenship papers so that he could represent the U.S. at the 1982 Olympics. Actually, they were really hoping that he could represent them in 1978, but that, the Congressman told the USFSA, was really pushing things. U.S. citizenship usually took seven years to finalize. The right word to the right people might be able to speed up some paperwork and make it five years, but a single year was out of the question. As a result, even though Igor won the 1978 U.S. National Championships (with so many 6.0s one newspaper compared him to Damian, the boy with the 666 tattooed into his skull from the then hit-movie, *The Omen*), it was the runner-up and 1977 Champion, Gary Gold from San Francisco, who went to the 1978 Olympics and finished in seventh place, very respectable for a seventeen year old at his first Games. But, not nearly as respectable as the Silver medal Igor won at the World Championships a month later. (He would have won Gold, the USFSA officials insisted publicly, if those crooked Russian judges hadn't all ganged up with the Polish, Czech, and East Germans against him).

Four years later, Igor did win gold, not just at the Worlds, but at the Olympics, as well. This time, however, his exploits weren't earth-shattering enough to merit the front page of *The Times.* Sure, it was a gold medal won for the U.S., their single one of those entire Games, but, it was only in figure-skating, after all. Not in a real sport, like, oh, say, golf.

And so, Igor had to wait over a quarter of a century to get his second front-page news story.

In the meantime, he retired from amateur competition, skated professionally for a few years, and then became a coach at the same Olympic training center that had once taken him in.

"To pay back a debt," he explained.

Aw . . . . everyone thought.

And, in the end, it was coaching, which, in November of 2005, brought a now forty-two year old Igor Marchenko back to Russia for the first time since his chilly desertion.

Igor's top student, the 2005 U.S. Ladies's Silver Medalist, Jordan Ares, had been invited, along with her teammate—2005 U.S. Ladies' Bronze Medalist, Lian Reilly, Gary Gold's top student—to skate in a "U.S. vs. Russia" made-for-TV event in Moscow.

At first, Igor refused to attend, exactly the same way he'd refused to attend any competition held on Soviet soil while he was an amateur, and on formerly Soviet soil once he was a coach. It wasn't until the Russian Skating Federation personally issued an invitation, a sort of "Come home, all is forgiven, Love & Kisses, Russia–P.S. We'll even let you see your family again, isn't that terribly nice of us?" missive, that he agreed to make the trip.

This news made the 24/7 Sports Television Network very, very happy. Sure, it was in their contract to cover the event anyway, but now, on top of the up-close-and-personal profiles they were planning to tell all along—Lian vs. Jordan, their final head-to-head before the 2006 Nationals, where, due to the retirement of Erin Simpson, the 2005 Champion, the U.S. Ladies crown was at stake—now, they actually had a naturally (as opposed to a manufactured) dramatic story to tell: "Igor Marchenko Comes Home for the First Time." Oh, this was going to be a tear-jerker, they could just feel it. The producers were already debating whether to use The Beatles' "Back in the U.S.S.R." or John Denver's "Take Me Home," for the primary background music. (Although everyone agreed that Neil Diamond's "Coming to America" should definitely be played when they recapped the part about his dramatic escape. That one was a gimme.)

Fortunately for the gag reflex of the viewing public, neither ditty came to be. The day of the American girls and their coaches's first practice in Russia, Igor Marchenko collapsed in Neaboknovenay Arena. He was dead before the ambulance got there—three and a half hours after it was called.

"Of course, Americans would get the most prompt service," the arena manager whom everyone seemed to simply call Shura, groused. "Special privileges only for Americans."

Lying face down and inert barely three feet away from the ice surface upon which his star-making competitive career first began, Igor Marchenko finally earned his second *New York Times* story.

This time, the headline read: "Murdered!"

Judging figure skating can be ice-cold murder.

Murder on Ice

A Figure Skating Mystery Series

by Alina Adams

When an Olympic judge is murdered, it is up to figure skating researcher Bex Levy to solve the crime before the trail turns cold.

"ALINA ADAMS NAILS THE TRIPLE AXEL."
—*MYSTERY READER*

"A LIKEABLE, DOWN-TO-EARTH HEROINE MAKES THIS A MUST-READ FOR COZY MYSTERY FANS WITH A FASCINATION FOR FIGURE SKATING."
—*ROMANTIC TIMES*

0-425-19307-1

Available wherever books are sold or at www.penguin.com

pc597